BETTER THAN HOME

BETTER *than* HOME

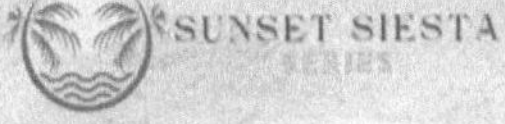

BETTER THAN HOME

Siesta Sunset Series

ERIN BROCKUS

Chapter One

HARPER

I INHALED the scent of raw lumber and possibility while ignoring the undercurrent of pure panic. Bungalow number four—full of potential, unfinished, and one of the reasons I couldn't sleep at night. The gutted space represented everything wonderful and terrifying about Siesta Sunset's resort renovation—opportunities wrapped in financial risk, dreams entangled with practical nightmares.

"Come on." I led my older brother Eli down the unfinished hallway, stepping carefully around a stack of drywall. "I wanted you to see the progress before your shift."

Sunlight streamed through the empty window frames, illuminating swirling dust motes and highlighting the gleaming light-gauge steel studs where walls would eventually stand. The exposed concrete subfloors echoed our footsteps, awaiting the hardwood flooring that would transform this skeleton into the luxury beachfront bungalow of my imagination. And Chase Ashworth's meticulous designs.

"Progress, huh?" Eli ran his hand along an exposed steel beam, his deep indigo eyes dancing. "It looked like a hurricane hit, and then someone sent in a wrecking crew for good measure."

I shot him a look. "That steel framing you're lovingly stroking isn't just for show, Eli. Chase designed it to withstand hurricanes. It's called *in progress*. Two weeks ago, this was just a concrete foundation."

"Ah, yes, the famous Harper Coleridge optimism." He grinned, the same effortless smile that charmed tourists into booking his dive excursions. My brother had perfected the sun-kissed beach bum look—tousled dark blond hair, perpetual tan, and an easy, humorous confidence that made everyone instantly comfortable. Today, he wore board shorts and a faded Sunset Siesta Dive Shop T-shirt, already dressed for his upcoming class.

I gestured toward where the bed would eventually be. "The windows will face the ocean. The bathroom plumbing is starting. And look—" I pointed to the far wall. "That's where the private deck will extend, with steps down to the beach. Or something like that. Chase is still working on the design."

Eli whistled low. "Fancy. I'm still getting used to the idea of our little family resort going all premium on us."

"We have to evolve or die." The weight of my general manager responsibilities settled on my shoulders like a lead balloon. "The Florida Keys might be paradise, but Sunset Siesta can't survive on nostalgia and charm alone anymore."

"Especially when the charm includes leaky roofs and air conditioners from the Reagan era."

I let out a wry laugh. "Tell me about it. I spent an hour yesterday placating the Hendersons in room twenty after their AC died. Again."

The resort's situation wasn't exactly dire, but it wasn't far off. Our ancestors had built something special here on Dove Key, but after Dad's disappearance fifteen years ago, Mom had struggled to keep things afloat. Now that she was stepping back, the responsibility fell mostly to me to keep the family legacy from crumbling beneath waves of deferred maintenance and outdated amenities.

Eli kicked at a scrap of wood. "You doing okay, sis? You've been looking tired."

"Gee, thanks."

"Not in a bad way," he amended quickly. "Just in a 'my sister is trying to run a struggling resort while single-parenting a kindergartner' kind of way."

I sighed, leaning against a half-constructed wall. "It's been intense. The construction crew hit an unexpected framing issue in bungalow two yesterday, which means more delays and probably more money."

"And the amazing nephew?" Eli's face softened.

A mental snapshot of my son flashed through my mind—his bright blue eyes always searching, golden brown hair a wild mess no matter what I did. And his energy? Boundless. "Finn's great. Except he announced last night that he has a part in the school play, which means costume-making falls to me, his hopelessly uncrafty mother."

"Sweet. What's the play?"

"Something about ocean conservation. He's a parrotfish."

"A parrotfish?" Eli's expression brightened. "Perfect! That kid's already obsessed with everything underwater. Must be genetic."

"He wants blue and green scales and a rainbow tail."

"Which is only right, you know."

"The play is the kindergarten class's major project. It's

not for several months, so at least I have some time to work on my costume-making skills."

"Tell you what," Eli said. "I'll help with the costume. I can be crafty when proper uncle duties motivate me."

I smiled, genuinely grateful. "You're the best."

"Of course I am," he replied with a mock bow. "I'll be proud uncle number one in the audience, front and center, embarrassing him with excessive applause."

The worry lines between my eyebrows relaxed. This was Eli's gift—making everything more manageable with his easy confidence and humor. Where I carried the weight of responsibility, Eli navigated life with a light touch. It had driven me crazy when we were younger, but now I appreciated his counterbalance to my constant stress. Though it still surprised me that he'd recently found the love of his life in our straitlaced, laser-focused accountant. They balanced each other and Jules had recently moved in with Eli.

He studied my face for a moment, then his expression shifted subtly. "So... back to the disaster area. Is my best friend making your life hell?"

And there was the other reason I couldn't sleep at night.

Chase Ashworth, award-winning architect, my brother's best friend since forever, and now—through a series of events that still baffled me—our family's business partner in this massive renovation project. Both Eli and Chase were a year older than me at thirty-five.

"Chase is doing precisely what we wanted him to do." I kept my voice deliberately neutral. "His designs are amazing, and he's been incredibly patient with our budget constraints."

"But..."

"No but," I insisted. "The fact that he invested his own

money into becoming a partner still feels like a small miracle. Without him, I'd be even more stressed about how much this is costing."

Eli looked skeptical. "That doesn't answer my question about whether he's making your life hell."

I sighed. "It's complicated."

Like the fact that every time Chase walked into a room, my heart did this irritating flutter thing that had no place in a professional relationship. Or how his quiet confidence and focus made me simultaneously calmer and more flustered. Or the way his sleeves rolled up to reveal forearms that—

"Define complicated," Eli prompted, interrupting my inappropriate mental tangent.

"Chase has a very expansive vision," I explained. "Sometimes that vision requires materials that cost more than the original budget for these bungalows. We debate. We compromise. It's the normal back-and-forth of any project."

"And?"

"And nothing."

Eli's eyebrow arched knowingly. "Harper, I've known Chase since we were kids. He can be intense when he cares about something. And he definitely cares about this project."

"He's been a rock," I insisted, perhaps a bit too forcefully. "Professional. Supportive. Understanding."

"Glad to hear it. If he steps out of line, let me know. I'll pound him to smithereens. Or send him diving with concrete shoes."

That made me laugh, bless him. "At least wait until we're finished with the renovations to do him in, okay?"

He hesitated, studying my face with unexpected seriousness. "You know I'm here if you need anything, right?

Even if it's just to take Finn for an evening so you can decompress."

The sincerity in his voice caught me off guard, and a rush of gratitude for my eccentric, loyal family suffused me. "I know. Thank you."

I turned back to survey the unfinished space. In my mind's eye, I could picture Chase's designs coming to life—the clean lines, the natural materials, the careful balance of luxury and authenticity. He understood what I wanted for the resort even before I could articulate it.

A complicated flutter ran through my chest. I couldn't deny Chase had become an unexpected highlight of my chaotic days, with his quiet confidence and dry humor. That somehow over the years, he'd gone from being Eli's brainy, meticulous friend to a successful, distractingly handsome architect. And since the resort remodel had begun four months ago, I swore he even smelled better, a combination of cedar and drywall that shouldn't have been as enticing as it was. But my life was complicated enough already. Besides, Chase had never given any indication that he thought of me as anything other than his best friend's sister and now his business partner.

Just then, the man himself walked through the unfinished doorway with a rolled set of documents tucked under his arm. Unlike my sawdust-covered self, Chase managed to be utterly composed amid the construction chaos—dark hair neatly styled, a crisp button-down with sleeves rolled to reveal those distracting forearms, and slacks that were somehow immune to the dust coating everything else in the building.

His hazel eyes, flecked with gold and green in the morning light, immediately found mine across the unfinished space. His gaze made my heart stutter in my chest. It held a quiet intensity reserved for buildings, blueprints, and occasionally, disconcertingly, for me.

"There you are." His voice carried that calm steadiness that had anchored our project through every crisis. "I was looking for you at the main office."

"Harper's giving me the grand tour of Sawdust Palace," Eli chimed in, crossing the room to greet his friend.

Chase's mouth twitched at one corner. "You like it? I call this style *Contemporary Destruction*. Very avant-garde."

Eli laughed, clapping him on the shoulder. "Slumming it today, Ashworth? You're usually holed up in your fancy office, drawing perfect lines or whatever it is you do."

"Someone has to prevent your sister from installing purple shag carpet," Chase replied, his eyes finding mine again with a hint of shared humor.

"As if," I protested. "My taste is impeccable."

"Yes, it is," Chase agreed with unexpected sincerity, and a rush of warmth engulfed me.

Eli looked between us with a barely contained smirk. "Well, I'll leave you two professionals to your... professional things. I've got a room full of future divers waiting to discover they can't clear their masks without panicking."

"Your confidence in your students is inspiring," Chase said.

"Hey, they've all come back alive so far, haven't they?" Eli headed for the door, then turned back. "Take good care of the project and the project manager, Chase. My sister works too hard."

Before I could protest this characterization, Eli was gone, his footsteps fading down the walkway that connected the bungalows to the main property.

Which left me alone with Chase amid the constant hum of distant construction and the soft whisper of ocean waves from beyond the half-built deck. I became hyper-aware of my appearance—dusty jeans, resort polo shirt with the embroidered sunset logo slightly tilted, brown hair pulled back in a hasty ponytail.

"I got the final renderings late yesterday," Chase said, breaking the momentary silence as he held up the rolled sheaf of documents. He moved to a makeshift table formed from sawhorses and a sheet of plywood. "And some material samples I'd like you to approve."

"Wonderful." My voice sounded overly bright to my own ears. I stepped closer as he unrolled a large, detailed color rendering of the finished bungalow.

My breath froze. His design was stunning, more beautiful than I had ever imagined from his hand-drawn sketches. The exterior featured storm-resistant concrete siding in a warm white tone, with crisp black trim and large windows that maximized the ocean view. A private deck stretched across the ocean side, with built-in seating and steps leading directly to the beach. The surrounding landscaping incorporated native plants that would provide both privacy and beauty.

"Chase," I whispered, moved by the vision he'd created. "It's perfect."

Something flashed across his face—pride, pleasure, something deeper I couldn't name. "You think so?"

"It's exactly what I wanted but couldn't articulate." I leaned closer, examining the details. "You've captured the essence of what makes Sunset Siesta special but elevated it to something new."

"That was the goal," he said, his voice warm. "Honoring the history while moving forward."

He pointed to various elements of the design, and I listened, entranced, as he explained each decision with the passion of someone who truly cared about creating meaningful spaces. The interior featured vaulted ceilings with exposed beams, large sliding doors that opened the living area to the deck, and a seating area.

"For the bathroom countertops, I'm thinking this." He produced a sample of polished quartz with tiny fragments of sea glass embedded throughout. The surface caught the light, sparkling with blues and greens that evoked the ocean beyond.

"It's beautiful," I murmured, running my fingers over the smooth surface. "Local?"

He nodded. "A craftsman in Key West. Costs a bit more, but the quality is exceptional, and it tells a story about this place."

"The ideal balance of practical and special," I agreed. "Our guests will love it."

"Speaking of guests, I've been thinking about the target market for these bungalows." Chase leaned in closer, his arm brushing against mine as he indicated the floor plan. The light contact sent a ridiculous tingle up my spine. I forced myself to focus on the plans, not on the way his presence filled the unfinished space. "These aren't just rooms. They're experiences. Honeymooners, anniversary celebrations, special occasions."

"Premium pricing. Which we'll need to offset the building costs." I hesitated, then added, "Thank you again for the investment. I know it was a risk."

Chase's expression turned serious, and his eyes held mine. "Not a risk. An opportunity. I believe in this place, Harper. And I believe in your vision for it."

Something unspoken passed between us, and I found myself wondering, not for the first time, what had prompted Chase Ashworth—successful architect with a fledgling firm here in Dove Key—to invest his own money in our struggling family resort. His twenty-five percent stake and cash infusion had made the renovation possible, but the business case didn't quite explain the passion he brought to every aspect of the project.

"Well," I said, breaking the moment before it became too intense, "your belief is paying off. These bungalows are going to save us."

I'd nearly had a coronary when he unveiled the design for four brand-new bungalows stretching along the far end of the beach. He'd kept the idea to himself until he was sure, then had lobbied hard for the unexpected project. And expense. I'd reluctantly approved it, but now that I saw the real potential, I was fully on board.

Chase nodded, turning back to the renderings. "The indoor-outdoor flow was key to the design. I wanted guests to feel connected to the beach and water even when they're inside."

"It's just right. Authentic luxury, not pretentious."

"Exactly." His smile was warm, appreciative. "You get it."

"We make a good team. Even when we argue about budgets."

"Especially then," he countered with a hint of humor. "Your practical constraints rein me in a little."

"And your insistence on quality saves me from my worst penny-pinching instincts."

Chase laughed, the sound rich and genuine in the bare space. "Remember the great light fixture debate of last month?"

"When you tried to convince me to spend three times the budget on custom pendants?" I shook my head, smiling despite myself.

"Well, design isn't just about aesthetics—it's about experience. How a place makes you feel."

"I get that. Which is why I love your idea for the countertops. I'm still not going for the pendants, though."

Our eyes met over the plans, and I was intensely aware of how this place made me feel. My earlier anxieties about budgets and timelines melted into something warmer, more complicated.

I cleared my throat and looked back at the renderings. "So, timeline for these bungalows?"

Chase shifted his weight, returning to professional mode. "Plumbing rough-in completes this week. Electrical next." He ran a hand through his hair, a rare gesture of uncertainty. "I'm a bit concerned about the windows. The supplier is backlogged."

"Can we expedite?" I mentally calculated what that might do to our already strained budget.

"I've been working on it. I have some connections from previous projects. I might be able to pull some strings."

"Chase Ashworth, using his considerable charm for the greater good of Sunset Siesta?"

His eyes crinkled at the corners. "Is that how you see me? Charming?"

The question caught me off guard, and heat flooded my cheeks. "I meant, uh… professionally speaking. You know, with suppliers and contractors."

"Ah," he said, his expression unreadable. "Of course."

An awkward silence fell between us, filled only by the distant sounds of hammering and the gentle shush of waves. I scrambled for something professional to say. "What about the fixtures for the bathroom? Did you decide on the matte black or the brushed nickel?"

"Actually," Chase reached into his messenger bag and

produced another small sample board. "I found an option I think you'll like better."

Our hands brushed as he passed me the sample—a beautiful, antique copper that would age naturally over time, developing character and color with each passing year. The metaphor wasn't lost on me.

"Oh my," I said softly, looking up to find him watching me intently. "I've never seen anything like this."

"I'm glad you like it," he replied, his voice lower than before.

The air between us thickened. Our shoulders brushed again as we both leaned over the plans, and this time neither of us moved away. The moment stretched, possibility lingering heavily in the sawdust-laden air.

"Harper!" someone called from outside, breaking the spell. "You there? The Hendersons are checking out and asking for you specifically!"

I stepped back, reality rushing in. "Duty calls."

Chase nodded, rolling up the renderings with careful hands. "We can review the rest of these later. Sounds like your magic touch is needed."

"That's what I'm afraid of." I mentally shifted into general manager mode.

As I turned to leave, Chase called after me. "Harper?"

I glanced back, caught by something in his tone.

"It's going to be worth it. All of this. I promise."

I nodded, believing him despite all my practical doubts, and headed back to deal with the Hendersons, the feel of aged copper and the memory of his arm against mine lingering like promises.

Chapter Two

CHASE

I TRACED my finger along the clean line of the cabana roof on the blueprint, a familiar satisfaction at the elegant simplicity of the design filling me. Sunlight streamed through the generous windows of my office, casting geometric patterns on the polished concrete floor. Six months ago, this building had been a forgotten relic just off Main Street in Dove Key. Now Latitudes Design breathed with possibility. My possibility. The soft jazz playing in the background couldn't quite drown out the low hum of anxiety that had been my constant companion since launching the firm, but the pride of seeing my vision take shape helped keep it at bay. At least most days.

The renovation plans for Sunset Siesta's pool area spread across my desk. I'd been staring at them for hours, making minor adjustments, checking measurements, and second-guessing placement. Six cabanas, spaced evenly around the free-form pool to form a cohesive whole. The custom-built concrete deck would make the area modern and welcoming. The Siesta Sunset project wasn't particularly large or complex by industry standards, but it carried weight beyond its scope. It was Latitudes Design's first major undertaking—my chance to prove that leaving the security of Patterson & Walsh hadn't been professional suicide.

I sat back, rubbing my eyes. The plans before me were solid. Better than solid. The designs balanced luxury with practicality, offering shaded retreats that would elevate the resort's aging pool area into something worth the premium rates we needed to charge. I knew the work was good. So why couldn't I stop fidgeting with the details?

The answer arrived unbidden, in the form of chestnut hair and warm brown eyes that practically glowed in the sunlight. Harper Coleridge. General manager of Sunset Siesta. Single mother. My best friend's sister. The woman I'd been carefully not thinking about for longer than I cared to admit. Years.

"Not helping," I muttered to myself as I reached for a drafting pencil.

I'd known the Coleridges most of my life. Eli had been my best friend since elementary school, which meant I'd grown up with his family by extension. I'd witnessed Harper evolve from an annoying kid sister to a confidently capable woman who radiated warmth and quiet strength. Never drawing attention to herself, she was simply, undeniably beautiful. I'd watched her navigate the shock of unexpected pregnancy and abandonment with a fortitude and grace that still astounded me. And I'd kept my distance because some lines weren't meant to be crossed.

The memory of Eli's teenage decree floated back. "My sisters are off-limits, man. Bro code. Don't mess with it." A stupid adolescent pact that shouldn't matter twenty years later.

But it did.

Especially when Harper's smile made my chest tighten.

I forced my attention back to the blueprint, looking for distractions in dimensions and material lists. A cabana on the north side needed a slight adjustment to its flowing drapes—nothing major, but worth noting before tomorrow's construction meeting. I scribbled a correction, losing myself in the familiar rhythm of problem-solving.

A soft knock pulled me from my concentration. Marilyn Wallace stood in the doorway, two steaming mugs in hand and an amused expression on her face. "You've been staring at those plans for three hours." She placed a steaming mug of coffee on my desk. "I figured caffeine might be in order."

I smiled gratefully and inhaled the rich aroma. "You're a mind reader."

"Part of the job description." She settled into the chair opposite me, her own mug cradled between her hands. At fifty-two, Marilyn radiated a calm competence that had made her my first and only choice when staffing the office. Her silver-streaked bob and practical attire projected the professional-but-approachable image I wanted for Latitudes.

"How's the Franson meeting looking?" I asked, taking a sip of damn good coffee.

"Confirmed for Thursday at two. She's bringing her husband this time." Marilyn's expression turned wry. "She mentioned he has *strong opinions* about the guest bathroom."

"No worries. Most people do." I smiled, a rush of gratitude rising. Six months in, and I still marveled at how she kept on top of it all.

"The contractor called about the Rivera kitchen," she continued. "The custom cabinets will be delayed another week. I've already adjusted the schedule and let Mrs. Rivera know."

"How'd she take it?"

"Better than expected. I sent over that 3D rendering you did of the finished space—it softened the blow considerably."

I nodded. Another crisis that Marilyn's diplomatic skills averted. "You know, when I hired you, I thought I was getting a receptionist. Turns out I got a miracle worker."

She waved away the compliment, but her smile showed her pleasure. "Speaking of miracles, have you made any progress with this?" She nodded toward the Sunset Siesta plans.

"Some." I rotated the blueprint so she could see the layout. "I'm considering shifting the placement of these privacy plantings. The current plan works, but if we move them here"—I indicated the new location—"we can create more natural screening without blocking the ocean view from the deck."

Marilyn studied the design, head tilted. "Makes sense to me. Though I have to wonder if you're overthinking beautiful cabanas because you're nervous about the project."

I opened my mouth to protest, then closed it. She wasn't wrong.

"It's your first major contract since opening Latitudes," she continued gently. "You're a partner in the business, and it's for people you care about. Of course you want it to be perfect."

"I know." I gestured vaguely, unsure how to articulate the pressure I felt without sounding ungrateful. "There's a lot riding on this."

"And the end result will be worth it."

Relief and appreciation mingled as I nodded. "Thanks, Marilyn. For everything."

"That's what you pay me for." She rose before pausing at the door. "And, Chase? The cabanas will be spectacular. Stop worrying."

After she left, I turned back to the blueprints with fresh eyes. Maybe she was right. Maybe I was overthinking this.

The notification sound from my computer interrupted my thoughts. I glanced at the screen, where a new email had appeared in my inbox. The sender's name caught my attention immediately. Harper Coleridge. The subject line read *Pool Renovation Materials Question*.

My pulse ticked up a notch. *Professional*, I reminded myself firmly. *This is a professional relationship.*

I clicked the email open. Harper's message was brief and to the point, asking about the possibility of substituting a different wood for the cabana framing. She'd seen something at another property that might work well and wanted my opinion. Simple. Straightforward. Nothing to warrant the way my heart rate had accelerated.

And yet.

I checked my watch. Just past eleven. The construction crew would be on site now, likely working on the footings if they were keeping to schedule. Harper would probably be there too.

I could reply to the email with my thoughts. That would be the efficient choice. The professional choice.

Instead, I found myself gathering the plans, then sliding them into a carrying tube. Some things were better discussed in person. Especially when they involved wood selections that needed to be seen in the right light. At least that's what I told myself as I headed for my SUV, plans in hand.

The construction site hummed with activity as I approached. The sharp tang of wet concrete mixed with salt air, a combination I'd always found oddly satisfying. Workers moved with purpose around the cabana footings, the percussion of hammers and drills creating a chaotic counterpoint to the steady rhythm of waves in the background. I spotted Harper immediately, clipboard in hand, deep in conversation with one of the foremen. Her wavy brown hair was pulled back in a ponytail, but the breeze had teased a few strands loose. Even from this distance, her focused intensity was evident in the set of her shoulders and the precise gestures that accompanied her words. Ignoring the way my skin heated up, I tucked the plans securely under my arm and headed her way.

The once-tranquil pool area of Sunset Siesta was transformed into an organized battlefield of construction materials and equipment. A separate section that moved depending on the work being done was kept open for guests, along with a free drink to minimize complaints. Eight weeks in, and the project was taking shape exactly as I'd envisioned thanks to good planning and better execution.

Harper noticed my approach and wrapped up her conversation with a nod to the foreman. She turned to meet me, a smile warming her delicate features. Her snub nose had just a touch of sun and her gorgeous cheekbones held a shade of pink that had nothing to do with makeup. "Chase. I wasn't expecting you today. Got my email about the wood?"

"I did." I unrolled the plans on a nearby table with an umbrella providing shade, then weighed the corners with small clamps I kept in my pocket for exactly this purpose. "Thought it would be easier to discuss in person. Show me what you had in mind."

She moved beside me, her shoulder nearly touching mine as she leaned over the blueprints. The faint scent of her shampoo—something citrusy and clean—momentarily derailed my thoughts before I pulled myself back to focus.

"Here." Harper pointed to the floor plan for a cabana. "I was at The Sandpiper last week, and I was drawn to the wood in their restaurant. It has this beautiful, variegated pattern that would tie in wonderfully with our existing wood accents at Driftwood Grill." She pointed toward the main resort restaurant and its screen of vertical planks framing the entrance. Then she handed me a sample board.

I ran a hand over the smooth surface, considering. "Coastal Blend, right? Good quality."

"The lumberyard is running a promotion right now. Thirty percent off for commercial orders over five hundred square feet." She glanced up at me, a hint of triumph in her expression. "Which we'd easily clear with six cabanas."

I raised an eyebrow, impressed. "You've done your homework."

"I'm not just a pretty face," she deadpanned, then smiled to soften the words.

"You've proven you're much more than that." The response came automatically, but I quickly redirected. "It's a solid suggestion. The Coastal Blend would work well with the overall aesthetic."

Harper nodded before turning back to the plans. "That's what I thought. It has these subtle grains running through it that would look great in the sunlight."

We spent the next few minutes discussing various options and placement details. Harper had an eye for design that went beyond mere aesthetics—she understood functionality, durability, and the practical needs of a busy resort.

"If we shift the service access point to this side"—she indicated a spot on cabana five—"it would be less visible from the pool deck but still give staff easy entry."

I evaluated the suggestion, mentally reconfiguring the layout. "That would work. Good catch."

"I've spent enough years watching servers struggle with awkward access points." She shrugged. "Makes more sense to design it right from the start."

"And that's why client input is invaluable." I made a notation on the plans. "You see things from an operational perspective that I might miss."

"Is that your diplomatic way of saying I'm picky?"

I looked up to find amusement dancing in her eyes. The sunlight caught the warm undertones in her hair, making it glow against her tanned skin. For a moment, I forgot we were standing in the middle of a busy construction site. I forgot how to breathe.

"I'd say discerning," I replied, my voice dropping a little. "It's a quality I appreciate."

Something shifted in her expression, a subtle softening, a flicker of awareness that mirrored my own. For a heartbeat, we weren't resort manager and architect, but simply a man and woman standing close enough to feel the warmth between them.

"And I appreciate a designer who listens." Her voice carried a hint of playfulness. "Instead of dismissing my operational concerns as irrelevant to the grand artistic vision."

"Sounds like you've dealt with some ego problems in the past."

"You have no idea. The last project manager we worked with actually said—and I quote—If you wanted practical, you should have hired an engineer." She rolled her eyes. "As if aesthetics and functionality are mutually exclusive."

I laughed. "On behalf of my profession, I apologize."

"Accepted." Her smile widened, genuine and warm. "You're definitely an improvement."

The compliment shouldn't have affected me as much as it did. I'd received plenty of professional praise in my career and from clients far more prestigious than a family-owned resort in Dove Key. But Harper's approval carried a weight that defied logic. I wanted to impress her, to see that light of appreciation in her eyes. It was a dangerous impulse for a man trying to maintain professional boundaries. Boundaries I wasn't sure I could keep if she encouraged me.

I forced my attention back to the plans, tracing a line with my finger. "I've been thinking about the privacy plantings. If we shift them six inches, we could enhance the screening without compromising the ocean view."

Harper leaned closer, studying the area I indicated. She nodded slowly. "I like that. And Finn would approve too. He's been very concerned about whether people can see him building sandcastles from the cabanas."

The mention of her six-year-old son brought a smile to my face. "Important design considerations from our youngest consultant."

"He takes his advisory role very seriously." Harper's expression softened the way it always did when she spoke of Finn. "Yesterday he informed me that all pool areas should have secret tunnels for escape routes."

"That's actually not the worst idea I've ever heard."

"Don't encourage him!" She laughed. "He already thinks you hang the moon since you let him *help* with the initial measurements."

I remembered that day clearly—Finn following me

around with a small measuring tape, solemnly recording numbers in a notebook that consisted mostly of creative spelling and stick figures. It had added an hour to my site survey, but the kid's enthusiasm had been contagious.

"He's a good assistant. Very detail-oriented."

"He gets that from me." Harper's voice carried a note of pride.

Our eyes met again, and this time the connection held. The air between us electrified, becoming charged with something neither of us acknowledged out loud. I was acutely aware of every inch between us—not enough for propriety, too much for what I wanted. Her lips parted as if she might say something beyond the professional discussion we'd been maintaining. My eyes automatically dropped to her generous mouth.

The chime of her phone shattered the moment. Harper blinked, then reached into her pocket with an apologetic smile. "Sorry, I should check this."

I stepped back, grateful for the interruption even as disappointment coursed through me. The distance helped clear my head, reminding me of all the reasons I needed to keep my distance.

She glanced at the text and sighed. "Kitchen crisis. Apparently, there's a disagreement about the new menu items that requires management intervention."

"Sounds urgent," I said, keeping my tone light.

"In the grand hierarchy of resort emergencies, food generally trumps construction." She tucked her phone away and met my eyes again, her expression firmly back in professional territory. "I'm sorry to cut this short. Are we good with the wood change?"

"Absolutely. I'll update the order specs this afternoon."

"Perfect." She gathered her clipboard. "I trust your

judgment on the planting adjustments too. Whatever you think works best."

I nodded, already missing her presence even though she hadn't left yet. "I'll have revised plans for you to review by the end of the week."

"You're the best, Chase." She reached out, her hand briefly touching my arm.

With that, she was gone, weaving her way through the construction zone with the confident stride of someone who belonged everywhere she went. The place where her fingers had touched my arm tingled through the fabric of my shirt.

Movement at the edge of the construction zone caught my attention. Ben Coleridge, the eldest sibling, sat at one of the undisturbed pool tables, hunched over what appeared to be flashcards and textbooks. His posture spoke of frustration—shoulders tight, one hand stuck in his light brown hair as he stared at the materials spread before him.

Before I could overthink it, I approached the table. Ben was so absorbed in his studies that he didn't notice me until I was nearly beside him.

"Double-checking drainage or dodging math?" I asked.

He snapped his head up, then snorted when he recognized me. "Neither. Trying to memorize acronyms that make absolutely no sense."

I glanced at the flashcards spread across the table, which looked medical in nature. "EMT training?" Harper had mentioned that he'd started taking classes.

He nodded, pushing the cards away with a grimace. "Turns out there's a lot more memorization than I expected."

Ben had always been the enigma of the family, the intense one who carried a rough, troubled history. Seeing him wrestle with textbooks under the Florida sun was relatable in an unexpected way. We were both trying to build something new under intense scrutiny, to prove we were capable of more than our pasts suggested. His struggle with acronyms wasn't so different from my struggle to balance budgets with vision, loyalty with desire. "What's giving you trouble?"

"All of it." He gestured at the scattered cards. "I've never been good at this crap. I learn by doing, not by staring at cards until my eyes bleed."

I set down my plan tube on the table, then picked up one of the cards. "SAMPLE—Signs/symptoms, Allergies, Medications, Past medical history, Last oral intake, Events leading to illness or injury." I read aloud. "Patient assessment framework?"

"Yeah." Ben's eyebrows flew up. "How'd you know?"

"Educated guess." I twitched a corner of my mouth. "But it makes sense as a systematic approach. Like a checklist."

He nodded slowly. "Yeah, that's it."

"I had to memorize building codes my first year out of school." I set the card down. "Hundreds of regulations that seemed completely arbitrary until I saw them applied in real situations."

"How'd you get through it?"

I considered the question. "I made it practical. Instead of trying to memorize abstract numbers and rules, I connected each code to an actual building element. Made them real."

The lines in his brow smoothed. "That might work. I've been trying to force them in by repetition, but nothing's sticking."

"It worked for me. Connect the acronym to the action. Visualize yourself asking a patient about allergies *while* you're thinking A. What does P look like when you're asking about past history? Make it tangible, not just letters floating in your head." I tapped the tube with its rolled-up plans next to me. "That pressure you feel? It's the same pressure I feel trying to ensure these designs hold up, literally and financially. We just have different acronyms."

His expression shifted, a flare of understanding replacing the frustration. "Make it real… Okay. That might work. I've just been hammering away with flash-cards, getting nowhere." He started gathering the cards, his movements less defeated, more purposeful.

"Everyone hits walls." I straightened and grabbed my plan tube. "It's how you get over them that counts."

He met my eyes then, a spark of the determination I recognized in Harper flaring briefly. "Appreciate the advice."

"Anytime." I hesitated, an unexpected urge to offer more encouragement taking over me at recognizing a kindred spirit in his struggle against self-doubt. "Look, Ben, for what it's worth… This EMT thing? It's impressive. Takes real courage to chase something that demanding, especially when it doesn't come easy."

Surprise widened his eyes again, and he seemed momentarily lost for words. We weren't close, despite my long friendship with his brother. Just two guys connected by Eli and now, unexpectedly, by the shared weight of trying to build something new.

"Yeah, well… Thanks," he mumbled, looking down at his books again, a faint flush rising on his neck.

I clapped him lightly on the shoulder, a brief gesture of support before stepping away. "Good luck with the studying."

As I walked toward the beach bungalows, the sounds of hammering and sawing welcomed me back to the familiar world of buildings and blueprints. My thoughts drifted between the two Coleridges I'd just encountered—Harper with her warm smile and professional competence, and Ben with his determined struggle to forge a new path.

Both of them, in their different ways, were trying to build something meaningful. Maybe that's why I felt drawn to them, beyond the complications of attraction or old friendships. We were all works in progress, reaching for something more.

Chapter Three

HARPER

TURQUOISE FELT WAS SURPRISINGLY hard to work with. I smoothed a piece over the table and tried again, the sequins catching and sticking to my fingers like stubborn glitter ants. I ignored the tension building in my shoulders and focused on gluing a rogue sparkle into place.

This was for Finn.

Everything was for Finn.

My son hummed a tuneless song from the other side of the table, his eyes soft as he lined up a row of seashells. The warm illumination of the kitchen lights caught on his brown hair and haloed his small, busy hands. His abstracted smile told me that his biggest care in the world was this parrotfish costume. Mine was keeping it that way.

The kitchen table was an ocean of felt, sequins, and supplies, a colorful chaos that was giving me hives. The faintly sweet scent of glue mixed with the last trace of baked chicken from dinner, settling into a weird, not-quite-appetizing aroma that reminded me of how uncreative I was. It was Finn's night to choose our activity, and he'd picked costume making, possibly in an effort to bankrupt me in glitter.

"Do parrotfish have teeth, Mom? Like super sharp ones?"

I smiled at his crayon drawing and the determined way he moved shells into a complex arrangement only he could decode. "I think they have more of a beak."

The sequin slipped again, and I thought briefly about Eli's offer to help. But I needed to do this. A small act of control in the bedlam of managing the resort while being a single mom. The gluey frustration in my fingers was oddly comforting, a tangible reminder that I was doing something for my boy. I wanted to be the kind of mom who was good at this. Who made him feel whole and loved and like he wasn't missing anything.

I triumphantly pinned the sequin to the felt and glanced up. Finn was trying to open a jar of glitter glue with his teeth.

"Hey, no biting the supplies. You already had dinner, remember?"

He giggled. "I wasn't gonna."

His enthusiasm was contagious, even if I was hopelessly outmatched by craft supplies.

He glanced at my part of the project and frowned. "Mom, are you sure parrotfish have big scales?"

"They're huge," I said, just as the last sequin fell from the felt. I huffed in mock annoyance. "They're just really hard to catch."

"I can help you," Finn declared, handing me an already sticky piece of blue fabric.

I took it from him, brushing a stray curl from his forehead with the back of my hand. "I know you can, sweetheart."

As we settled into the project, my thoughts wandered to the pile of invoices waiting on my desk at work and the email from the window contractor explaining the delays in the new bungalows. My head ached at the memory of my day, and I focused again on gluing a row of shimmery sequins, willing myself to enjoy this pocket of time with Finn.

Chase flashed through my mind, that disconcerting combination of competence and pure masculine appeal. His calm certainty as he walked me through the pool reno plans, the brush of his arm against mine as we huddled over the wood sample for the cabana frame. His quiet intensity as he smiled at me in that way he had, like I was more than the sum of my obligations. It had been so long since I'd felt that pooling heat in the belly, that delicious shiver over the skin, that I was surprised I was still capable of it.

Though we certainly weren't without our frictions. We'd butted heads multiple times over designs, materials, and schedules, over my desire for practical and budget-friendly warring with his preference for artistic and expensive. The weird thing was that the disagreements only heightened the connection between us. The interaction at the pool flitted through my head again. Was I imagining that moment between us? That frisson of heat, flaming hot out of nothing?

"What's next?" Finn's bright and eager voice pulled me back, and I smiled at him.

"We've got a way to go with this. What do you think?"

He pondered for a moment, lips pursed in a comically thoughtful expression. "The rainbow tail!"

I reached for the rainbow shimmer fabric. "That sounds perfect."

We worked together, a slow rhythm of cutting and

gluing and adjusting. I let Finn's delight guide me, and the rest of my worries faded like the soft, gluey light that filled the kitchen.

Finn gave the instructions, moving sequins around the fabric. "Right there, Mom! No, a little more. Right—no—yes! Right there!" He bounced with each word, nearly falling off his chair. I grinned at him, and the warmth of his enthusiasm melted the icy edges of my stress.

"How's that?" I exhaled, letting the layers of anxiety slip off my shoulders. Even if I was underqualified and overwhelmed and unable to stop everything from sliding into disarray, Finn's confidence in me was all that mattered.

"Are you going to sew on the big scales?" he asked, pointing at the package of needles I bought in a futile moment of ambition.

"Think I'm going to cheat and use more glue." I laughed as I reached for the adhesive. "How about this one? Extra strength. It's a mom's best friend."

"You're my best friend." He smiled, and my heart squeezed at the absolute, uncomplicated way he loved me.

"We're a great team. No doubt about it. No parrotfish can stand against us."

A line of sequins slipped out of place, and I nearly knocked the whole damn thing to the floor in my eagerness to fix it. Finn just laughed, the sound like little bells.

"I meant to do that." I carefully lined up the blue scale.

"Sure you did, Mom."

We sat in comfortable silence for a few minutes, a soft calm settling between us. I thought of the day Finn was born, how tiny and fragile and impossibly perfect he was. I promised myself I would never let him feel abandoned, that he'd never doubt how much I loved him. I'd made that mistake with his father, and I couldn't bear the thought of it happening to Finn.

The resort, the costume, all of it seemed like proof. Proof I could do this.

I worked on the last few scales, trying to keep my growing frustrations in check. Even if it was lopsided and covered in glue, the parrotfish costume was *ours*. And if I handed the mess over to one of our housekeepers and expert seamstresses for reinforcement, that was just suitable managerial delegation, right?

Finn scooted closer to inspect it, his breath hot on my neck. "Can I put on the head?"

"Sure thing." I helped him into the silly cap I picked up at the costume store, his smile filling the room.

He scrambled back, doing a dramatic spin. "Ta-daaaaa!"

I held up the tunic, the garish rainbow and sticky scales somehow looking more right than anything I'd ever made.

"I'm going to be the best parrotfish EVER!" Finn shouted and crashed into me with a hug.

I laughed, letting the sound chase away the rest of my anxiety. This was what mattered. This was the one thing that wouldn't fall apart, that I wouldn't fail at.

The costume wasn't perfect, but this moment was close enough.

THE NEXT MORNING, the sounds of hammering and drilling filled the air around the resort's two-story Room Block One. All our guests were installed in the still unrenovated, seafoam green Room Block Two across the pool deck, safely out of the demo zone, though not necessarily the noise. The simple room block had proved one of the first battles Chase and I had negotiated. He wanted to do a grand total reno and remodel, where I favored a staged, one-floor-at-a-time approach. My idea would be less expensive and his would be safer.

In other words, our interaction on this issue encompassed our dynamic completely.

In the end, I won that particular battle, and we were proceeding with demolishing the second floor while the first waited below. And I just kept my proverbial fingers crossed that no major issues would show up on the ground floor. Otherwise, our timeline might get hosed.

I picked my way through the dust and debris of a guest room that currently looked nearly as skeletal as one of our beach bungalows, a familiar tightness settling in my chest. The pressure was back with a vengeance, and I hugged my clipboard like a lifeline.

As I approached, Chase's voice cut through the noise like a thread of sanity. I ignored the skip of my heart and the annoyance that followed it, quickening my pace toward him and the foreman.

"Harper, over here!" The foreman in charge of the room block remodel, Joe, waved me over to where he and Chase were already standing in the bathroom. Impatience radiated from the architect. The tangled mess of pipes around them looked about as promising as the growing acid in my stomach. Joe had sent me a text asking me to come over ASAP, but it looked like I was the last one to arrive at the party.

"Okay, here I am. What's up?"

Joe pointed with his chin at the bare studs behind the shower, the corners of his mouth pulled down in a scowl that came with news he knew I wouldn't want to hear. "I'm not gonna sugarcoat it. The copper's worse than we thought. All the corrosion's a real mess."

A mess. That was putting it kindly. The wall behind him was opened up to reveal a labyrinth that even I could recognize as corroded pipes. Everything I didn't want to deal with was literally staring me in the face.

"Can you fix it?" I asked, already knowing the answer would involve more money, more time, more of everything we couldn't afford.

"Depends on how you want us to go at it." Joe shot a glance at Chase, and I had to work to keep my face neutral. Was he in on this with Joe already? "Option A— we replace the worst sections and patch the rest. Quickest way to keep the project going. Minimal disruption. Block Two won't feel a thing."

The noise and disruption complaints from Block Two had already piled up in my inbox. The last thing we needed was another issue with guests. "And Option B?"

"Full pipe replacement for the entire section," Chase said in his deep voice. "Costs more, takes longer, but we won't have to worry about this happening again."

I could feel his eyes on me, but I kept my focus on Joe, the weight of indecision pressing down on me. "What kind of delay are we talking about?"

"At least a week, maybe two," the foreman answered.

"Weeks!" I echoed, unable to mask my frustration. Every delay added another complication, another layer of pressure. I needed time we didn't have and money we couldn't spare. "And the cost?"

"More than patching it, less than doing it twice." Chase's steady voice cut in before Joe could respond. I met his gaze, and the quiet intensity in his eyes made my heart trip.

"This is going to put us even further behind, Chase." My voice rose to match the tension. "The pool, the bungalows… We're already stretched so thin."

He unfolded a tablet, the screen lighting up with a diagram of the pipes. "This is the only way to do it right, Harper." His tone was maddeningly certain, and he moved closer to show me the details. "Patching is a temporary fix. It will fail eventually."

"So will our bank account if we keep sinking money into delays." I tried not to notice his strong, sexy hands once more. But my own certainty was unraveling, his logic chipping away at it. I wanted to be reasonable, but I also needed to keep the resort afloat, keep the chaos manageable. "We have guests right there." I stabbed a finger toward Block Two. "Wouldn't replacing everything involve shutting down the water to both blocks?"

Chase nodded. "Yes. But only for a day." He had a way of becoming even more focused when things blew up around him, of almost disappearing into the disaster of the moment.

I squared up to him. "Oh, great! It's not just the cost. I'm already drowning in complaints. Without the water being shut off!"

Joe cleared his throat loudly and slunk out to the main bedroom, clearly eager to let us duke it out on our own. The tension between Chase and me was as thick as the dust that surrounded us.

"We have to think long-term," Chase insisted, holding out the tablet like a judge's gavel. "Patches are just a way of throwing good money after bad. It only prioritizes short-term convenience over the full investment." The last word hit like a well-aimed punch, reminding me of his stake in all this. The partnership I couldn't quite believe was real.

My frustration boiled over. "Investment? Are you accusing me of being careless?"

He ran a hand through his neat hair, leaving a trail of

grit. That alone told me how upset he was. "I'm saying you need to look at the bigger picture. You're risking the integrity of the entire renovation to save a few bucks."

"I'm risking—" My hot, angry burst echoed over the noise as I stepped closer. "We're tackling too much at once! The new beach bungalows, the room remodels, and the pool reno. And you're expecting me to just go along with your plans without any regard for the day-to-day reality I'm dealing with."

His eyes flashed with a mix of frustration and something deeper, something that mirrored the uncertainty in my own heart. "It's not my plans I'm worried about. It's yours. You're too afraid to commit to this."

The suggestion of fear behind my decisions, of hesitance to embrace the changes, was infuriating. "That's not fair." My words came out as a growl. "You think this is easy for me? That I'm not drowning in all of this? We need to patch the goddamn pipes, not replace them."

Chase took a breath, his jaw tense. "I already gave in once, Harper. With the cabanas? I agreed to go with your suggestion on the wood framing to save money. All I'm asking is for you to give me the same consideration here."

"It's not the same at all!" I exploded. "This affects everything! The budget, the schedule, our guests…" My words came out in a rush, fueled by the heat of feeling cornered and unheard.

"Exactly!" Chase's frustration matched mine, his eyes fierce and unyielding. "It's not just about saving money now. It's about making sure everything doesn't fall apart in six months."

"Six months?" I threw my hands up, disbelief and anger swirling together. "We'll be bankrupt in six months if we keep going like this."

"Or we'll be thriving," he countered, his determination

cutting through all my defenses. "If you trust me enough to do this right."

Trust. The word hung between us like a challenge, daring me to cross a line I wasn't sure how to navigate. Trust had always been my issue. My heart pounded with the weight of it all—his expectations, my fears, everything that felt impossible to reconcile. The worst part was how much I wanted to believe him, how much I craved the certainty in his voice.

I stared at him, my frustration mingling with a magnetic pull I couldn't ignore. His broad shoulders and strong hands, the way he stood so sure of himself, made me want to scream and melt at the same time. Why did he have to be so infuriatingly right? So impossible to resist?

The personal tension between us simmered beneath the professional disagreement, threatening to spill over in a way I wasn't ready for. Hell, neither of us was. The set of his jaw declared the hurt behind his own anger, and it only fueled my need to prove him wrong.

We glared at each other over the chasm of copper and conflicting priorities. Neither of us willing to bend, to admit defeat. The dust and noise felt like nothing compared to the tumult between us, and both of us were too damn stubborn to back down.

Chase snapped his tablet shut with a finality that sent a shiver through me. "You know what? Do what you want. But don't say I didn't warn you."

He turned sharply, leaving me with my growing resentment and a sense of something fragile crumbling between us. I watched him go, a ridiculous urge to cry overwhelming me. The weight of everything bore down on me, and I struggled to keep my head above the rising tide. I stalked off in the opposite direction. The air was thick with unresolved tension and the debris of all we weren't saying.

Chapter Four

HARPER

MY CAR'S engine rumbled as I stared at the familiar, beautiful house and braced myself for another argument. It was past 9:00 p.m., but I knew Chase would be in his home office, surrounded by blueprints and sketchbooks and enough architectural ambition to keep him awake long past midnight. The plumbing issue had been a festering wound all day, and I wouldn't sleep until we ripped off the bandage and bled it dry. Finn already had a sleepover at Mom's for tonight, so I had nothing preventing me from coming over. And I didn't want to call or text about this. I rehearsed my compromise one last time as I walked to the front door and rang the bell. He answered quickly.

"Harper? D-didn't expect to see you," he stammered, surprise etched across his face. He leaned uneasily against the doorframe, barefoot and undeniably sexy in jeans and a navy T-shirt. I tried not to notice that.

"I know, but this is important, Chase." I crossed my arms, not letting him distract me. "So I came over to see you in person. We need to talk about the Block One plumbing realistically."

Shifting his broad frame, he led me inside. "Funny, I thought that's what we were doing all day."

I ignored him, my steps echoing against the immaculate wood floors. I'd been in his house before with Eli, but now I saw it with new eyes. The living room was precisely what I'd expect from a talented architect. Lovingly restored, beautiful floors. Modern furniture that screamed understated elegance yet also looked inviting. My irritation with him mixed with the stupid warmth that grew hotter every time I looked at his beautiful, chiseled face, creating an emotional Molotov cocktail I was afraid could explode at any moment.

So why did I come over here in person instead of calling?

I couldn't remember now.

He motioned to the open door of his office. "Let's go in here. I've been working tonight."

"I should have brought my battle armor," I muttered.

"Yeah, well," he called back, meeting my eyes, "I left my white flag at the studio."

I followed him into his office and took a long inhale. This had to stay professional.

The room smelled like paper, ink, and Chase. Clean. Precise. And just messy enough to show he'd been working hard. Blueprints of the resort renovations covered his wide mahogany desk. His hair was mussed, his jawline stubbled, and if I weren't already annoyed with him, the whole thing would have been disgustingly attractive. It still was, and that was part of the problem.

"We need to fix this before it throws the entire schedule off." I planted myself by his desk, standing like I might refuse to leave.

"Fixing it is the whole idea." He joined me, leaning on

the desk with infuriating casualness and keeping his voice even. "Replacing the pipes now saves headaches down the line."

I shook my head. "Chase, the budget's already tight, and ripping everything out means we'd have to close the entire block. It's too disruptive."

"It's disruptive for a week, Harper, not for the rest of the season." His voice was as cool as the room, his eyes never leaving mine. "And the water will be off for less than a day. Patch jobs won't last. You're sacrificing the long-term health of the resort."

"Or maybe I'm prioritizing our guests' comfort and payroll!" I snapped.

He crossed his arms, which highlighted his muscles. Damn him. "This isn't about saving a few dollars today. It's about preventing a catastrophe tomorrow. Do you fully understand the risks here?"

The words stung, and I glared at him. "You think I don't understand? Easy for you to say from your ivory tower! I'm the one dealing with complaints and staff, not sitting pretty in a design studio!"

"Really?" His brows shot up. "Because from where I'm standing, you're doing a pretty good job running the show."

I ignored his compliment. "Maybe because I have to fight for every inch! We're going way over budget."

"And I've been fronting the money for the overruns, if you recall." His icy, precise tone grated on my nerves. So did the fact that he was taking a lot of the financial risks.

"Yes, sir." I snarled. "You have the money. You make the decisions."

He stood up and stared daggers down at me. "That's not what I meant at all."

"There's got to be some sort of compromise besides

ripping out all that copper. It got replaced only a decade ago!"

"And the contractor did a shitty job on that section. I'm sorry, but this *is* the compromise. Otherwise, I'd suggest replacing all of it, Harper. The whole building. This isn't just a disagreement. It's a fundamental issue with the project, and I thought we were on the same page about these things."

"You're so inflexible," I shouted back, stabbing my finger in his chest. "You're designing for an architectural magazine, not a real-world resort!"

"I'm trying to make sure you—we—still have a resort ten years from now," he growled through gritted teeth, the volume of his voice rising.

My anger erupted, fueled by exhaustion, attraction, and the rising fear that he was right. I stepped right up to him, refusing to back down. "Maybe you don't trust me to handle this!"

He stared at me, his hazel eyes flashing. "Maybe you're trying to control everything because you can't stand not knowing the outcome!"

His words hung in the air like the Florida humidity, thick and unavoidable. He was so close I could feel the heat from his body, his clean scent invading my senses, my anger mixing with something else entirely. The whole thing was overwhelming, the air crackling.

The expression on his face was determined, intense, and I couldn't tell if I wanted to kiss it or slap it.

Both.

I wanted both.

And then, suddenly, I couldn't tell which was which because his mouth was on mine.

He'd moved so fast I hardly saw him coming. And all that frustration, simmering attraction, and boiling tension between us ignited. My head spun from the force of his mouth. Our kiss wasn't gentle—it was a collision. Tongues clashed, hands gripped, clothes were wrenched aside. There was no air, no pause. Just weeks and months of wanting unleashed all at once. His lips were firm, insistent, angry. The taste of him was everything I'd been trying to fight. Buttons and boundaries blurred. My tank top ripped as he tugged it over my head.

I gasped against his mouth, his hands on my bare skin at last. "Yes! Don't stop."

I fumbled with the button on his jeans, then yanked his shirt up over his head. He backed me against the desk, the wood cool against my thighs as I pulled him closer, both of us frantic, all logic and restraint gone. My bra came next, the straps snapping, sliding down my arms. It joined his shirt somewhere on the floor.

"Harper," he breathed, hoarse and rough. His mouth moved from my lips to my throat, his hands roaming over me, pulling, gripping, squeezing, like he was making sure I was real. His touch burned through me, frantic and impossibly intense.

My mind reeled as I remembered who I was, who he was, who I thought I was supposed to be. He wrenched the jeans from my legs, and it all spun away again, the hard reality of my life evaporating like steam against his skin. Chase was here. And I wanted this. More than anything.

He lifted me and set me on the desk, leaving me bare to him, not an inch of clothing left. I should have been embarrassed. I should have been anything but what I was —desperate, gasping, clawing at his pants. But he was relentless, hungry, catching my mouth in his again, stifling the tiny cry that slipped out of me as I got his jeans and underwear off his hips. They slid in a heap to the floor, and he kicked them aside.

As his body came into full breathtaking view, my breath caught, and my hands slowed. Jesus. Hard and ready, he was… huge. I hesitated, thrown back into my own head, caught between wild anticipation and fear. He must have seen it in my eyes, in the way my body stiffened under his hands. He paused, his breath ragged, his gaze searching mine with sudden concern.

"Hey," he murmured, brushing hair back from my face. "You okay?"

I swallowed hard. "I haven't been with anyone since… since Finn's father." My voice sounded strange in my own ears, shaky and unsure, and the laugh I barked was even worse. "I'm not sure I even remember how."

He stilled above me, then let out an almost relieved laugh. His eyes softened with something more than just heat before he pressed a gentle kiss across my jaw. "You don't need to worry about that. We'll figure it out together."

And then he showed me just how much he meant it. His hands were slow now, tender as they moved over my skin with reverence and care. He whispered my name like a promise against my neck, trailing kisses down my throat until I melted beneath him. My earlier panic faded into something else entirely.

He stroked the hair back from my face, his touch gentle as if he was calming a startled animal. Then he smoothed his palms down my arms, pausing, offering me a way out. "Better now?"

The smart thing would be to stop. To walk away. To remember all the reasons why this was a disaster waiting to happen.

But the smart thing had nothing to do with what I wanted.

And God, I wanted this. I wanted him.

"Yes."

"You're so beautiful." He ran his lips over my collarbone, his breath sending a hot shiver through me. He went on, the words almost too quiet to hear, the sound of my name mingling with sweet, unexpected things that melted me from the inside.

Any last thread of reluctance dissolved. I nodded, a silent plea for him not to stop, never to stop. He smiled against my neck, the feel of it turning my knees to water.

I moaned as his mouth traveled down my chest, as his hands explored me with more care and patience than I'd known in years. Maybe ever. Reverence and hunger mingled in every touch, in every kiss, drawing out every forgotten piece of myself. My body responded to him in ways I thought I'd locked away. In ways I thought I didn't deserve to feel again.

Chase's mouth found my breast, and I gasped, arching into him. His tongue was a slow tease, circling, tasting, sending sparks through every nerve. He took me deeper, sucking hard, his hand kneading the other with a perfect rhythm that made my head spin.

It was too much. Not enough. My fingers gripped his silky hair, holding him there as everything but the feel of him faded away. The way he touched me was so focused, so intent on making sure I knew how much he wanted me.

My heart raced as he switched sides, his mouth relentless, pulling me back from the edge of my own hesitation. Each tug and stroke shot straight to my core, lighting up every inch of skin. I felt wild under his hands, every breath a plea for more.

I'd never been so aroused in my life.

The fear of what this might mean vanished, replaced by an urgent, throbbing need for more of him. He groaned, trailing kisses over my abdomen, letting his mouth and hands rediscover parts of me I'd abandoned to motherhood, work, and responsibility.

"God, Harper. You have no idea how long I've wanted to do this."

That shocked me for a moment, but soon I was lost in the sensation again. He found sensitive spots, lingering with fingers and lips until I gasped. His grip on me shifted, intense but careful, knowing, building heat upon heat.

"Oh, Chase," I whispered, my voice unsteady, begging for what only he could give me, wanting him more than I'd ever wanted anything. "I want you so much."

He kneeled as I lay on the desk and parted my legs with his hands, not to surrender but to claim and consume and make me his. A soft whimper tore from my lips as his mouth found me, unrelenting, devouring, leaving no inch unexplored. It was a reverent act and a wild one, a true meeting of need. His tongue was agile, unyielding, teasing in relentless circles, flicks, and strokes that left me gasping, making me forget who I was. Making me remember what I needed. His fingers joined in, working a magic so intense, so overwhelming, I could hardly breathe, every movement bringing soaring tension to a new peak. The world narrowed to nothing but the feel of him between my thighs, a rising, aching pleasure that should have been unbearable but wasn't because he made it bliss.

Too much. Too good. Too long since I'd craved anything the way I craved him right now.

He groaned, the sound indescribably intimate, then increased his pressure, his pace. He coaxed and teased with his lips, his tongue, his clever, skillful hands, until I was half-mad with wanting.

I shuddered and my hands flew to his shoulders, my voice ragged and desperate as I clung to him, as he held me on the razor's edge of ecstasy. "Chase—oh God, Chase!"

His hands held me steady as I shattered against his mouth, my body arching wildly, his name on my lips. It had been so long, and the feeling was so overwhelming, I cried out, shocked and blissful, unable to hold anything back. He didn't let up, sending me flying until I nearly sobbed with the intensity of it, the years of self-denial coming undone all at once.

He kissed his way back up my body as I came down from the high, as my breath returned in shallow, shuddering gasps. My heart pounded in my chest, and I felt him against me, hard and ready, and knew I needed him again. I swept a file folder onto the floor and barely saw the papers flutter out.

"Please," I said, the word urgent and pleading. He rose above me, his eyes dark with desire. "I need you."

In one smooth motion, he grabbed his wallet from the pocket of his jeans. The condom was in his hand in an instant, and he rolled it on with a speed that made me ache for him even more. I stared at the long, thick length of him poised above me, and all I wanted was for him to fill me. To feel him inside me. No more fear.

He moved between my legs, watching my face for any sign of hesitation. There was none. There was only need.

My breath hitched as he entered me slowly, inch by inch, his size almost too much. Almost. I gasped at the impossible fullness, the rightness of it, stretching and surrounding him. He kissed me slowly, letting me feel everything, letting me adjust to the newness of him, and then he moved.

We found a rhythm that was more than anything I could have prepared for. More than I'd imagined when I lay awake at night, trying to banish the thought of this from my mind. I clung to him, all control gone, his name leaving my lips again and again as he thrust into me, demanding everything, giving everything.

He slid his hands under my ass, knocking a set of blueprints off the desk. I wrapped my legs around him, and he filled me so completely I could only moan in response, meeting his movements and surrendering to the mindless frenzy of it. There was only us, and I couldn't stop, amazed at how perfectly we fit together. He drove into me hard, almost too fast, knowing exactly what I wanted, knowing what I needed, his voice hoarse in my ear, telling me not to hold back, not to be afraid, to take this, take all of it, all of him.

I lost track of everything, every sense overwhelmed as I reached another dizzying high, the pressure inside building once again, coiling, snapping loose. This climax was powerful, electric. I bucked wildly against him, gasping his name, releasing everything at once.

He gripped me fiercely, chasing me to the peak, lost in the sensation of us. We flew together, and I felt him let go, a long, broken moan that was all I'd wanted to hear. He followed me over the edge, and the pleasure was blinding. We crashed down together, all the tension gone, and he collapsed on top of me, his breath hot against my neck.

We lay tangled in the aftermath, surrounded by the mess we'd made, panting and sweat-slicked. The air was thick with the scent of sex, with the reality of what we'd done.

Chase lifted his head, smoothing my hair back, his expression unreadable. His eyes searched mine, dark and intense, and he whispered two words, "Stay tonight."

My heart slammed against my ribs. Finn was safe with Mom. Tomorrow, this would change everything. But tonight…

I nodded.

His body relaxed against mine, and he smiled. "I'm glad we talked this through."

My returning smile lit me from within. "Oh, I don't think we're done with the conversation just yet. Maybe we should talk more in your bedroom."

Chapter Five

CHASE

I WOKE to sunlight streaming across familiar yet unfamiliar territory—my own bedroom but somehow altered. The sheets clung to my legs, the pillow next to mine bearing the gentle indent of another head. I took a deep breath with closed eyes. Harper's scent lingered in the fabric, a mix of coconut shampoo and something distinctly her, making my chest tighten with the memory of her body against mine. For a moment, I lay still as if any movement might disrupt the delicate evidence that last night had actually happened.

Then reality crashed over me like a rogue wave. Harper Coleridge had been in my bed.

Was no longer in my bed.

I bolted upright, scanning the room. Her clothes from last night weren't scattered across my polished floor anymore. The bedroom door stood ajar, letting in the faint aroma of… coffee?

Jesus. This was real.

I rubbed a hand over my stubble, memories flooding back with startling clarity. Harper's unexpected visit to discuss the latest resort renovation plans. The way our attempt to resolve the argument had somehow veered into personal territory. And then…

My stomach dropped as the full implications hit me. I'd slept with my business partner. Not to mention my best friend's sister.

I'd broken the cardinal rule of my thirty-odd-year friendship with Eli, the half-joking, completely serious pact we'd made in high school that his sisters were permanently off-limits. But here I was, in the aftermath of making Harper Coleridge very much on-limits. Part of me wanted to believe that Eli would understand. He'd grown a lot over the past year and found his own love. But another part had to wonder if that would only make him more protective than ever. Crossing my oldest friend felt like standing on a trapdoor, wondering not if, but when the ground would drop out from under me.

Then there was Harper. Even if Eli didn't kill me, there was no escaping the fallout at work. I'd crossed every professional boundary imaginable with the general manager of my biggest project.

And God help me, I couldn't bring myself to regret a single second of it. After we stumbled up here, our second time had been almost a reverse of the first. Slow, tender, explorative touches and kisses built into frantic, explosive, gasping surrender. Both times had been all-encompassing.

I pressed the heels of my hands against my eyes. What the hell was I thinking? I wasn't. That was the problem.

"You're overthinking this already, aren't you?" Harper had whispered against my shoulder sometime in the dark hours, her voice knowing and warm against my skin. "Stop it and just relax for now."

I'd been transparent even then. She saw right through me.

Forcing myself out of bed, I felt oddly vulnerable in my own space. The polished surfaces and strategically chosen furniture stared back accusingly. This house, with its flawless organization and deliberate aesthetic, had been my refuge—a controlled environment where everything had its place. No messy emotions, no uncertainty. But now Harper had been here and changed the very air, leaving invisible fingerprints on everything.

I pulled on a pair of jeans and a gray T-shirt, conscious of choosing something casual, as if dressing for work might somehow make this morning after more awkward than it already promised to be. The bed remained unmade behind me, a rumpled reminder I couldn't bring myself to erase yet.

My feet carried me down the hallway toward the kitchen, but I paused at my home office doorway. More evidence of last night's transformation—blueprints for the Sunset Siesta renovation spread haphazardly across my usually pristine desk, a guest room render on the floor and weighed down by Harper's sandals. The sight sent another jolt of memory through me, of her kicking them off in a frenzy. More papers were strewn across the floor along with my shirt.

After inhaling a huge, long breath, I continued toward the kitchen where the coffee scent grew stronger.

Harper stood with her back to me, dressed in last night's clothes but barefoot, her chestnut hair pulled into a messy knot at the nape of her neck. She was frowning at my thrumming espresso machine like it was a puzzle she was determined to solve. The morning light through the kitchen windows caught the highlights in her hair, the curve of her cheek.

For a second, I watched her, this woman who had somehow wholly untied me. She looked beautiful in a way that made my heart stop and start all at once. Hair unkempt, no makeup, just Harper. A gorgeous woman not trying, or needing, to be anything else.

She must have sensed my presence because she stiffened slightly before turning around, coffee mug clutched in her hands like a shield.

"Hey," she said, her voice tight with forced casualness.

"Morning," I replied, aiming for normal and missing by a mile. "I see you figured out the espresso machine."

She glanced down at the mug as if surprised to find it there. "Sort of. It made some threatening noises at me but eventually surrendered. Hope you don't mind."

"Of course not." I moved into the kitchen, hyperaware of the careful distance she maintained between us. The air felt charged with all the things we weren't saying. "I, uh, saw your shoes in my office."

She blushed. "Right. I should grab those." She turned back to the espresso machine. "Do you want one too? Since I've already conquered this unnecessarily complicated beast." She seemed relieved to have something to do with her hands, something to focus on besides me or the elephant-sized awkwardness filling my kitchen.

"That'd be great." I leaned against the counter at what felt like a safe distance.

Harper nodded and grabbed another mug from the open shelf. Her movements were methodical as she positioned it under the spout, her brow furrowing in concentration. A mechanical hum filled the kitchen, a welcome buffer. We stood in painful silence, the machine rumbling softly in the background like it was mocking our discomfort. Eventually, she turned around and handed me the mug. The rich scent rose in the air but didn't cut the tension.

"Harper—" I started.

"Chase—" she said simultaneously.

We both stopped. I gestured for her to go ahead.

She took a deep breath. "We probably need to talk about last night."

"That's what I was going to say." I spun the mug around, needing something to do with my hands. "Listen, about what happened—"

"It was unexpected," she cut in gently but firmly as her brown eyes finally met mine. "And complicated. Incredibly complicated. You're partnering with my family on a major renovation. Your best friend is my brother, who, like my other brothers, doesn't like to admit I'm a fully grown woman. And most importantly…" She paused. "There's Finn to consider. I have to think about what any relationship would mean for him."

The word *relationship* hung in the air between us. I hadn't even gotten as far as labeling what this might be. "I understand," I said, though I wasn't sure I did. The depth of her concerns made me wonder if she was looking for an easy exit. "But before we go any further down the 'all the reasons this is a bad idea' road, I need to tell you something."

She tilted her head to one side, waiting.

"I don't regret a single moment of last night. I-I've wanted to be with you for years." The words tumbled out with none of my usual precision. I forged on before I could lose my nerve. "Since college. You probably don't even remember—you were dating someone, I think—but you argued with me about sustainable architecture being soulless, and I'd never met anyone who challenged me like that. I was blown away, and at that moment you stopped being

Eli's sister and became a separate woman. A very attractive woman."

Her eyes widened, lips parting in surprise. "What?"

"I never said anything because of Eli's ridiculous *hands off my sisters* rule," I continued, rubbing my neck. "And honestly, I figured you wouldn't be interested in someone like me. You've always been…" I gestured vaguely, searching for words. "You're Harper. Everyone loves you. You hold that whole place together. I'm just a guy who draws buildings and overthinks everything."

"Are you serious?" Harper set her mug down with a definitive click. "You actually thought I would turn you down? Chase, you're—" She scanned me from head to toe, her expression incredulous. "Look at you. You're successful, talented, kind. Not to mention fall-down-and-faint gorgeous. Half the women in Dove Key would kill to be standing in my place right now."

Heat crept up my neck. "That's… not been my experience."

"Then you haven't been paying attention." Her voice had softened, but she quickly shook her head as if clearing it. "But that's beside the point. The timing couldn't be worse. You're working with my family. The resort project is getting more complicated by the day. We've already shown this is a pretty stressful time."

"I know." I wanted to add a super-sized, gigantic *but*. Instead, I kept silent, my tongue tied up.

"And there's Finn," she continued. "He's already so attached to you. If we started something and it didn't work out…"

I nodded, sagging under the weight of her words. "I get it. The professional complications alone are enough to make this a terrible idea. I've built my career on being reliable, ethical. Getting involved with a client goes against everything I've stood for." I set my coffee mug on the counter and sloshed some over the side. "Except we already crossed that line, didn't we?"

A small, shaky smile lifted the corner of her mouth. "Yeah. We sure did."

I smiled back, helpless to resist. "I need you to know that what happened last night wasn't typical for me, either. The, uh, jumping into bed part."

Finally, her smile steadied. "Well, like you said last night. We figured it out." Her eyes flicked to the clock on my kitchen wall, and resolution washed over her features. "I need to get back to Finn. He had a sleepover at Grandma's, but I told her I'd pick him up by eight."

My heart sank, but I nodded. What had I expected? That we'd solve this over coffee?

"I think…" She paused, choosing her words with care. "I think we both need some time to figure out what this means. Where we go from here. If we go anywhere from here."

Her voice was steady, but fear lurked in her eyes, the same uncertainty that clawed at my insides. She turned to leave, and panic surged through me. I couldn't let her walk out without knowing one thing.

"Harper, wait." My voice sounded rough even to my own ears. "Do you regret it? Last night?"

She paused, hand on the kitchen doorframe. When she turned back, her eyes searched mine with a look that made my breath catch. She shook her head. "No. I don't regret it at all. And I'm glad you said you didn't either."

I didn't hesitate. "It was the best night of my life."

Another small smile, this one reaching her eyes. "I thought it was incredible too. I'll get my shoes. And then I really have to go."

I nodded, then she disappeared down the hallway.

Soon after, the front door closed with a quiet click, and I was alone. The scent of her perfume lingered in the air. The memory of her taste haunted my lips.

I leaned against the counter, staring at the empty space where she'd stood. Desire and dread battled for dominance in my chest. I wanted her, had wanted her for years, but the potential fallout loomed like a storm on the horizon. My business, my friendship with Eli, her family's trust, Finn's well-being… all hanging in the balance.

One night had rewritten the plan, and I wasn't sure I knew how to read the new design.

Chapter Six

HARPER

THE ROAR of a circular saw ripping through plywood was the soundtrack to my mounting anxiety. I stepped over a tangle of electrical conduit snaking across the floor of Room 1208, my shoes kicking up clouds of fine gray dust that coated my capris and settled grittily on my skin. Bare studs framed the space where luxurious guest rooms would eventually stand, but right now, Room Block One felt less like progress and more like a battlefield casualty. Sunlight streamed through the empty window frames, illuminating the chaotic dance of airborne debris. It was organized chaos, theoretically, but the sheer scale of the simultaneous renovations—this block, the new bungalows, the pool complex—felt overwhelming today.

Because boy, had things changed.

I hugged my project clipboard, the hard edges digging into my ribs. Plumbing. That was the mission. Settle the damn copper pipe issue with Chase because we hadn't exactly gotten around to it the other night.

And there he was. Standing near the gutted bathroom entryway and appearing utterly composed while deep in conversation with Joe, the foreman. He gestured toward the exposed pipes, his movements precise, his voice calm but carrying authority even over the din.

My stomach did a complicated flip, a mix of lingering desire, residual frustration from our unresolved argument two days ago, and the sheer awkwardness of facing him after… well, *after*. The memory of our night at his house was a persistent heat beneath my skin, a secret that felt too big to contain. We hadn't really spoken since that clumsy morning-after coffee. He'd been at his office all day yesterday, while I had done all my usual juggling here.

Seeing him now, so focused and *normal*, made the intensity of our encounter almost surreal. Had that really been me, losing all control on his desk? Had it been him, his usual reserve shattering into raw passion? Because that night had been unlike anything I had ever experienced.

I took a steadying breath to remind myself of the stakes. This wasn't just about navigating awkward personal territory. It was about the resort, the budget, the schedule. I needed to be General Manager Harper Coleridge right now, not… whoever that wild, reckless woman at his house had been.

As I approached, his hazel eyes lifted and met mine. For a heartbeat, the professional mask slipped on his end too. Awareness flickered there, a spark of shared memory, before it was quickly shuttered behind his usual calm focus. But that brief moment was enough to send warmth flooding my cheeks, reminding me just how exposed I felt. Joe nodded to me as he headed toward the other side of the room, leaving me alone with Chase.

"Morning," Chase said, his voice even, betraying none

of the turmoil that was roiling inside me. His gaze held mine for a fraction longer than necessary.

"Hello," I replied, matching his professional tone, though my heart hammered against my ribs. I gestured toward the tangled mess of pipes revealed in the opened wall and dove in. "Seems we got, uh, sidetracked the other night before we actually solved anything."

A ghost of a smile touched Chase's lips, a shared acknowledgment of the colossal understatement. "Sidetracked is one word for it. My desk may never forgive us."

I couldn't help the small laugh that escaped me, tension easing a touch at his willingness to admit the absurdity. "Yeah, not the expected thing, for sure. So"—I took a breath, forcing myself back to the issue at hand—"since we failed miserably at resolving the plumbing situation then, are you ready to make a call on the copper now?"

"Lead the way." His expression turned serious again. "But I want to say that my recommendation hasn't changed. The only responsible long-term solution is replacing the affected sections."

I nodded. I'd spent hours yesterday distracting myself by agonizing over the cost estimates, the potential delays, the impact on guests in Block Two. But after seeing the extent of the corrosion again in stark sunlight, Chase was right. Patching it would be like putting a cheap bandage on a gaping wound.

"I know," I conceded. "I reviewed the revised costs again this morning. You're right. Patching it is too risky. We'll replace the affected section."

Relief flashed across Chase's face, quickly masked by professional approval. "Good. It's the right call, Harper. I know it stretches the budget—"

"But it's necessary," I finished. I met his gaze directly. "And I want to say I'm sorry about... the argument.

Before. I shouldn't have yelled or implied you weren't considering the practicalities."

His expression softened. "Hey, I wasn't super diplomatic myself." He rubbed the back of his neck in a familiar gesture that made my stomach flutter inappropriately. "I'm sorry too. Things got heated. Professional disagreements don't have to get personal."

The irony wasn't lost on me. Things between us couldn't have gotten more personal.

A wry smile touched my lips. "Right. Not personal at all."

We shared another look, a silent understanding of the monumental line we'd crossed. Then we were both laughing. It was the kind of laughter that felt like a truce. Like clearing the air and getting past the awkwardness.

Chase leaned back against a stack of drywall, the shared laughter still warming the air between us. He picked up a stray wood shaving, turning it over in his fingers, his expression shifting from amusement to something more thoughtful.

"Speaking of budgets and things not going as planned." His tone was casual but with an undercurrent I recognized as Architect Chase. "This pipe situation today…" He gestured vaguely toward the opened wall. "It's a good reminder that Room Block One might be hoarding a few more surprises for us."

I sobered a little, but the earlier ease lingered. "Let's hope not. After these pipes, I was hoping we'd caught the worst of it for a while."

He gave a short, wry laugh. "Remember our big debate about phasing the renovation in there? Doing the top floor first, leaving the ground floor to spread the cost?"

I remembered it well. "Vaguely." A smile played on my lips. "Something about me being a budget-minded pragmatist and you being a purist who wanted to X-ray every stud before we even ordered drywall?"

"Something like that," he conceded, a reluctant grin tugging at his own mouth. "My point is, that phased approach, while financially sensible, still makes the architect in me twitch."

I nodded, aware he had a point. "So, on a scale of *minor inconvenience* to *sell a kidney*, where are we on your professional worry-meter for that?"

Chase met my eyes, and the humor faded, replaced by a familiar, steady seriousness. "Let's just say I'm glad we're making good progress on the bungalows and the pool. Keeping the contingency fund healthy helps me sleep at night." His face took on a speculative, slightly wolfish expression that made something squirm deep inside me. Then he flashed a small, reassuring smile, the kind that recognized the risk but didn't dwell on the fear. "But there's no point in borrowing trouble. We'll handle whatever comes up."

The casual way he said *"we'll handle whatever comes up"* relaxed something in me, a quiet confidence that mirrored the easy understanding that had just bloomed between us after the pipe argument.

"We will," I stated confidently. "With you overseeing everything, how can we not?"

"So..." Chase cleared his throat, that earlier shared humor returning to his eyes along with a new, more searching intensity. "Where do we go from here?"

The question hung in the air, heavy with unspoken meaning. Was he talking about the pipes? Or us? My breath caught. "Professionally? We replace the pipes," I said carefully, focusing on the immediate task.

"What about... personally?" he pressed gently, his gaze holding mine.

I glanced around the chaotic room, at the exposed studs and dangling wires, feeling utterly exposed myself. "I don't know, Chase." The honesty felt raw, vulnerable. "Maybe we can get together later this week? Talk things through properly? Somewhere that isn't… here."

Hope flared in his eyes, bright and unmistakable. "Yeah. Okay." He sounded relieved, almost boyish. "Whenever works for you. Just let me know."

"I will," I promised, though my mind was already racing with the logistics and potential pitfalls of such a conversation.

I focused back on the plumbing disaster, needing a distraction, and my arm brushed against his. The contact was brief, accidental, but it sent an electric jolt through my system. I inhaled sharply. It was absurd how a touch could obliterate all the distance I was trying to maintain, crumbling my resolve in an instant. Did he feel it too? The air between us was thick enough to slice, filled with so much leftover tension it was difficult to breathe.

I lifted my gaze to his, where the same surprise, the same flare of heat, was reflected in his eyes. Professionalism felt like tissue paper against this magnetic force. I wanted to step away, reestablish distance, but my feet were rooted to the floor.

Every rational thought battled with a desperate urge to close the gap between us. Chase rocked slightly on his feet as if he wasn't sure whether to rebuild his cool detachment or give in to whatever was happening. This pull between us was as impossible to ignore as it had been at his house. My heart pounded in my ears, each beat a reminder that I was in dangerous territory. It was impossible not to remember the way we'd come together so fiercely, so unexpectedly, the desk digging into my back, his hands on my waist, pulling me impossibly closer.

He swallowed hard, a quick flicker of intention in his eyes, like he was about to say something important. But no words came. His gaze dropped to where we'd touched, his expression one of unguarded desire.

Had I really thought we could shove everything that had happened into a neat little drawer and forget about it? Now, standing this close, I couldn't even pretend to be unaffected. Heat pulsed in my cheeks again, mirroring the flush on Chase's face. Whatever was happening between us was dangerous, unpredictable. Like standing in a lightning storm.

"Harper…" My name sounded almost like a question. Hearing him say it sent another thrill through me. He looked as thrown off balance as I felt.

I tried to think straight, to focus on the practical. My gaze drifted over the raw edges of the drywall, anything but him. But it refused to focus, instead drawn straight back to his face. "Yes?"

Chase watched me for another long moment, his eyes searching. I tried to steady my heartbeat, but his presence was like gravity. Instead of pushing him away, I felt myself leaning toward him.

His eyes darted toward a newly drywalled closet near the bathroom entrance, a small space offering the only semblance of privacy amidst the demolition. He cleared his throat. "Need to check the framing in here real quick. Come take a look?" His words came out deeper, huskier, and sent a molten throb through my core.

Even as my logical brain screamed *No! Bad idea!*, my body overruled it. I jerked a nod, unable to trust my voice.

He stepped into the confined space, the sharp scent of raw pine filling the air. After making sure no one was looking our way, I followed with my heart threatening to burst from my chest. He reached back and pulled the temporary plastic sheeting partially across the opening, cocooning us in dim, dusty intimacy. The roar of the construction site faded to a muffled hum.

We stood inches apart. Close enough to feel the heat radiating from his body, close enough to see the slight tremor in his hand as he pretended to inspect the wall.

"Chase, what are—"

He didn't answer with words. His hand came up, calloused fingers surprisingly gentle as they cupped my cheek, his thumb brushing away a smudge of dust. His touch was electric, grounding, and unsettling all at once. I leaned into it instinctively, my eyes fluttering closed for a dizzying moment.

That was all it took.

His warm, firm mouth covered mine and silenced any further questions. This kiss wasn't fueled by anger like the first. It held a different kind of urgency. A seeking, a questioning, a desperate need to affirm that the connection we'd forged in the heat of the night wasn't an anomaly.

I responded without hesitation, my own need overriding caution. My arms wrapped around his neck, pulling him down, my body molding against his strong frame. This felt dangerous, reckless, and utterly right. His mouth was insistent, exploring mine with a confidence that tore straight through me. He parted my lips, and our tongues met in a deep, searching kiss that tasted of coffee and desperation and something undeniably right. I deepened the kiss, my hands sliding up into his silky dark hair. He felt solid, real, anchoring me even as my world tilted on its axis.

His hands slid down my back, finding the curve of my waist, pulling me flush against his hardening arousal. And I sure remembered *that*. A whimper escaped my throat, a sound of pure, unadulterated want. He shifted, pressing me gently against the rough, chalky drywall of the closet.

This is a terrible idea, a tiny voice screamed in the back of my mind. *In a construction zone. During work hours.*

But the feel of his body against mine, the intoxicating taste of his mouth, drowned out all reason. I arched against him, needing more, needing—

BZZZZT. BZZZZT.

The insistent vibration against my hip startled us both. We sprang apart as if electrocuted, breathing heavily, eyes wide and locked. His phone. Reality crashed back in, harsh and unwelcome.

I smoothed my hair. "You'd better check that."

"I…" He started, then grabbed his phone and frowned at the screen. "It's a text from Marilyn. Confirming the meeting we have shortly with a new client."

I nodded as I tried not to focus on his swollen lips. "Right. Work."

He looked down at me, his eyes still dark with lingering desire, a muscle ticking in his jaw. "Later this week, then?"

"Yes," I promised, my voice steadier this time. "We'll talk." My own professional responsibilities beckoned— invoices to approve, staff schedules to finalize, a resort to run. Anything normal. Anything that didn't make me feel like the earth itself was askew.

He gave me one last intense look, a silent promise hanging in the air, then pushed aside the plastic sheeting and stepped back into the noisy reality of the construction site.

I leaned back against the closet for a moment after he was gone, my legs shaky, my lips tingling. What in God's name had just happened? I'd come here to settle the plumbing issue, and somehow we'd nearly combusted in a dusty closet.

Taking several deep, centering breaths, I smoothed down my polo shirt, tucked stray hairs back into my ponytail, and forced myself to walk back out into the controlled chaos. Thank God none of the workers were paying any attention. Professionalism was my armor, and I needed it now more than ever. As I hurried toward the main lobby, one thought echoed in my mind.

Later this week.

Chapter Seven

CHASE

THE AFTERNOON SUN glinted into the conference room of Latitudes Design, making the white walls appear even whiter, almost like a scene from an art gallery. The screen behind me displayed the final guest suite renderings, a slick 3D walk-through that played like a Pixar short. Tom Franson studied the design as if it were his own child winning a gold medal, while his wife relaxed in her chair with a bright smile. Landing their contract was more than just a professional win. It was proof that Latitudes Design was on its way. Marilyn floated through the room, expertly corralling stray papers. A rush of satisfaction went through me, and I calculated the start date in my head. The mental exercise helped me keep from thinking about Harper. Or Eli.

"We really nailed this," I said, guiding the Fransons through the last few details. I pointed to the screen, emphasizing Tom's prized workspace. "See how it integrates without sacrificing any of the living area? A seamless transition between productivity and relaxation."

"Impressive." Tom nodded with enthusiasm. "You understood what I wanted better than I did."

Marilyn placed a final copy of the contract in front of him, her timing impeccable.

Tom leaned back and eyed me like I'd just turned water into wine. "This is exactly why we went with you, Chase. You're a man of vision and action."

Beside him, his wife glanced up, her smile warm and appreciative. "It's lovely, Mr. Ashworth. I knew it would be. You've brought it all together so beautifully."

"We've already started coordinating with the structural engineers, so permitting should progress quickly," I continued, trying not to sound too much like a salesman. "Construction will be underway soon."

A well of relief mixed with pride surged through me, a validation of every late night and second-guessed decision. The anxiety that had haunted me since the firm opened lifted just a little, like mist burned away by the morning sun.

Marilyn collected the final signed documents, her calm professionalism adding a sense of completion to the moment. "We look forward to starting this project," she said with a graceful nod. "Thank you for your trust in Latitudes Design."

The Fransons left, their footsteps echoing down the hall like the soundtrack of my success. I watched them go, enjoying the comforting weight of a job well done.

Marilyn lingered for a moment, the hint of a smile playing on her lips. "That was almost too easy. You're setting the bar high, Chase."

"Maybe next time, I'll try juggling fire," I joked,

already feeling the shift from business to personal as I watched her softly latch the door behind her.

I leaned back in my chair, alone in the sunlit conference room, and the mental dam I'd built around Harper broke free. My mind wandered back to that unexpected, intense night. Not just the argument or the furious first kiss, but the moment *after*. When I'd pushed her against the desk, ready to lose myself entirely, and she'd stiffened. When she'd seen me naked and ready. Her eyes, usually so direct and confident, had widened with a sudden flash of something I hadn't expected—vulnerability? Fear? It had jolted me, stopping me cold. It was more than concern at my size. Then she'd spoken the words, something raw and honest about how long it had been. Years. How she wasn't sure…

The admission had hit me hard. *Years*. She'd been alone, guarding herself, raising Finn, managing that resort, and I'd almost charged right past that fragile trust in my own urgency. A sharp wave of protectiveness had washed over me, followed quickly by a surge of something fiercely possessive, almost primal.

I was the first in years.

I would make this right for her.

I would be careful.

I forced myself to slow down then, gentling my touch, whispering her name, needing to erase that fear, needing her to *choose* this with me, not just be swept away by the heat of the moment. And the way she'd melted at last, the tension easing from her shoulders, her eyes meeting mine again with a dawning trust that made my own breath catch…

Goddamn.

And then seeing her completely unravel, hearing that raw, beautiful cry torn from her throat as she shattered against me... Jesus, it had been humbling. Powerful. Witnessing that release after so long was a different kind of intensity altogether, something that went beyond mere physical pleasure and took root deep in my chest, both exhilarating and terrifying.

And now, that memory—her vulnerability, her stunning release—only amplified my worry. This wasn't just sex. This was something else. Something terrifyingly real.

I pushed away from the conference table, the smooth glide of my chair on the polished floor echoing in the sudden quiet. I walked to the window, staring out at the familiar Dove Key landscape without really seeing it. Because my mind had traveled back to Room 1212 this morning.

Getting Harper to agree on replacing the copper pipes had felt like a victory, not just for the project's integrity, but for *us*. It meant she trusted my judgment, even when it complicated her budget and schedule. The relief that washed over me when she conceded had been immense.

And then, the apologies. Stilted at first, then dissolving into that shared, unexpected laughter. It had felt like breaking through a layer of ice, finding something warmer, more real underneath.

But then... the closet.

Even now, hours later, I couldn't quite believe I'd done that. What the hell had possessed me? Right there, surrounded by raw lumber and drywall dust, with hammering echoing just feet away... we'd nearly lost ourselves again. Thank God I'd gotten that text.

I ran a hand over my face before whispering, "A closet. On an active worksite. Jesus."

It defied every rule of professional conduct I'd ever adhered to. It defied basic common sense. Yet, remembering the feel of her lips, the soft gasp against my mouth, the sheer rightness of holding her… a thrill shot through me, overriding the logical panic.

This *thing* with Harper, whatever it was, wasn't going to be compartmentalized. It wasn't going to stay neatly within the lines I usually drew around my life. It was messy, complicated, and incredibly potent. All the things I tried to avoid, all the things I had no clue how to navigate.

I couldn't wait to see her again. The thought was a persistent fire, licking at the edges of my ordered life. A deviation from my precisely planned trajectory. A beautiful, terrifying deviation.

But fear clung just as fiercely. Harper was more than just a tempting unknown. She was a mother, a professional ally, a pivotal part of my world and Eli's. Her history was more complicated than the blueprints I drew up for a living. Finn's father had left her the moment he found out she was pregnant. As far as I knew, she'd never heard from him again. Which was undoubtedly for the best—any man who would do that to his woman and child didn't deserve them.

I weighed the risks, logic fighting with emotion in a tug-of-war that left me frayed and exhausted. She was everything I craved but told myself I didn't need, a thrilling challenge to my sense of control. And maybe the only person who understood the high stakes as well as I did.

The meeting with Eli tonight loomed large in my mind. A simple get-together at my place for drinks that was anything but simple. Not telling him wasn't even an option. I was an awful liar, and even withholding the truth made me horribly uncomfortable. I imagined the disappointment in his eyes, the confrontation. But I needed his perspective, his acknowledgment, maybe even his permission before this spiraled out of control.

His old warning came back to haunt me. A pact sealed

with a high school promise—his sisters were off-limits. "You break it, I break you." His words had hung somewhere between truth and humor, but his eyes had been dead serious.

I stared at the clock, my life unfolding in dizzying, exhilarating chaos.

I ARRANGED the bourbon glasses for the third time, angling them just so on the walnut side table. The evening air hung heavy with jasmine and salt, a typical Keys combination that usually soothed me. Not tonight. The string lights overhead cast soft illumination across my deck, creating the illusion of calm that contradicted the storm in my chest. Any minute now, Eli would arrive, and I'd have to tell my best friend that I'd had mind-blowing sex with his sister. Well, maybe not quite in those words. I took a deep breath and poured two fingers of bourbon into each glass, watching the amber liquid catch the light. The ice clinked against the sides like a countdown.

The restored house had been my passion project for years—a 1920s conch house with good bones and terrible updates that I'd painstakingly returned to its original charm while adding modern conveniences. The deck had been my final addition, a place to unwind after long days at the office. Usually, sitting here as the sun dipped toward the horizon brought me peace. Tonight, it felt like waiting for my own execution.

I swirled the bourbon in my glass as the sunset painted the sky in streaks of orange and pink. A gentle breeze stirred the palm fronds overhead, their soft rustle a counterpoint to the crickets starting their evening chorus.

The sound of flip-flops slapping against the concrete

path announced Eli's arrival moments before he appeared, grinning and carrying a small paper bag as he opened the solid wooden gate. He stopped just inside the gate, taking an appreciative glance around the deck and the back of the house, all illuminated by the new landscape lighting I'd installed last month.

"Place looks good as always, man," Eli said, moving toward the chairs. "So, fend off any frantic calls from magazine editors or millionaires begging you to sell it lately?"

Eli wasn't just joking. The painstaking five-year restoration of the cottage *had* won a state preservation award. It was listed on the local historic register and had been featured in *Coastal Living* and even a small spread in *Architectural Digest* after I finished the kitchen. That kind of attention inevitably brought offers, usually polite inquiries forwarded by Marilyn, but Arthur Albright, whose beachfront place on Little Torch Key I'd redesigned a couple of years back, had cornered me at a charity event last Christmas, half-joking but completely serious when he said all I needed to do was ask my price and he'd take it.

"Ha. I'll take all the publicity I can get." I laughed, shaking my head as Eli dropped into the chair opposite mine and reached for his glass. "Albright practically offered me his firstborn for it again last month. But no, I'm staying put. Too much sweat equity in these walls."

"His loss," Eli said easily, taking a generous swallow of bourbon. He set the paper bag on the table between us. "Speaking of people staying put, I brought some key lime cookies Jules made. She thinks they'll pair well with bourbon, which sounds disgusting to me, but what do I know? I'm just the guy who drinks beer from a can."

Despite my anxiety, I had to smile. Eli had the unique ability to dispel tension without even knowing it existed.

Tonight, he wore a faded T-shirt from some dive shop in Bali, cargo shorts that had seen better days, and his ever-present flip-flops. His perpetually sun-bleached hair and easy smile projected his usual carefree demeanor.

"Jules let you out on a school night?" I teased, falling into our familiar rhythm despite the weight sitting on my chest. "Must have signed a permission slip."

"Please. Jules does not tell me what to do." He took a sip, then added with a grin, "She merely makes strongly worded suggestions that I choose to follow because I value my life and access to her."

"How is domestic bliss?" I asked, leaning back in my chair and trying to appear relaxed. "She moved in, what, a month ago? And neither of you has killed the other yet. Impressive."

"It's good. Really good, actually." His expression softened. "You know how she alphabetizes the spice rack? Turns out, I find that weirdly hot."

I laughed. "You've changed, man. The Eli I used to know would break out in hives at the mere mention of cohabitation."

"The Eli you used to know was an idiot," he countered, raising his glass in a mock toast. "Though Jules would argue that not much has changed. Yesterday she found my wetsuit dripping in the bathtub instead of on the deck rack she installed specifically for that purpose."

"And you're still alive to tell the tale? She must really love you."

"Miracle, right?" He grinned, then took another sip of bourbon, eyeing me over the rim of his glass. "But enough about my domestic triumphs. What's going on with you? And don't say nothing because you've adjusted those coasters at least four times since I sat down."

I froze, caught in the act of nudging a coaster into

exact alignment with the edge of the table. For all his laid-back demeanor, Eli had always been perceptive. It was what made him such a good dive instructor—that ability to read people, to sense when something was off.

"That obvious, huh?" I abandoned the pretense, setting my glass down and leaning forward.

"Okay, spill it," Eli said, his tone shifting from playful to concerned. "You look wound up tighter than a drum. What's up?"

I took a deep breath, then a long swallow of bourbon, welcoming the burn as it slid down my throat. I'd rehearsed variations of this conversation all day, but now, facing Eli, all my prepared phrases abandoned me.

"There's something you need to know," I said in a voice that was steadier than I felt. "About Harper and me."

Eli went still, his glass halfway to his lips. An expression I couldn't quite read crossed his face—not quite surprise, not quite understanding. He set his glass down. "Go on."

"We…" I faltered, then pushed forward. "The other night, she came over here to discuss an issue we're having with the pipes in Room Block One. Something happened between us."

Eli didn't blink, didn't move. His silence compelled me to continue.

"We kissed. Well, a lot more than that." I didn't elaborate, knowing Eli wouldn't want details. "It wasn't planned, but it happened. And I can't stop thinking about her, Eli."

I braced myself for anger, for the protective brotherly rage I'd feared. Instead, Eli remained unnervingly calm, studying me with a perceptiveness I rarely saw from him. "You and Harper? Huh. At least you both got some action."

"I was half-expecting you to tackle me," I ventured, uncertain of this measured response.

Eli picked up his glass again and took a deliberate sip. "Would it make you feel better if I punched you? Because I could do that if it helps."

The deadpan delivery made me choke on my bourbon. "No, that won't be necessary."

"Good, because I just had my nails done." He flexed his fingers dramatically. Then his expression became serious, the joking façade dropping away. "Listen to me very carefully, Chase. Harper isn't just another woman. She's been hurt before. Badly. Finn's father walked out when she told him she was pregnant. Didn't even stick around long enough to see his son born."

I nodded, absorbing the gravity in his tone.

"She had to rebuild her entire life around being a single mom. Everything she does, every decision she makes, is with Finn in mind. That kid is her whole world." He leaned forward, his eyes locking with mine. "If you're just looking for something casual, or if you're not sure what you want, you need to walk away now. Harper and Finn deserve stability, not complications."

"I'm not looking to hurt her," I said quietly. "I honestly don't know what this is yet, Eli. It caught me off guard. But I respect her too much not to treat her right."

Eli studied me for a long moment. "You know, you two are a lot alike. You're both responsible to a fault, both put everyone else first." He shook his head. "Your timing sucks, though. Even worse than mine and Jules's. Congrats."

"So… you're not going to kill me?"

"Not today." Eli picked up his glass again. "Harper's a grown woman who makes her own choices. I don't get a vote. But she's also my sister, and Finn is my nephew, so I get to say this once—if you hurt her, I will absolutely make your life miserable in creative and painful ways."

"Understood." That leaden weight lifted from my

chest, even as a new one settled in its place. Eli's blessing came with expectations—to be worthy of Harper's trust, to consider Finn in any decisions I made.

"Besides," Eli added, "you two are some of my favorite people. If you can make each other happy, who am I to stand in the way? Just… be careful. There's a lot at stake."

"I know." I swirled the remaining bourbon in my glass, watching the ice shift. "I'm going to talk to her, figure out what we both want."

"Good." Eli nodded, then reached for one of Jules's cookies. "Now can we please talk about something else? I'm gonna need you to spare me the sordid play-by-play of you and my sister. I guess that might become a new rule between us."

I laughed, relief washing through me. "Fair enough. How about those Hammerheads?"

We fell into an easier conversation after that, discussing everything from the upcoming dive season to my latest projects. By the time he left a couple of hours later, things between us felt mostly normal again—our friendship intact, if somewhat altered by this new dimension.

I remained on the deck after Eli's departure, nursing a third bourbon and staring into the darkness. The night had descended fully around me. Crickets and distant waves provided a soundtrack to my thoughts.

Eli's reaction had been better than I'd feared but brought with it a deeper responsibility than I'd anticipated. His understanding wasn't permission to pursue Harper. It was a trust I couldn't betray. I thought about her, about Finn, about the complicated path ahead if we decided to see where this attraction led. And we needed to consider not just our own feelings but the potential impact on Finn, on the renovation project, on the complex web of relationships that connected us.

Chapter Eight

HARPER

"YOU THINKING Sea Breeze or Gulf Water?" Chase's voice vibrated through the bare walls of the bungalow's shell as he held out two paint chips. My chest tightened when I met his gaze. The flecks of green in his irises held me captive. I bit my lip and touched a finger to the Gulf Water.

He smiled, the same one that had me in bed with him after years of pretending there wasn't an itch to scratch. "Good choice. I prefer that one too."

"I thought you weren't one for blues."

Chase shrugged, leaning closer than necessary to examine the sample. "Maybe they're growing on me."

He was certainly growing on me. I swallowed hard, trying to shift back to the safety of our professional relationship, but Chase was already dismantling that wall with a sledgehammer.

"It's easier to work together now," he said, both playful

and probing. "Now that we've cleared up those… plumbing issues."

I rolled my eyes but couldn't stop a laugh. "You're never going to let me live that down, are you?"

"Not a chance." Then his smile fell, and he dropped his eyes quickly to the ground. "Actually, there's something else I need to tell you."

My stomach flopped disconcertingly. "What?"

He hesitated, clearing his throat like the words were stuck in there. "I, uh… I told Eli last night."

My heart skipped. "About us?"

He nodded, wincing a little. "I didn't want to keep it from him. He's my best friend, Harper. And I know we agreed to talk later, but I want to keep this going. You and me."

The initial shock melted into a mix of emotions that tangled inside me—relief that the cat was out of the bag, anxiety about Eli's reaction, and a sense of elation expanding like a balloon. Because I'd also given up on us going back to what we'd been before. "Me too. How did it go?"

"He took it better than I expected."

"That's a good sign." My mind was still spinning at this new reality. It figured that Chase would feel the need to be honest with Eli. And that wasn't at all a bad thing as far as I was concerned. I had way too much experience with a man who couldn't handle the truth right in front of him. "I guess with Eli knowing, that's one down."

Chase stepped closer, his eyes searching mine as if trying to gauge how much trouble he was in.

I tilted my head. "What exactly did he say?"

Chase rubbed the back of his neck, looking both amused and exasperated. "A lot about treating you right and kicking my ass if I didn't."

A relieved laugh bubbled out of me. Of course Eli would play the overprotective brother. "And he was okay? Really?"

"Once he was done warning me, he seemed fine. But you and I both know we can't keep this a secret. Not if we want to see where it goes."

I nodded, relieved to have the truth acknowledged. "We can't pretend nothing happened. Or keep sneaking around like teenagers."

"I can't have any more hidden closet meetings," he said, a flush creeping up his neck.

A laugh tumbled out of me. "That was your idea, remember?"

He rubbed his chin, looking adorably sheepish. "Not the image I'm going for."

"Or me," I agreed. "We need to act like the professionals we are at work. Save other things for other times, maybe?"

"Maybe we try a real date instead of our usual room-under-renovation meeting?" His suggestion was hopeful and warm, the playful spark in his eyes grounding us.

"Okay. No more pretending. And we agreed to get together later this week, so how is Friday night for you?"

Chase's grin widened, the kind that made my heart do ridiculous things. "Friday works. No paint samples or construction dust allowed." He reached out and squeezed my hand, a simple gesture that held the complexity of everything we didn't need to say. "And don't worry. I can handle your brothers."

"That makes one of us," I muttered, but his confidence was contagious.

I followed him to the door, the shift between us like a breeze clearing away storm clouds. As we stepped outside, I spotted Austin, Braden, and Ben clustered around a newly planted section of hibiscus and palm trees. The sight of them gathered like that twisted my stomach into anxious knots.

Chase caught my eye, his expression a mix of encouragement and empathy. "Looks like you're up."

"I guess so. See you Friday, then?"

He stroked my arm, a light, lingering touch. "I'll pick you up at six."

I realized I had no idea where we were going. "What should I wear?"

His smile turned wolfish, and I had to laugh. Then his expression softened as he looked me up and down. "I want to take you somewhere nice. Wear whatever you think is appropriate."

Somewhere nice? My wheels were already spinning, mentally going through all my mom clothes and finding nothing appropriate. I might have to dig into the very back of the closet. "I'll be ready at six. See you later."

I smiled and broke away, focusing on the three figures ahead. Austin leaned against a palm tree, his rugged face and intense gray eyes taking everything in with a quiet, reserved presence. His arms were crossed, a subtle shield against the world. Next to him, Braden shifted impatiently and checked his watch, probably eager to get to Tidal Hops for the day. His hair was a shade lighter than Austin's and Ben's but darker than Eli's. His easy grin matched his energetic blue eyes and restless ambition. Ben stood slightly apart with one arm resting on the handle of a shovel, his observant gaze missing nothing. The image of them together should've been intimidating, but I'd never backed down from the brotherhood before.

Taking a deep breath, I walked purposefully toward them. They turned as I approached, the noise of construction fading. Their attention felt like something physical, the manifestation of the secret I was about to unload.

"Morning, Harper." Braden's voice carried a teasing lilt. "Did you bring us breakfast?"

I held out my empty arms. "Does it look like it? You're all grown men, you know. You're on your own."

Austin nodded hello but remained silent. His gaze shifted pointedly past me toward the bungalows, then back to my face, a single eyebrow lifting almost imperceptibly. He hadn't missed Chase and me emerging from Bungalow Four. Damn his fisherman's eyes. He saw everything.

Ben shifted position, his expression thoughtful. "Did you come to rescue us or recruit us?"

"Maybe both," I said.

"How's the bungalow construction going?" Austin asked.

"It's going well," I said, my voice steady and determined. "Which brings me to why I came over here. Chase has already talked to Eli, and I wanted you to hear it from me. Chase and I started seeing each other. Uh, romantically."

The words hung in the air, and I watched as they landed.

Austin's reaction was subtle but immediate. His gray eyes narrowed, not in anger, but in sharp assessment. A vertical line appeared between his brows—concern, maybe? Or just his default state of guarded evaluation. He shifted his weight but said nothing, his silence a heavy blanket of unspoken thoughts. Typical Austin. He'd process it internally before saying anything out loud.

Ben, predictable in his own quiet way, met my gaze steadily. His evaluation was swift, his decision seemingly made in an instant. He gave that slow, deliberate nod I knew so well. "Chase is a good guy. You could pick worse."

Then he added the inevitable Coleridge caution, "Just… be careful. Lots of complicating factors here." His acceptance, quiet but firm, felt like solid ground beneath my feet. He trusted Chase, or at least trusted my judgment enough not to interfere immediately.

Braden, however, reacted as I might have predicted Eli would have, minus the immediate threat of bodily harm to Chase. His grin exploded across his face, wide and full of surprised amusement. "Seriously?" He barked a short laugh, shaking his head. "Wow. Took Ashworth long enough."

I blinked, thrown by his enthusiastic lack of concern. "Huh?"

"Are you kidding?" Braden scoffed as he picked at his Tidal Hops T-shirt. "The way you two have been dancing around each other? The arguments over faucet finishes? Total foreplay, sis. Obvious to everyone."

Heat flooded my cheeks. "We have *not* been—"

"Oh, please," Braden interrupted, waving a dismissive hand. "The tension was thicker than the stout I brewed last week. Austin saw it, right?" He nudged our notoriously pensive middle brother.

Austin shrugged, his expression unchanging and offering no confirmation or denial.

"See?" Braden declared triumphantly, apparently taking Austin's silence as agreement. "Anyway, good for you guys. Chase is solid. Good business sense too, investing like that." His focus had already shifted, characteristically, to the practical, business implications.

While I appreciated his lack of drama, his easy dismissal felt odd. It was almost *too* casual. Did he really not see the potential complications? The minefield of mixing family business with a relationship involving Eli's best friend? Or did he just assume Chase, being successful and stable, was automatically a "good catch" and therefore uncomplicated? It felt like he was skipping over the emotional risks entirely.

"It's… complicated, Braden," I said quietly.

He shrugged again, already glancing back toward Tidal Hops. "What isn't, with this family? Look, as long as it doesn't mess up the renovation timeline or my beer delivery schedule, I'm good. Just try not to have any dramatic breakups in the middle of the brewpub, okay?" He winked, then clapped Ben on the shoulder. "Gotta run. Those kegs won't clean themselves." With a final jaunty wave, he headed off, leaving me with Austin and Ben.

Ben gave me another quiet nod. "Maybe Eli and Jules getting involved kind of broke the ice on these kinds of relationships. But he'd better do right by you. Just say the word, and I'll rearrange his face for him." He picked up his shovel and went back to inspecting a newly planted hibiscus.

"I hardly think that will be necessary," I said with as much dignity as I could muster under the circumstances.

That left Austin. He pushed away from the palm tree, his gaze fixed on me as we walked away. "You okay?" he asked gruffly, the two words carrying more weight than Braden's entire monologue.

"I think so," I admitted honestly. "It's… new. And scary."

"It's your business. But don't let it distract you from all that's going on around here." A pause, a shift in his expression. "Or get hurt again."

I chewed my lip, sensing the warning beneath his words. "How about we take a walk down to your boat?" I suggested, hoping to bridge the distance between us.

"Sure."

As we made our way toward the dock, I thought about

how much Austin had changed, how the fun, easygoing brother of my youth had become this introspective, sometimes downright curmudgeonly man. He used to laugh with a freedom that matched the ocean he loved, but I was afraid those days were behind him now.

Line Dancer sat tied to the pier, the resort's fishing charter boat that mirrored its captain. Everything about it was tidy and efficient, from the coiled ropes to the spotless deck. Austin stepped on board, waiting for me to join him.

A mix of frustration and hope knotted in my chest. "So that's it? You're not going to say anything else?"

His eyes shifted to mine, then out to the water. "Chase has got it together. He's not like Dad. Or Jarod."

I let out a breath. It wasn't a ringing endorsement, but it was something. "No, he's not." And I had a feeling reminding myself he wasn't Finn's dad was going to be a common refrain for me.

He looked at me again, a hint of a smile pulling at his lips. "Just don't expect me to babysit while you two are off having sex in some fancy new resort bed."

I laughed, the sound carrying over the water. "Fine. I've got plenty of others to ask."

His smile steadied, and lightness spread through my chest. When Austin smiled, it changed his whole face, like the sun breaking through a cloudy sky, a glimpse of the brother he'd once been. "Finn's welcome on my boat anytime. You know that."

"I do. Thank you. He loves going out on the water with you."

"When are you gonna tell Mom?" he asked, a knowing look in his eye.

"Once I survive telling everyone else."

"I think she'll be okay with it." He leaned against the

railing, relaxed now. "You and Chase are the responsible ones. I didn't blame her for being furious at Eli."

I shook my head and smiled. "Yeah, but look how that came out."

We stood in companionable silence for a moment, the waves lapping against the hull. At last, I felt like maybe everything was going to be okay. Or at least manageable.

"I guess Brenna is next on the list," I said.

Austin nodded, then picked up one of the huge rods and inspected the reel. "You know where to find me if Ashworth steps out of line."

As I walked away, I pulled out my phone and dialed my little sister. She was between Austin and Braden in the birth order. Her voice came through bright and cheerful. "Harper! What's up?"

"Could I come over to the bookshop?" I asked, the need for a sisterly sounding board growing stronger. She could offer advice that would never even occur to our brothers. "I've got something to talk about."

"Of course," she said without missing a beat. "I'll brew a fresh pot of tea."

"Perfect," I replied, feeling a touch lighter. We hung up, and I made my way to the parking lot, bracing myself for round two of the Coleridge confession tour.

"… so I just came from telling Austin, Braden, and Ben about us," I finished, picking nervously at a loose thread on the cuff of my resort polo shirt as I leaned against the checkout counter of Bookshop in Paradise.

Brenna just stared at me, her iced tea halfway to her lips, those warm green eyes wide with surprised assessment. She'd kept quiet during my long-winded explanation. For a long moment, the only sound was the low hum of the shop's air conditioner. Then, slowly, a wide, knowing smile spread across her face.

"Chase?" she finally breathed, setting her tea down carefully on a stack of order forms. She tilted her head. "Actually, yeah. That sort of makes sense, doesn't it?"

Relief prickled under my skin, surprisingly potent. "You think so? Because right now it feels completely unhinged."

Brenna laughed, that soft, musical sound that always felt like coming home. "Well, you *are* a Coleridge. Unhinged is kind of our baseline." She came around the counter and leaned back against it beside me. "But there have been some serious sparks and tension between you two."

"God, now you sound like Braden. We have *not* been…" I started, then trailed off because, honestly, who was I kidding? "Okay, maybe there's been some underlying… professional friction."

"Uh-huh." Brenna smirked. "Friction. Is that what we're calling it?" She nudged my shoulder playfully. "Sounds like this… friction between you two was pretty good."

I sighed, letting some of the bewildered energy settle. "Better than good. Amazing. And he's just so easy to be around. It's completely illogical. He's Eli's best friend. He's our business partner now. The timing is objectively terrible. There's no other way to put it." I threw my hands up slightly. "And yet, when I'm actually *with* him, arguing about plumbing or hovering over blueprints, it just… clicks. It feels easy somehow, comfortable, even when we're disagreeing. Which makes absolutely no sense."

"Since when does anything involving attraction make logical sense?" Brenna asked wryly. She took another sip of her tea. "So, it feels easy and comfortable, even though it's complicated and messy. Sounds about right."

"Is that supposed to be reassuring?"

"Maybe." Her smile was warm now, full of genuine affection. "Look, Harper, you've had your life locked down tight for years. Finn first, resort second, everything else—especially you—a distant third. Maybe it's okay for something illogical and messy to feel good for a change?"

"But the complications are real," I insisted. "Do you want me to recount them again?"

"Okay, okay, breathe." Brenna held up a hand. "Yes, the complications are real. They always are. I married Hunter! The Markham name alone was practically a declaration of war in our family." She shuddered theatrically. "You can't let the complications overshadow the good stuff. And there's obviously good stuff."

"Yeah. Plenty." I smiled, unable to help it. "We're going on a real date on Friday. Away from the resort."

Brenna's eyes lit up. "See? That's progress."

"It is nice," I agreed, a flutter of anticipation mixing with the nerves. "It's just scary. It's been so long."

"Of course it's scary," Brenna said gently. "Jumping back in after… well, after everything, it's always scary. And Chase isn't exactly low-stakes, given the circumstances." She paused, her gaze thoughtful. "But, Harper, don't let the *what-ifs* ruin the *right now*. You like him, don't you?"

I nodded, unable to deny the warmth spreading through my chest at the thought of his reassuring yet very sexy gaze, his unexpected humor. "Yeah. I really do."

"And he clearly likes you. So, go on the date. Have fun. See what happens when you're not covered in sawdust or arguing about copper pipes." She nudged me again. "Stop trying to plan the next ten years based on one explosive night and a potentially great date."

Tears I hadn't expected pricked my eyes, blurring the colorful book covers surrounding us. It wasn't profound advice, maybe, but it was exactly what I needed—permission to just be in the moment.

"You think it could actually work?" I asked.

"I have no idea," Brenna admitted with a shrug. "Nobody ever does at the start. But this is Chase. He's a good guy, Harper. Steady. Kind. Maybe a little too controlled for his own good sometimes, but straight up. And from what you just told me"—she smiled softly—"it seems worth finding out, doesn't it?"

I pictured his smile, the way his eyes crinkled at the corners, the surprising tenderness he'd shown me after my initial panic. The easy way he was with Finn. Yes, it was worth finding out.

"Okay," I said, taking a shaky breath and finally returning her smile. "Okay. I'll stop catastrophizing. For tonight, anyway."

"That's my sister." Brenna gave my arm a squeeze. "Now go figure out what you're going to wear."

I felt lighter leaving the bookstore than I had arriving, the anxieties still present but now overshadowed by a burgeoning sense of excitement and curiosity. A real date. With Chase Ashworth. Maybe this ridiculously complicated situation could lead to something wonderful.

Chapter Nine

CHASE

AFTER KNOCKING on the front door, I fiddled with my tie, shifting from one foot to the other on Harper's front porch. The door flung open, launching my stomach to my throat when I saw her standing in the doorway, and I forgot how to function. Her chestnut hair was styled and loose around her shoulders, subtle makeup enhancing her already striking features. She wore a dress in the exact shade of wow.

"Hi," I managed, my voice not obeying basic laws of sound. "You look incredible."

She blinked in surprise, then let out a small laugh. "You're not too shabby yourself."

The dress was a deep emerald that made her eyes a richer brown than I'd ever seen them. And the way it hugged her curves, just enough but not too much, made me want to stare for way longer than what was probably acceptable. She shifted from one leg to the other, and I realized I was still staring. I needed to pull it together.

I wanted this to be perfect. Different from work. Different from family. Different enough that there was no mistaking it for anything but what it was—a real, actual date. "I can hardly wait to show you off. How about a little dinner?"

Her cheeks flushed. I couldn't tell if it was the humidity or the compliment that caused it, but either way, it was a nice contrast against the green of her dress. "Dinner sounds lovely. Should we go?"

I nodded, knowing my voice would probably betray me if I spoke again. As she locked up, I took in the small, screened-in porch. It was cluttered but cozy, with potted plants mingling with Finn's toys and some practical but mismatched furniture. What was it like to come home to a place like this, filled with warmth and life?

We reached my SUV, and I opened the passenger door for her. She glanced at my hand as I offered it, almost like she was surprised, but then took it. Her touch sent a jolt through me. "Thank you," she said, settling into the seat.

As I got in on my side, the only sound was the smooth hum of the engine and the sultry voice of superstar singer Sutton Vale singing one of her ballads. I hadn't felt this kind of tension since high school prom. Back then, it was sweaty palms and not knowing where to put them. Now it was realizing how much was at stake.

"So," I said, trying to break the silence as we pulled out. I turned the distraction of the radio off. "What is Finn up to?"

"Spending the night with Aunt Brenna and Uncle Hunter," she replied, her eyes catching mine. "He's very excited."

"Glad to hear it." I smiled, relaxing slightly. "I might not be able to compete with an ex-Special Forces soldier, but I'm not too bad at reservations."

"Are you bribing me with dinner, Ashworth?" she teased, leaning back in her seat.

"Maybe. You're worth it."

We fell into a more comfortable silence, the kind that doesn't need to be filled because it isn't awkward—it's just nice. My SUV's sleek interior was a contrast to her lived-in porch. It was all polished and organized, much like my life until recently.

She broke the silence as we drove over the causeway, nodding to a billboard for Calypso Key Resort featuring Orchid Restaurant and its executive chef, Stella Markham. The restaurant was famous as one of the best fine dining places in the Lower Keys. "Trying to impress me with the competition?"

I couldn't hide my grin. "Uh-oh. Does it ruin the surprise?"

"On the contrary, I'm intrigued." She looked back at me, eyes sparkling. "Especially since I have a cookbook authored by Stella in the cottage."

I shrugged like it was no big deal. Like I wasn't trying hard on every conceivable level. "I thought a change of scenery might be nice. Somewhere we can be just us. Not General Manager Coleridge and the Architect."

"That sounds perfect," she said softly.

It was like she was letting her guard down in stages. As we parked at Calypso Key Resort, the last bit slipped away. We ambled down a softly lit path to a pale pink, one-story building overlooking the western edge of the small island. The place was stunning, low-lit and elegant, the hum of conversation subdued but vibrant. We were shown to a secluded, prime table on the patio overlooking the water, lit by soft candlelight and surrounded by potted orchids. The scent of the sea mingled with something floral and sophisticated.

"This is incredible." Harper glanced around. "Thank you."

We relaxed in our seats, and the feeling was everything I'd hoped for. More. Orchid was a crown jewel kind of restaurant, and it showed. The attentive service and pristine setting were flawless. But it was the contrast to our normal days that made this so special. No interruptions. No expectations. Just the two of us, away from everything and everyone we knew.

A server in black slacks and a neat white shirt and apron appeared, and I ordered wine, hoping I didn't screw it up. As he disappeared, I realized I was leaning across the table, hanging on Harper's every word as she described the menu with an unexpected passion.

I was seeing Harper without the constant demands of life pulling at her from every angle, and she was mesmerizing. Her laugh was full and relaxed as she told me about Finn's latest escapade.

They offered a selection of catch of the day specials and we each ordered one. Her animated expression as she shared an anecdote about a younger Braden chasing Eli around with a blowtorch and a bottle of gin during Driftwood Dragon Weekend made me want to prolong the night indefinitely.

"I don't remember seeing you this laid back," she mentioned after brushing a lock of hair from her face. "Is this a new thing?"

I took a sip of the heady red wine, pleased with my choice. "I don't know. I'm pretty sure Eli would say I'm wound tighter than a steel cable."

"I beg to differ. You're not wound tight, just steady."

"Which is worse?"

She eyed me. "I find steady very sexy."

It struck me then. How much I wanted this. Wanted her.

As we ate our salads, the conversation inevitably turned to the renovation. But there was no trace of tension, no butting heads over different visions. I wanted to know more, how she was really coping. I studied her face. "How do you feel about taking on a loan after all?"

Originally, my partnership and investment were designed to avoid external financing. But it hadn't worked out that way after we decided to renovate multiple areas at once to speed up the overall project.

She was quiet for a moment, thoughtful. "Honestly? Worried at first. But it was the only option, and with you onboard…" She paused to meet my eyes, sincerity obvious in hers. "I feel like we might actually pull it off. Thank you for believing in us."

I swallowed, trying to mask how deeply her words impacted me. How much they meant. I couldn't look away from her. "I didn't invest just to help. I invested because I knew you'd make it work. We'd make it work."

Before she could respond, our entrees arrived, a flawless presentation of fish fresh from local waters.

"Oh, wow. This looks incredible," she said, examining her plate.

"I told you this was a bribe."

She laughed again, the sound everything I wanted this night to be.

I was about to change the subject when Stella Markham herself came over to our table. "Harper Coleridge, the busiest woman in Dove Key." Her voice was friendly and assured. In her mid-thirties, with dark hair pulled back, Stella had a confident energy that was vibrant and alive even under the restraint of a crisp chef's coat. "I saw you from the kitchen and thought I'd say hello. What brings you all the way over here?"

Harper grinned, standing to give Stella a hug. "Chase does," she said, full of pride and something else I couldn't quite pin down. "We've got him all tied up with the resort renovation, but I've corralled him into a break."

Stella's eyes flicked to me, sizing me up with the expert precision of a head chef dissecting a challenging dish. "So, you're the man behind the project everyone's talking about."

"Chase Ashworth, Latitudes Design." I briefly rose to shake her hand. It couldn't be a bad idea for a Markham to know my firm's name.

"I'll have to take a proper tour when it's all said and done." She then nodded toward our steaming entrees, her professional focus returning. "How is everything looking?"

Harper leaned forward, her eyes shining as she took in her plate. "Stella, it looks absolutely incredible. We haven't even taken a bite yet, but the presentation alone is breathtaking."

A spark of passion ignited in Stella's eyes, transforming her from a sharp businesswoman to an animated artist. "You both made excellent choices. My father actually brought those in himself this afternoon. Harper, your snapper was line-caught just off Sombrero Reef around two o'clock. It's pan-seared with that citrus-herb butter. It should melt in your mouth." She turned to me, pride evident on her face. "And Chase, your dorado was speared by him near the old freighter wreck, the *Benson*. We're serving it with a citrus-mango salsa and coconut rice tonight. Both are about as fresh as it gets without eating it on the boat."

The way she spoke about the fish and the direct

connection to her father was why I loved having local connections like this.

Stella shot us both a smile. "But enough yammering. I'll let you both enjoy your dinner." She gave Harper another quick nod, then to me. "Nice to meet you, Chase. Perhaps when Sunset Siesta is finished, Calypso Key will need to hire you for our *next* big project to keep up."

She grinned, a flash of humor, then with a final, "Enjoy your night," she was gone, disappearing back toward the hum of her kitchen as smoothly as she'd arrived.

I tried not to read too much into her final statement or how much a big contract like Calypso Key Resort could mean to a new firm. Instead, I concentrated on the exceptional dish in front of me. Each entrée was a gastronomic marvel, each bite bursting with flavor. The presentation alone was worth the drive, with vibrant seasonal vegetables and artful drizzles of sauce that made the plates look like they belonged in a food magazine. As I savored the first mouthful, I knew my instincts were right. This was the kind of date we needed, and I felt a smug sense of accomplishment at having pulled it off. Harper gave a contented sigh after her first taste and beamed at me from across the table.

As the candles winked and the night grew darker, we split a dessert, some decadent chocolate thing that made me mentally add a mile to tomorrow's run. Harper leaned back with a touch of the whipped cream on her upper lip. I couldn't resist the urge to wipe it away, then lick it off my thumb with a wink at her.

She smiled brightly and a soft, slightly flustered laugh escaped her. She quickly looked down at her water glass, tracing the condensation with a fingertip. "I have a confession." Her voice was quieter now, as if testing the waters. She lifted her gaze, her eyes searching mine. "When you mentioned noticing me when you were in college…"

I held my breath, suddenly wary. "Yeah?"

"Well," she continued, drawing the word out, "it wasn't entirely one-sided."

My heart gave a distinct thump against my ribs. "It wasn't?"

She shook her head. "There was this one time, right after you graduated. You, Eli, and I were grabbing beers at Conch Republic after work. I couldn't have been more than twenty-three. Eli was going on about wanting to rearrange the dive shop—you know how he gets these grand, impractical ideas."

I snorted. "Vaguely involving duct tape, cardboard, and ignoring basic physics?"

"Exactly. He described his new layout, very detailed for Eli. I thought it wasn't half-bad. But you just… scowled." She laughed at the memory. "You told him it would create a bottleneck. That there wasn't enough room for both fins and BCDs on that wall. So you pulled a pen from your pocket, grabbed a napkin, and just drew. So fast. Your hands…" Her voice trailed off for a second, her gaze distant. "They were so strong, moving the pen, but the lines you made were so precise, so delicate. You sketched out the entire optimal flow, the counter placement, storage solutions… basically the exact layout that's still there today. All in about ninety seconds on a bar napkin."

She looked back at me, her expression earnest now. "I was completely enthralled. Watching your focus, the way your hands knew exactly what to do, creating something smart and functional out of Eli's chaos. I'd always seen you as Eli's quiet, brainy friend. But in that moment, I saw something else. Competence. Confidence. Capability. It was…" She searched for the words. "Really attractive. I never forgot it."

I stared at her, momentarily speechless. I recalled arguing with Eli about dive shop layouts over beers countless times, but the specific incident was lost to me. To think she'd not only remembered it but seen *me* that way back then…

I cleared my throat, aiming for lightness to cover how much her admission affected me. "Wow. All that from a napkin sketch? Guess I should have carried more napkins around back then."

Her smile remained, but she shook her head to let me know she'd seen through me. "Never sell yourself short, Chase Ashworth. There was always more to you than just being Eli's quiet friend."

Her confidence in me, stated so simply, hit hard. It spread deep inside me, a validation I hadn't known I was seeking. I held her gaze, our shared history, the newly revealed mutual awareness stretching between us like a tangible thing.

"Thank you, Harper."

She reached out and placed her warm hand on mine. "No, thank you, Chase. I needed this. It's been a long time since I just felt like Harper. Not Manager Coleridge or Finn's Mom. Just… me." Her voice was soft, vulnerable. It was the sound of her walls coming down completely.

"You should always feel like you," I said, flipping my hand over to lace our fingers together. "You deserve nights like this. And more than once in a blue moon too."

Her eyes held mine across the flickering candlelight, filled with a deep, quiet seriousness that mirrored the sudden intensity in my own chest.

"Ready to head back?" I asked finally, the question a reluctant surrender to the clock.

She nodded slowly, a soft, luminous smile touching her lips. "Yes. I think so."

As we stood and pushed back our chairs, the quiet intimacy of the moment lingered. My hand found her back as we walked through the elegant dining room, a simple gesture of belonging and protection I didn't pause to analyze. Dinner might be over, the plates cleared, the wine bottle empty. But for us, the night had barely begun.

Harper's cottage door clicked shut behind us and the world seemed to exhale. We left our shoes by the entrance, side by side like they were made for each other. It was hard to say what changed when we walked inside. Maybe it was the lamps casting a more intimate light, the lingering scent of cinnamon, or just being here in her space. It was less dinner and more date, less nightcap and more staying over. Harper poured us drinks as we settled on the sofa, drinks that felt unnecessary when the air was already thick with possibilities.

This time, I didn't worry about what to say. I could tell by the way she fit herself against my side that she wasn't concerned either. Her dress spilled like emerald water across the cushions, catching the soft light. The dress might have been incredible, but she was spectacular.

"So," she said, her voice teasing, "how long do you think it'll take before the entire island knows about this?"

"About us?" I asked, pretending to be shocked. "I thought I was just your architect."

"Is that what you're calling it these days?"

"I'm a man of many talents." There was a lightness between us that wasn't there before, an unspoken acknowledgment that tonight had changed things in ways we hadn't even started to explore.

She laughed, the sound easy and full of promise. "I noticed. You're also a very good date planner."

"I aim to please."

"In that case"—her lips curved into a smile that made my pulse race—"I'd like to book another one."

"Consider it done." I set my drink down, drawn to her in a way that made everything else feel secondary. The resort. The renovation. My entire life on Dove Key.

She shifted closer and her gaze locked on mine. "Look at you, Mr. Confident," she whispered, her breath warm against my cheek. "Not nervous at all anymore."

"Wouldn't go that far. I've had plenty of nervous moments the past few months."

She stroked my arm. "Jumping ship from a steady job to open your own firm can do that to a person."

"I tried to get through to my folks that I wasn't happy being a corporate minion, but they weren't pleased with the switch."

"I'm sorry they didn't support your choice." She shifted sideways to see me better. "You never really talk about them."

"That's because they make me look emotionally open," I said, keeping it light but honest.

"That bad?"

"Yeah." I paused. "Never what you'd call… passionate. They have a pretty loveless marriage, ruled by inertia."

She nodded like she understood. "Mom is sort of that way, but for different reasons. I've been afraid of ending up the same way. Afraid to want anything beyond the resort and Finn."

An ache tugged in my chest, hearing her open up like this. It was both a relief and a connection, knowing she had similar doubts and fears. I wanted to say something that would tell her she wasn't alone. Something that told her how much tonight meant to me, too.

"I'll say it again," I said as I brushed my knuckles over

her cheek. "You deserve nights like this a lot more than just once in a while."

She stared at me, and I saw the flicker of hope she was trying to hold onto.

"You really think we can do this?" Her words were almost a whisper, as if speaking too loudly might shatter the fragile possibility between us.

"Yeah," I said, pulling her closer. "I really do."

Her lips met mine and the brush of skin felt like everything sliding into place. Like we were the only two people in the world, the kind of kiss that said things words couldn't.

We were standing before I knew it, our hands tangling and reaching, guiding each other. She led me to the bedroom in a blur, a soft rush of color and taste. And raw desire. I'd never wanted anything more than to make her feel how I did.

Seen. Real.

The room faded as we moved together. It was more than a moment. It was a choice.

I woke first. Soft light filtered through the curtain, painting Harper beside me. Her hair spilled over the pillow like the start of a perfect day. Her breath was slow, her face soft and unguarded.

I'd grown up in a house where emotions were as rare as snowstorms in the Keys. My parents didn't fight, didn't cry, didn't laugh. Just a steady monotone of existence. I learned early to keep things under wraps. How else was I supposed to act? It worked fine when my life was all about jobs and architecture, but Harper was different. She made me want more than fine, and I wasn't sure how to accomplish that.

My heart was a contradiction of speed and weight,

each beat echoing the undeniable shift between us. I could lose myself in this, in her, and it scared me. It scared me because I wanted it.

Because I already knew how much it would hurt if it slipped away.

Chapter Ten

HARPER

I FLEXED my toes in the sand of Siesta Sunset's beach, absorbing the sun-warmed grains as Finn shot past me. He dragged Chase toward the water's edge by the hand, his bright green snorkel and mask bobbing like antennae. Chase, relaxed and effortless in board shorts—not to mention breathtaking—glanced over and waved at me.

It will be fine, I reminded myself as I lifted my hand in return. Nothing like diving headfirst into a casual family outing with the man who'd haunted my thoughts and my body since our date at Orchid two weeks ago. And in that time, Chase had slowly introduced himself into our lives. Now it was time for the next step—melding together.

As Finn let go to dash along the shore, I studied Chase's easy demeanor. My heart did a little squeeze, hope and anxiety wrestling each other like the WWE. I'd sat Finn down the day after our date at Orchid and explained that Chase and I had become *very special friends*, and that Finn would be seeing him more. My sweet boy's face had lit up like I told him he'd won a year's supply of LEGOs. And now this fun snorkeling and beach trip was a test of my heart's ability to handle this not-so-casual outing. I recalled Brenna's words to relax for once and enjoy the moment. At the time, it had seemed such an easy thing to do. And I had, both during the date and the night after.

Especially the night after.

"Chase, look!" Finn crouched to poke at a patch of seaweed or maybe a washed-up sand dollar. He had his explorer face on—intense, delighted, ready to share his findings. Chase hunkered next to him, never rushing.

"Ready for your briefing, troops?" Eli's voice carried over the waves. He was striding toward us in bare feet and his dive instructor persona, a towel slung over one shoulder like a sash. "Okay, Ashworth. Currents are negligible, visibility is excellent. Primary hazard: six-year-old with excessive enthusiasm." He fixed Chase with a look, all mock-seriousness. "Rule number one: Don't let him try to snorkel upside down to look at crabs. Rule number two: Don't lose my nephew. Rule number three: Seriously, don't lose him."

Chase grinned. "Got it. Protect the nephew at all costs."

Shading his forehead with his hand, Eli inspected the reef visible below the rippling surface. "Don't go out too far. Little dude might get tired out."

"Eli," I said and even managed to keep from slugging him. "I have taken my son snorkeling multiple times on this very reef. More than you."

"Doesn't mean you know what you're doing," he muttered.

Finn started giggling. "You're silly, Uncle Eli."

Folding his arms, the dive instructor stared down at my son. "What's our rule?"

Finn arranged his face in a polite enough expression. "Diving or snorkeling is fun, but it's also very serious."

"My man!" The two high-fived.

"I think we got the important details," Chase interjected before Eli could derail us any further. "Anything else, Captain?"

"Yeah," Eli said, turning to me with a teasing glint in his eye. "Sure you don't want me to chaperone? Make sure you guys don't get lost down there?"

Chase and I exchanged a glance, and the laugh we shared eased some of the knots in my chest. "Get lost!" I said as Chase added, "Go find Jules."

Eli left us with a satisfied smirk, his lanky stride carrying him back up the beach. I shook my head, grateful for his antics and the noticeably reduced tension in my shoulders. I didn't want a chaperone. I wanted a chance. Maybe Eli's protective big-brother act had been a little over the top, but it reminded me what was on the line.

"Come on, come on!" Finn's voice was a bubbling fountain of enthusiasm, and even the Florida sun couldn't match his brightness.

I gave him an okay signal as I lowered my mask onto my face. "Looks like we're ready!"

We waded into the gentle sea, and the clear turquoise water wrapped around our legs. The surface shimmered like a jewel. Finn splashed ahead, a blur of yellow rash guard and excitement. "I see fish already!"

Chase fell in step beside me, and the nearness of him sent another round of thrills through me. Especially after he held a steadying hand to my lower back. "This was a good idea."

"Finn certainly thinks so. Hold up there!" When Chase and I caught up, we dipped under a wave, the water warm and clear. It felt like diving into more than the ocean—like diving into hope.

The world beneath the water was otherworldly, bright, captivating. Chase and Finn were ahead of me, their silhouettes darting like two overgrown fish. They moved in tandem, Chase pausing to point at a green sea fan, Finn practically vibrating with delight. I hovered a little behind, caught in the pull of watching them fit so naturally.

It was the exact kind of family outing I'd never let myself imagine. Even though I'd initiated it, being here now felt surreal, like a movie I'd watched but wasn't supposed to be in. Yet there they were—Chase and Finn, both absorbed, moving together in a dance as old as my fears.

A glimmer of blue parrotfish caught my eye, its scales reflecting the sunlight filtering through the water like living stained glass. The fish darted between coral formations, its beak-like mouth nibbling at the reef. I kicked my fins, moving closer to where Chase and Finn were examining a cluster of sea anemones.

I tapped Finn's shoulder and pointed toward the vibrant fish. His eyes widened behind his mask. When we surfaced a moment later, he sputtered with excitement.

"Mom! Did you see how blue it was? And its mouth looked like a parrot!"

"That's why they call it a parrotfish, buddy," I said, pushing wet hair from my face.

Finn's grin was infectious. "It's just like the fish costume I'll wear in the play. Mrs. Rodriguez said I could be the lead parrotfish! Chase, did you see it?"

Chase treaded water beside us, water streaming down his face. "Sure did. I think there's a pufferfish down there too."

We ducked our heads down and watched the brown-

and-white puffer trundle along the reef. I let myself fall behind them just so I could observe as the sun bathed my back in warmth.

A sputter of bubbles interrupted the thought. Finn's mask had leaked, filling with water, and he screwed his face up. Chase grabbed him, and we surfaced together. Chase fiddled with the strap, which had loosened, but couldn't thread it back in.

Before I knew it, I was there, gently nudging Chase's hands away. I reseated the mask with a practiced touch. "There you go."

Chase watched me as we treaded water, his expression one of appreciation and something else—something that made me believe this could really work. His smile met mine, and my heart did another one of those squeezes. It was the briefest of exchanges, but in it, I felt the possibility of a future. It was terrifying and exhilarating and so, so real.

He winked. "I know when to give way to the real pro."

We snorkeled our way back toward the shore, and the hopeful, fragile feeling expanded in my chest. When we walked out of the water, the sand was cool and powdery beneath our feet. We headed down the beach after Finn, a flutter of uncertainty still lodged in my chest. This day, this feeling—both seemed as precarious as the sandcastle that was next on the agenda. And yet, for the first time in a long time, I felt like it was worth the risk.

The sun hung high, casting short, sharp shadows as we kneeled around our sandy construction site in front of the bonfire area we Coleridges hung out at periodically. Buckets and shovels dotted the sand, evidence of our big plans. Finn, the enthusiastic foreman, issued orders. "More water. The tower needs shells!"

Chase saluted playfully. "On it, Chief!"

Finn directed traffic as I placed my latest batch of shell decorations on our wobbly towers. "Chase, you build the bridge. Mom, we need more!" His voice held no doubt that we'd keep up with his big vision.

Chase was right in his element, adjusting and reinforcing, drawing Finn into every decision. "These turrets need a wider base. See? We don't want them toppling over, do we?" He moved with energy, his sandy hands never resting.

"They won't do that." Finn laughed, scooping and patting and imagining a world where this creation was a castle fit for a king—no, an emperor.

We worked side by side, Chase's knee brushing mine, his eyes finding mine with that new, wonderful familiarity. Our gazes held for a long, beautiful moment. We broke into smiles that felt as wide and bright as the sky above us. I stood and went for more shells, the wind carrying Finn's constant chatter. He included Chase in everything, without pause or pretense, as though Chase had always been here.

Finn's giggle erupted as a turret caved under the weight of its ambition. "Uh-oh, better fix it." He handed Chase another bucket.

"Structural integrity," Chase said with a straight-faced nod. "Very important. Don't worry, we've got this."

I let myself sink back down next to them, smiling at the small, earnest face before me.

"It's almost done, guys." Finn scooped more sand out of the moat. "We have to hurry before the waves get it!"

The waves. They came in, and they washed away. It was all so wonderfully, beautifully simple, and yet I couldn't shake the fear that it wouldn't last, that Chase would see how messy and complicated it could be and walk away. Worse, I feared the pain if Finn got attached and then lost this. I didn't know how to protect him from it. From this fragile happiness.

Our castle was sprawling, detailed, full of little touches. An intricate and delicate thing. We decorated the towers, bridges, and walls. We laughed when it fell, and we laughed when it stood tall.

Finn took off down the beach, searching for more shells to add to his stockpile.

Chase leaned in and gave me a quick kiss. "I'm having a blast."

"Me too." I smiled, letting myself believe it was that simple.

He tipped his head toward the castle. "I think we're going to end up with a masterpiece, you know."

"Of course, with you on the job. I heard you talking about structural integrity."

"Hey, it's important." He pulled me close, his touch easy and familiar. "I like seeing you like this. Relaxed."

"I like feeling like this."

We watched Finn as he zigzagged along the shore, stopping to pick up anything that caught his eye.

"He's a great kid," Chase said. "You've done an amazing job with him."

Warmth spread through me at his words. "Thanks. He really likes you."

His hand found mine again. "The feeling is mutual."

Finn came running back, arms full of treasures. "Look! I found the best shell ever!" He held it up triumphantly before adding it to our creation. Eventually, we had enough structurally sound towers and turrets decorated with shells.

Finn pressed a small piece of driftwood into my hand. "The flag! Put it on the biggest tower."

"Let's do it together," I said, and the three of us planted the makeshift beach flag and declared victory. The warmth spread through me again, as fragile as the castles we built and as intense as the sun overhead.

I sat with it, this mix of longing and fear. Chase and Finn, side by side, already looked like a team. Like family. My hand went to my heart, resting there as if to keep it from breaking out and getting ahead of itself.

Sandcastles weren't meant to last. But oh, how I hoped this would.

Chapter Eleven

CHASE

I STOOD at the edge of bungalow one's foundation, staring at the muddy puddle that had no right to exist. The afternoon squall had stopped half an hour ago, leaving behind that particular Keys humidity that made my shirt cling to my back like an overeager dance partner. This innocent-looking collection of rainwater was becoming my nemesis. Third time in two weeks, same spot, same problem. And I couldn't figure out why.

"How long's it been sitting like this?" I asked, though I already knew the answer.

Bill, the foreman for the bungalow project, shifted his weight, mud caking his work boots. "Since the rain started. Hasn't budged." Lifting his baseball hat with one hand, he gestured with it toward the adjacent bungalows. "Rest of them are dry as a bone."

I nodded, frustration building in my chest. All four bungalows were now fully framed, and their storm-resistant skeletons promised the luxurious accommodations that would soon draw visitors to Sunset Siesta. All of them perfect, except this one.

Bungalow one sat a bit lower than its neighbors, near a patch of dense, untamed brush that marked the property edge. According to my plans—plans I'd reviewed, revised, and refined until they were flawless—water should flow away from the foundation, not pool against it like an unwelcome guest refusing to leave.

I pulled my tablet from my bag and opened the grading specifications, scrolling through the detailed topographical survey of this section. "The grade is set for a two-degree slope away from the foundation toward that natural drainage area." I pointed toward the brush line. "Water shouldn't be collecting here at all."

Bill wiped sweat from his cheek, leaving a smudge of dirt. "Well, something isn't right. We followed your specs to the letter."

"I know you did."

And that was the problem. If the issue wasn't in the execution, it had to be in the planning. My planning.

I glanced past the construction site toward the beach, where a family was packing up their belongings as the late afternoon sun cast long shadows across the sand. Just last weekend, I'd been down there with Harper and Finn, building what Finn had declared was the most awesome sandcastle in the universe.

It had been easy, being with them. Natural, even. The way Harper teased me when I took the turret construction so seriously, or how Finn's laughter rose above the sound of the waves. We fit together somehow, despite my having zero experience.

Sandcastles were simple. You built them, the tide came in, they washed away. No expectations, no pressure, no persistent puddles undermining your professional competence. Too bad I wasn't building one with them right now.

"Maybe we need to regrade this whole section," Bill suggested, breaking into my thoughts.

I shook my head. "Let's not jump to solutions yet. We need to understand the problem first."

I examined the puddle, crouching down to get a better look at how the water was interacting with the terrain. My jeans were already spotted with mud, so I didn't bother trying to stay clean as I pressed my palm against the soil near the foundation.

The earth felt unusually compact, almost impervious. "The water's not penetrating the soil here the way it should." I stood, moving toward the brush line, checking the slope. "It should be flowing that way, toward the natural drainage."

I turned back to my tablet, flipping between the current grading plan and the original topographical survey. Nothing jumped out. The calculations were sound, the execution precise. I paced, trying to see what I was missing. I'd designed dozens of properties in coastal areas, accounting for drainage issues far more complex than this. The puddle seemed to mock me, reflecting the darkening sky above.

Standing water against a new foundation wasn't just an aesthetic issue. It was a potential structural problem waiting to happen. In the Florida Keys, with our particular challenges of high water tables and hurricane threats, proper drainage wasn't a luxury. It was essential. And beyond the practical concerns, there was my reputation to consider. Latitudes Design was still establishing itself, and the Sunset Siesta renovation was my highest-profile project to date. I thought of Harper, of the trust she'd placed in me. Hell, that the whole family had placed in me.

I stood and brushed the mud from my hands onto my jeans. The Keys sunset was beginning to paint the sky in vivid oranges and pinks, but I hardly noticed. "We need to solve this before we can move forward with the exterior on this bungalow," I said more to myself than to Bill. "I'm not having water damage issues down the line because we rushed past this."

Bill nodded, his expression a mix of respect and frustration. I knew the crew was eager to maintain their timeline, but some things couldn't be rushed. Quality wasn't negotiable.

I took a deep breath, the heavy, humid air filling my lungs. "Let's get some soil from this specific area and compare it to samples from the other bungalow foundations. I want to see if there's a detectable difference." I glanced at my watch. "We've still got some daylight. And I want to take another look at the historical property surveys, see if there's anything we missed."

Bill nodded, the resignation of a long day getting longer evident in his posture. "Whatever you say, boss. I'll grab the sample kits from the truck."

As he walked away, I turned back to the puddle, staring at it as if sheer force of will could make it reveal its secrets. The water reflected the dimming sky.

A movement on the beach caught my eye—a tall figure walking with purpose toward us, the distinctive stride immediately recognizable as Austin Coleridge's. Unlike the rest of us, who'd been sweating through the humid afternoon, Austin looked at ease in the Keys heat, his movements efficient and unhurried. He approached bungalow one, those observant gray eyes of his immediately focusing not on me or Bill, but on the puddle itself, studying it with an intensity that made me wonder what he was seeing that we weren't.

Austin stopped a few feet away, his gaze shifting from the puddle to the dense brush near the bungalow and back again. He didn't offer a greeting, just stood there, taking in the scene with quiet assessment.

"Hey, Austin," I said, breaking the silence.

"Afternoon. Looks a little wet around here."

"Yeah. Dealing with a surprise drainage issue."

He nodded once, acknowledging my explanation without commenting on it. Up close, I could see the slight weathering of his skin from years on the water, the careful way he held himself—observant, self-contained.

"We've got a persistent puddle that won't drain," I continued, gesturing toward the water collecting against the foundation. "According to the plans, the grading should direct water away from the foundation toward that natural drainage area in the brush, but something's not right."

Austin's focus remained fixed on the land rather than the puddle itself. After another moment of silent observation, he spoke. "Ground's always been soggy right there, especially after a storm." He nodded toward the thick tangle of vegetation at the property edge. "That's where the old well pump house sat. Before the '35 hurricane knocked it all to hell."

I blinked, processing this unexpected information. "Pump house?" I opened the site plans on my tablet and scrolled to the survey of this section. "There's nothing documented there, just overgrown vegetation slated for clearing later." I turned the screen toward him, showing the topographical survey. "See? The current drainage plan should work. There's a natural slope that should carry water away from the foundation and into the existing drainage corridor."

Austin glanced at the tablet with minimal interest, then looked back at the actual land. He rubbed a hand over his dark stubble, obviously thinking. "Plans wouldn't show rubble. I doubt there's any record of that old pump house anymore. Hurricane flattened the shed, but the foundation's probably still under there. Granddad likely just pushed debris into the hole and let the brush grow over it."

Before I could respond, Austin stepped decisively toward the dense vegetation. He paused at the edge, looking back at us. "Let's have a look."

Bill shot me a questioning glance. I nodded and followed Austin, ducking under low-hanging branches as we pushed a few yards into the thicket. The air felt even thicker here, trapped beneath the canopy of tangled growth, carrying the earthy scent of damp soil and decaying vegetation.

Austin stopped and used his boot to clear away a patch of fallen leaves and vines. "There." He pointed down.

I crouched for a closer look. Where I'd expected to find only soil, I instead saw the unmistakable edge of crumbling concrete and ancient timber, barely visible beneath decades of accumulated dirt and plant matter. Austin pushed aside more debris, revealing more concrete and what looked like rusted metal—the skeletal remains of the pump house Austin had mentioned.

"Holy shit," Bill murmured behind me.

"Back then, they didn't haul stuff away—too much work. Just pushed what was left into the hole and let nature take over."

I reached down, brushing dirt from a piece of concrete as my mind put the pieces together immediately. "So this is acting like a dam, blocking the natural water flow from the bungalow site."

Austin nodded. "See how the land slopes away past this point?" He indicated the natural contour of the ground extending beyond the hidden foundation. "Water should flow down there, but this junk is holding it back."

I stood. No wonder my calculations hadn't accounted for this. I drew a breath, already envisioning the solution. "We need to excavate this area. Clear out the debris, restore the natural drainage path. Maybe add a French drain to ensure proper flow away from the bungalow foundation."

Bill nodded, relief evident on his face. "So we don't need to regrade the whole damn area."

"No," I confirmed. "We just need to address this specific obstruction. This explains everything. Go ahead and take off for the day, Bill."

With relief on his face, the foreman headed out.

I turned to Harper's brother. "Man, I'm glad you walked by. This has been eating me alive for weeks now."

Austin's expression remained neutral, but there was a hint of satisfaction at having the answer nobody else had seen. "Excavate this stuff, and water will drain properly." He said the words simply as if the solution were the most obvious thing in the world. Which, to him, it probably was.

"Thanks. Seriously. You pinpointed exactly what we were missing."

A glint of surprise crossed his features as we walked back to the worksite—so brief I almost missed it—before he gave a small nod of acknowledgment. "You're doing good work here," he said after a moment, his eyes sweeping over the framed bungalows and grounds beyond. "The resort needed these changes. Everybody around here is always so scared of changing anything. Looking forward to seeing how it turns out."

The compliment, delivered in Austin's matter-of-fact tone, carried more weight than an effusive endorsement from someone else might have. This wasn't a man who offered praise lightly. And he had his own wealth of experience regarding building.

He glanced toward the pier where his fishing boat, *Line Dancer*, was docked. "You fish at all, Ashworth? Or just dive with Eli?"

"No time for either lately," I admitted. Between establishing Latitudes Design, overseeing the Sunset Siesta renovation, and spending what free time I had with Harper and Finn, leisure activities had taken a back seat.

Austin nodded toward his boat. "Water's been good lately. Tell Harper maybe you two ought to come out on *Line Dancer* sometime. Feel free to bring the little guy too. Can't let Eli indoctrinate him too much."

Warmth that had nothing to do with the humid Keys air filled me. The invitation wasn't just casual conversation. It was an offering, a gesture of acceptance from the most reserved of the Coleridge siblings. Then again, he had reason to be. "I'd like that a lot, Austin. I'll talk to her."

Austin gave a final curt nod, his expression unchanged save for a softening around the eyes. Then he walked away, his tall figure silhouetted against the golden late light as he headed back toward the resort grounds.

I'd come to the Sunset Siesta project armed with expertise, with carefully drawn plans and precise calculations. But I hadn't accounted for the history embedded in the land itself. History that wasn't documented in any survey or blueprint, but lived in the memories and experiences of people like Austin.

I stood and stared at the puddle, my mind making connections beyond the immediate construction problem. Relationships were like that too. You could analyze and plan, but without understanding the hidden foundations, you'd miss crucial context. Understanding Harper meant understanding not just who she was now, but the hidden foundations that had shaped the woman—her role as Finn's mother, her place within the Coleridge family, her deep connection to this resort.

I glanced back toward the pier where Austin's boat was docked and considered his invitation. It wasn't just a fishing trip he was offering—it was a chance to see the Keys through his eyes, to understand his world in a way that couldn't be conveyed through casual conversation.

As I walked back to bungalow one to make notes for tomorrow's excavation work, a new appreciation for the complex interconnections between the land, the resort, and the family that had shaped it over generations settled in. The renovation wasn't only about updating buildings. It was about honoring that history while creating space for new chapters.

And I was part of that story. A partner in the resort, yes. But now with Harper, something more.

Chapter Twelve

HARPER

CHASE and I stood side by side, going over countertop samples for the new pool bar as if we hadn't been tearing each other's clothes off every chance we got for a month now. I acted like the heat from the renovation wasn't making the same daydream all too real. Like his teasing smile and those intense, flashing eyes weren't adding to my already sweaty mess of an afternoon.

"The speckled one goes with the cabanas, don't you think?" I tried to focus, wiping construction dust off my arm as we stood under the partial shade of an umbrella.

Chase ran his fingers across the granite sample. His nails were clipped short, practical, and his tan was from actually working outside. God, his hands were beautiful.

"It has character."

I snorted. "You always say that when you mean 'it's not my favorite, but it'll work.'"

Chase pointed to a darker block of quartz. "I think this one brings out the tones in the cabanas better. Plus, this quartz is impervious to weather. Great for outdoor settings."

I studied the piece in his hand, nodding slowly. "Good point. You might be onto something. It does have a nice contrast with the wood. You win this round."

His lips curled into that grin again, the one that made me think things I wasn't supposed to think when I was focusing on the job. "Glad we agree."

I shifted the umbrella with my foot to block the afternoon sun. The construction was less chaotic today—framing for the cabanas was already well underway with my Coastal Blend wood of choice, and the sounds of saws and nail guns filled the air.

I took a drink from my ever-present thermal water bottle. "Good thing you're finally convinced. Otherwise, I might have changed my mind about the stools again."

Chase rubbed the back of his neck. "Only once?"

I remembered the last meeting, how we'd gotten stuck on decisions that were more complicated than I'd thought they would be. Not as complicated as kissing him in a half-finished closet, then trying to pretend it hadn't happened, but still. I smiled, mostly at myself. "Fine. More than once. But I like the light blue for the pop of color, even if it was a last-minute change."

"You made the right call." Chase picked up a catalog. "Worst case, they don't get delivered on time, and everyone has to stand at the new pool bar. It'll be fine."

"I want more than fine—" A loud noise caught me off guard.

It was his stomach.

"You need to feed that thing." I frowned. "It's louder than Eli's dive boat."

Chase laughed. "Guess I should've stopped for lunch."

"You didn't eat anything?"

"I was running late," he said with a casual shrug. "Didn't have time."

"You know, there are very professional, well-trained kitchen staff at Driftwood Grill right over there. You should've said something. How are you going to make it through the rest of the afternoon?"

"Depends. I've had a craving all day." He leaned close. "And not just for you. You know anyone who's good at making a grilled cheese?"

I had to laugh. "I'm practically a professional."

"Oh yeah?" Chase crossed his arms, the movement drawing my attention to his biceps. "The kids' menu at Driftwood?"

"Hardly." I straightened my spine, trying to look serious. "It's all about technique."

"Really? Let me guess. Classic cheddar?"

"Yes. On sourdough," I replied firmly. "It's all in the toasting."

He gave me an exaggerated nod, clearly skeptical. "You don't get bored using basic ingredients like that?"

"Are you calling me basic?"

"I'm saying I have taste buds."

I shoved his shoulder with mine. "Nothing wrong with a classic, you know."

"Pretty sure I can beat it. What do you think? Gruyère?"

"You would like that," I said with a teasing grin. "Or maybe something unnecessarily complex, like raclette or aged goat milk or whatever, just to make sure I know you put more thought into it than I do."

Chase grinned. "Don't forget the artisanal bread."

I narrowed my eyes. "Don't tell me you actually think you can make a better grilled cheese than me."

"There's only one way to find out." He shifted closer,

making the fine hairs on the back of my neck stand at attention. I caught my breath, ignoring the pleasant flutter in my chest. "Are you up for it?"

"I don't know." I dragged the words out as long as I could. "You're not scared I'll win?"

"I'll take my chances."

"You should know. I'm not above playing dirty."

Chase raised his eyebrows, looking amused. "I like the sound of that."

"You're on. Don't cry when I beat you."

He smiled. "I won't if you won't."

"We'll see." I shot him an answering grin. "Since you're about to fall over from hunger, let's have this cook-off tonight."

"Just tell me where. Think Finn would like to referee?"

"He'd love to." I pictured Finn holding up scorecards, drawing cartoons in the corner of the table. "But Mom's got him for the night."

"That's convenient," Chase said. I pretended not to notice the slightly hopeful look he gave me. "So?"

"So your place. You've got that fancy, modern kitchen. It's like an architect designed it for you or something."

"Harder to burn grilled cheese with a proper stove." Chase put his hand between my shoulder blades as we moved from under the umbrella. "When can you be there?"

I checked my watch, surprised how late it was. "After I hit the grocery store. Can't win a challenge without the right ingredients."

"Think you can find anything fancy on Dove Key?"

"If I can't"—I slung my tote over my shoulder—"I'll improvise. Don't worry. I'll find you some fancy cheese."

"I'll be ready." He glanced at his watch. "Say five?"

I nodded, pushing my hair out of my face. "Better not be a sore loser."

"Pretty sure that's my line. Should we place bets?"

"Nah, I'd feel bad taking your money. See you soon?"

He grinned. "Can't wait."

I was still thinking about that last smile, still half in work mode, half out, when I drove to Island Market. A pang of guilt hit me, knowing the only reason we could do this was because Finn was with Mom. I still hadn't told her about me and Chase, and now it felt like an overdue bill. I promised myself I'd talk to her soon.

Until then, I had a grilled cheese battle to win.

THE FRONT DOOR WAS UNLOCKED, and I let myself in with the groceries. Clean lines and expensive furniture. So different from my own cluttered, cozy cottage. There wasn't a crayon mark in sight, no stuffed animals peeking out from the couch cushions. The main room flowed seamlessly into the kitchen, and the walls were painted the kind of neutral gray you found in the *contemporary style* section of a paint store. Yet the shade also held a touch of the gentle blue of deep Gulf waters. Everything felt deliberate. Perfectly placed, perfectly organized. I was already starting to wonder how Chase and I ever fit together.

But somehow we did.

Chase's kitchen was as architecturally impressive as his office. Gleaming stainless-steel appliances reflected the recessed lighting, set against beautiful white quartz countertops veined with subtle gray. The state-of-the-art efficiency of it all, the sheer *flawlessness*, should have felt intimidating. This whole house was like that—the kind of meticulous, award-winning restoration people talked about, the one featured in *Keys Style* last spring. Everyone knew Chase

Ashworth didn't just design beautiful spaces. He *lived* in one. And I had no doubt the place was worth a small fortune. It should have made me feel hopelessly out of place, a splash of chaotic color in his exactly curated world. But strangely, standing here with bags of cheese and bread, I didn't feel like an intruder. That was true of all his designs I'd seen. He made spaces that were modern and functional yet still retained the essence of what they were meant to be.

Maybe it was the man, not just the house.

He came in from the back deck as I unpacked the groceries. "Look at that. You found the fancy stuff."

"It wasn't easy." I held up the small, imported package. "I think the people at Island Market have started taking bets on my buying habits."

Chase laughed. "If you're buying gruyère now, they'll be thinking you're moving up in the world."

"Maybe I am." I took out a loaf of something called pain de campagne, wrapped in a paper bag. "This was the most ostentatious bread I could find. Knock yourself out."

"Nice job." He moved closer and brushed a kiss over my lips. "Finn keeping Helen on her toes?"

Lips tingling, I lined up my sourdough and block of aged cheddar. "They get along famously, and both look forward to his sleepovers there."

He eyed the spread on the counter. "You've got this all planned out, don't you?"

"I like a competitive edge. Don't want to give you too much of a head start."

Chase opened his fridge and removed a carton of butter. "What makes you think I need it?"

"Let's see," I said. "Artisan bread? Fancy imported cheese? From your shopping list, I'm betting you've got a game plan."

"I do. What do you call that?" He nodded toward my plain, grocery-store sourdough.

"A classic. Only thing left to figure out is how badly I'm going to beat you."

"Keep dreaming, Coleridge."

He turned on two burners, and I let the smell of melting butter and browning bread do the talking for me. My whole body was in anticipation mode, half-focused on the food, half-focused on him. We cooked side by side, navigating the commercial cooktop like a kitchen choreography—bumping shoulders, reaching past each other, easy and fluid. Chase measured precisely, using his recipes like a road map to the immaculate sandwich. I went by taste, sneaking bites of cheese and pretending not to notice him watching.

"Shouldn't you have bought more of this?" I popped a chunk of gruyère in my mouth. "For practice?"

"You're a sore loser, huh?"

"I meant for you." I pretended to pout. "Not me."

He shifted closer. "Nice try."

His closeness, his calm, the fact that he wasn't nervous about being this domestic, made it hard to think straight. We laughed. We cooked. We teased each other until the kitchen smelled like golden perfection.

"Do we need to find a judge?" I held my plate and admitted, if only to myself, that his stove was a wonder of the world. "Or do we just admit you lost right now?"

Chase raised an eyebrow, nodding toward the back deck. "Let's settle this. Before you change your story."

We stepped outside, and it was like entering another world. The salty air, the distant sounds of the ocean, the way his dark yard gave way to stars. The patio was softly lit, a stark contrast to the bright precision of the kitchen. A few simple string lights hung in long lines, giving the entire space a private, secluded feel.

"Jasmine?" I said, breathing deeply. "I thought you weren't into the whole floral thing."

"I make exceptions." Chase lowered himself onto the deck seating instead of the glass table, making the outdoor couch look smaller. More intimate. "Ready to eat?"

We tasted each other's sandwiches like we were considering life-or-death decisions, but neither of us had the guts to call the winner. I faked a grimace. He took a second bite of mine, just to make sure it was a fluke. In the end, we declared a tie.

"Next time," he said, "we'll let Finn decide."

"That's not fair. He'd pick you just because you put more than one kind of cheese on it."

"Smart kid."

After dinner, we relaxed and I had to smile at the hidden lighting under the deck. The ocean air made everything softer, more like a dream than anything else. I tucked my legs under me, resting my head against the back of the couch. The deeper part of this—the reason I couldn't stop thinking about—made its way to the surface. "Chase?"

"Mmhmm?"

"This isn't the kind of place I thought I'd end up."

He paused. I could feel him weighing his words. "The deck or the grilled cheese?"

"Neither." I sighed, surprised by how easy it was to talk to him, to admit the truth that I'd barely let myself consider. "After Finn, I wasn't sure I wanted this. A family. Stability. Jarod—" I stopped. I hadn't meant to go there, to say more than I'd already said. "I didn't think about the future the way you do. I plan all facets of the resort and my homelife with future projections all mapped out, except when my heart is involved."

Chase's arm stretched behind me, pulling me closer. "Because of Jarod?"

"I thought we were happy." I shifted against Chase, not moving away, but finding a comfortable spot, finding the words that fit with what I hadn't said yet. "He was the kind of guy I thought I'd always be with. On paper, we made sense. Got along great, similar interests."

Chase traced a slow line down my arm with his thumb, waiting. He didn't rush me. Didn't push for answers.

"I told him I was pregnant." The words felt both far away and all too real, like they'd been locked up so long they didn't belong to me. "And all the color drained from his face."

Chase exhaled, a low sound that said more than words.

"I knew we weren't madly in love." I wondered how much I'd tell before I couldn't keep my own emotions in check. "But I thought there was enough. More than enough. I thought he cared about me, even if he wasn't crazy about the idea of a kid. I thought he'd come around to the idea of being a father. Instead, he split. And now I don't know how to trust anyone."

Chase shifted beside me, pulling me in tighter.

"Not just Jarod." I swallowed hard. "I don't know how to trust myself. I'm scared I'll never find a relationship where I get both—a partner and a father for Finn. I don't want to drag anyone into a life they don't really want."

Chase paused, and I was terrified I'd said too much. "That sucks."

"It sucks?"

"Yeah. He was a coward and a total shithead."

I waited. "You don't think it's stupid of me?"

"Of course not." Chase's voice was low and sure. "You're the one who got hurt."

"But—"

He cut me off. "I'm still here, aren't I?"

"Why?"

"Because," he said, holding me close, "I know how it feels."

"To get pregnant?" I snuggled against his side, my voice teasing, not wanting him to hear the wobble in it. "Impressive."

He laughed, a quiet sound that hummed through me. "No, to see something you thought was normal, then discover it wasn't at all like you thought."

I took a deep breath. "What do you mean?"

"My parents," he said. "They are all I've ever seen. Careful tiptoeing and silence. No heat, no passion. Just… there. When I got a little older and saw that other parents weren't like that, it kind of shook the foundation under me."

"And you're worried you'll be like that?"

"It's not how I want to end up."

"How do you want to end up?"

"With this." I felt him smile, and it broke something open inside me. "With something real."

"I should be scared, and I am. Taking a chance after what happened."

He nodded, leaning in closer. "Shouldn't I be scared, too?"

"Depends," I said, my lips brushing his. "Can you handle losing grilled cheese contests?"

He laughed and held me tighter, giving me all the answers I needed right then. The breeze picked up, blowing my hair into my face. I swept it away, pushing aside the doubt that always came with the past. This time, I had reason to hope it would stay there.

Chase leaned his cheek against my head. "I consider it a minor miracle, but my sister found happiness. Lacey wasn't as affected by our parents as I was. She and Daniel have a happy marriage. I miss her sometimes."

"You don't see her much?"

"Less since she got married. They live over in Big Pine Key now." He shrugged, but there was a hint of melancholy in his voice. "I get it, though. She's happy."

"And you're not?"

He tilted his head and kissed me softly as if to prove otherwise. "Getting there."

I smiled against his lips, letting myself believe what he was telling me. That we were both getting closer to something we'd never had before. We kissed again, longer this time, and the warmth of him seeped into every corner of doubt I'd ever had.

His hands moved slowly, tracing down the lines of my back as he pulled me into his lap. I shifted, straddling him on the couch as we lost ourselves in each other and the night. This was it. This was what I'd been too scared to imagine. The world fell away, leaving only Chase.

His skin against mine.

His heart against mine.

Chapter Thirteen

CHASE

THE WORLD COLLAPSED to a single point of contact where her hips touched mine. A kiss—deep and demanding—filled the void, our tongues moving in rhythm. I didn't even realize I'd slid my hands into Harper's hair until I felt her sigh into my mouth. I pulled back, breathless, her face a gorgeous portrait of desire. Then she gripped my shirt with a groan and kissed me hard. She pressed against me, and a sound was ripped from my throat. Helpless, needy. The kind of sound I'd never made before and didn't think I ever could unless it was her making me do it.

We'd talked so much over dinner, laid it all bare, but this—God, this—was like stripping away the last defenses. I felt the slight shift in Harper's weight, the tautness of her muscles as she pushed against me, and every other thought burned away. My hands slid down her back, grazing her skin as she arched into me with a moan. I wanted her so badly it made me dizzy.

"Maybe we should go upstairs?" My voice was rough, almost a plea. She pulled back, her eyes finding mine, lips swollen and shiny, her face open, a little wild.

"Chase…" Her breath caught on my name, and she shook her head, not to refuse but to insist. Her fingers found my hair, and her mouth curved with a promise. "Right here. Right now."

My pulse exploded, relief and hunger colliding in my chest. I eased her down, the couch soft beneath us, the cushions wide enough for two if we didn't mind being tangled. She shivered when I skimmed my hands beneath her shirt and pulled it off, exposing her to the night air. The sight of her bare skin made me reckless with want, and I dipped my head, tasting her neck. She was warm and perfect against my tongue.

I reached her lips again, caught the sweet noises she made as I covered her. One of us shifted, then the other until we were a messy pile of limbs. We ended up with me on my back and her on top. She sat up, and a bolt of heat seared through me at the look she gave me.

"You're incredible," I murmured, awed. I'd meant it about what was between us, the way she made me feel—unraveled and exposed but completely right—but her flush deepened as if I'd complimented her body. As if the two things weren't so deeply tied I could never separate them. She kissed me, a slow slide of lips and tongue that grew greedy fast.

Then her hands were at the waistband of my shorts. She undressed me deliberately, while I lay under her and fought for air. Thought turned liquid, poured from my head to somewhere lower, where it turned molten. Her fingers were warm and her motions assured as she pulled my shirt off. The sharp sound of a zipper, metal on metal, cut through the heavy night air. A wicked smile appeared when she saw my face. The cool night met my skin as she pushed my shorts over my hips and made me shudder. She grabbed both my hands and sat me up again with the cushions warm against my back.

Then she dropped to her knees, and all my thoughts evaporated at once.

"Shit." I ran my hands through my hair, then pressed the heels of my palms against my eyes. I groaned when I felt her tongue, like I'd been starving for this, for her, forever. Her mouth, her hands. Everything about it was desperate and exactly right, and I didn't know how long I could last. Didn't care as long as she kept going.

With a playful glint in her eyes, she looked up at me and teased, "I hope I can fit all of you in my mouth."

A taunt that felt like it would undo me even before her lips wrapped around my shaft and took me in, hard and close. "God, Harper."

Everything about it, about her, was incredible. It was more than I could handle. More than I could hold on to. Then she took me deeper, the world splintering around the edges.

Just when I thought I couldn't hold on a second longer, she slowly withdrew. A flash of teeth in the moonlight as she scrambled for my wallet and grabbed a condom. She sheathed me quickly, confidently, and I couldn't take my eyes off her. It was the sexiest thing I'd ever seen—the softness of her body as she stripped off her clothes, the smoothness of her skin in the moonlight. She climbed back onto the couch to straddle me, her legs on either side of mine.

"Come here." My voice sounded wrecked. She leaned down and kissed me as she guided me inside, not giving me time to get my breath before she stole it.

"Oh, Jesus," I choked.

Immediate pleasure, a white-hot bolt of it. I swore again and held her hips, feeling her thighs tense as she adjusted and began to move. She rode me slowly at first, controlling the pace, her fingers gripping my hair. I was dizzy with how much I wanted her, so badly it felt like falling. I held her tighter, careful to draw it out, feeling every shift of her hips as if it were happening in slow motion. I wanted this to last, to go on until we shattered into pieces so small we couldn't be found.

Then her nails scraped my shoulders, and she whispered my name in a way that almost destroyed me. She lifted up, impossibly graceful, her head tilted back. I pulled her to me, bracing her back, arching into her.

"You feel so good." My voice cracked, half-wild. "So impossibly good."

She moaned as I thrust up to meet her. Slow and easy became fast and urgent. She gave back every bit of it and more. I drove deeper and heard her gasp, saw her eyes glaze, felt her body shudder. More than I'd dreamed of having until she was suddenly there, raw and unguarded and *mine*.

Her breathless words sent me spiraling at the intensity of it all. Wanting her so badly, feeling her everywhere, never wanting it to stop. My skin tingled, too tight all of a sudden. We were moving together, fast, frantic, nothing between us except the desperate need to be closer, closer, to hold on until everything broke apart. And then to hold on even tighter.

We came undone, our release filling the night with a different kind of heat. Loud. Primal. It was like stepping into the sun, all light and impossible fire. A bright, dazzling flash that left me blind and spent, melted. All I could do was ride it out, each thrust sending a shock of pleasure through me until the stars collapsed and we went still.

Harper's head rested on my shoulder. My hands were shaking a little as I held her. I felt her breathing, felt the damp warmth of our skin pressed together, felt the stretch of silence as we sat in the moonlight, spent.

Felt it all in a way that terrified and thrilled me.

I buried my face in her hair and inhaled deeply, tickling at the slight prickle of it in my nose, licking the softness against my lips. As intense as everything had been, there was a shock of something even more powerful. The shock of rightness. Of being right where I needed to be, where I was supposed to be.

"You think the neighbors heard?" Harper's voice was muffled against my shoulder, thick with laughter. "Or did we scare them off the island?"

I laughed with her, feeling it rumble through both of us. "Pretty sure they're calling the National Guard right now."

She pulled back, her eyes bright and teasing. "Should we tell them it was just an earthquake?"

"Ah, let them figure it out."

"Hmm." She pretended to consider. "That could be fun."

I grinned. She made me feel like a kid who'd just found his favorite toy under the Christmas tree. "You're trouble, you know that?"

"And you can't resist it." She kissed me, quick and playful, then snuggled closer.

"Isn't that the truth."

We stayed wrapped up in each other until the air turned cool against our skin and we had to move inside. In the cool night of my bedroom, we made love again. Slower this time and sweeter. After, we fell defenseless into sleep.

· · ·

THE PRE-DAWN LIGHT filtered through my bedroom window, painting the walls with a hushed glow. I blinked at the ceiling, the weight of Harper's head on my shoulder, her hair soft against my skin. It was like waking from a dream that didn't end, a warmth that filled my chest with an ache too deep to name. Her lips parted in sleep, a faint whisper of breath against my neck, and I couldn't help but stare.

I lay there, hardly breathing, hardly daring to move. Harper shifted a little, burrowing deeper, her breath a slow and steady rhythm that calmed me even as my mind raced and whirled.

At how deeply I'd let her in, despite all the reasons not to.

How deeply I wanted to.

How I wouldn't be able to stop even if I tried.

I remembered every word we'd spoken over dinner. Jarod and how unsure I was about everything. Her laugh, the way she touched my hand as if it were the most natural thing in the world. I thought about her on my deck, the easy domesticity of her passing me a bottle of beer, the heady, unfamiliar warmth of our conversation. The intense connection when we made love. The strength of it, the sheer, breathtaking magnitude. Nothing about last night had been casual or fleeting. My feelings had crossed a line I'd never expected. Exhilaration shot through me, sharp and almost painful in its intensity.

Love.

The word echoed in my mind, no matter how hard I tried to shut it out. It was foreign. It was immense. It was terrifying. But I knew it was there, even if I wasn't ready to say it, even to myself.

The stillness of the morning hung around us, but I couldn't find stillness in my mind. Everything was in motion. Everything was changing. I thought of my parents' marriage. The cold… boringness of it. How I'd promised myself I'd never have anything like that. I'd never wanted a relationship with this much heat and depth, not until Harper, not until I felt it with her and knew what I was missing.

I thought of Finn, his laughter as he dragged me down the beach, the happiness on Harper's face when she watched us. I thought of the resort and the way she moved through it like it was an extension of her heart. I thought of Eli, the complicated knot of professional and personal ties that would make anything between us difficult, messy, maybe impossible.

But what I thought of most was the way this woman made me feel. Alive. Seen. More real than I'd ever been. The world had been carefully ordered before her, a blueprint written in clean lines and simple plans. Now it was a mess of colors and emotions, vibrant, unpredictable, terrifying. I wasn't sure what to make of it. I wasn't sure what to make of myself.

I loved it. I hated it. I couldn't get enough.

Chapter Fourteen

HARPER

MY BROTHER BRADEN was sampling a batch of IPA behind the bar, a pen behind his ear and his focus so tight he didn't notice me slip through the brewpub's door. The place was uncharacteristically quiet, the only noise a low hum of the cooler unit and the scuff of my sandals on the floor. Normally, I'd find this morning, pre-opening stillness relaxing. The time when the place was holding its breath and waiting to explode with laughter, life, and chatter. But my mind was a churning mess of giddy uncertainty and confusing happiness, a persistent tension that even the brewpub's expectant tranquility couldn't shake. I was there to hash out some menu ideas with Braden for an upcoming beer-pairing dinner at Driftwood Grill.

Then I saw Ben, slumped over a corner table with his schoolbooks spread in front of him. His coffee steamed at the edge of the table, untouched. I made my way over, watching him as he stared out the window like it was a magic portal that might free him from his torment. That was unlike him—he usually dove into challenges like a dog chasing a stick. I pulled up a chair across from him, glancing down at the book he'd been rattling a pen against. It was a two-inch-thick guide to human anatomy.

"Hey, you," I said gently. "Taking a study break?"

He started, blinking as he looked up at me. I was met with green eyes full of clouded frustration, the usual quiet intensity replaced by an expression of doubt. My heart gave a sisterly squeeze at the sight.

"Not quite," he said, attempting a weak smile.

As I sat with Ben and saw him struggling, my errand with Braden faded into the background. "You look about ready to throw that textbook into the ocean." I wasn't just teasing. There was a note of knowing understanding in my voice. I'd felt this way about my own life before.

Ben sighed and leaned back in his chair. His expression held a flicker of defeated humor, like he knew he was letting the situation get to him but couldn't help it. "Wouldn't be the worst idea. This stuff just isn't sinking in, Harper. Why am I doing this to myself?"

I leaned in, resting my chin in my hands as I watched him fidget with a stack of notes. Frustration oozed from his movements, the doubt eating away at him.

I wanted to find the right words. Something that would cut through the academic struggle and hit at the heart of what was driving him—his desire to help, to be more than just the bad boy of the island. "Ben, you remember that guest who fell and hurt his leg by the pool last year? You were the first one there, totally calm and talking to him, keeping everyone else back until help arrived. That's instinct. That's what matters."

"So?" He looked at me, a mix of skepticism and consideration in his eyes.

"You're the most determined person I know," I added.

"When you decide to do something, you don't give up. This is hard, yeah, but you can do hard things. You always have."

The words hung in the air, and I could almost see him processing them, trying to reconcile the truth of what I said with the noise in his own mind. It felt like I was speaking to both of us, trying to reassure him—and myself—that we could handle our separate challenges.

Ben's eyes dropped back to the book, the anatomy charts and diagrams looking impossibly complex and dense. I knew that feeling. It was the same way my heart felt when I thought about Chase and the future.

"Maybe you're right," he said, though the words came out uncertain. I could sense a tiny shift in him, like a stone nudged out of place in a stream, altering the flow of water around it.

"Trust me," I said. "This isn't about memorizing everything overnight. It's about sticking with it, pushing through, and coming out the other side. I know you can do that."

Ben didn't answer right away, but the corners of his mouth pulled upward just a little. A subtle shift in his posture followed—a quiet loosening of the tense set of his shoulders. It was like watching a tightly wound spring slowly release, bit by bit. His hand moved to the flashcards and flipped one over. He studied it with a new focus, and the words that had seemed to mock him minutes ago appeared to take on a different light.

Warmth rushed through me, like the nurturing side of me had wrapped around us both. Helping Ben brought clarity, a reminder of the strength that came from perseverance. My heart still danced with that messy, happy chaos over Chase, but supporting Ben anchored me to the present, making the uncertainties feel more manageable. "You can do this, Ben. I believe in you."

"Yeah. I sure hope so." His eyes met mine. The stare was quieter than his usual bravado, but there was something even more reassuring in its subtlety. He might not have been effusive in his thanks, but the way he returned to his work was all the affirmation I needed. Then he really looked at me. "Thanks, Harper. You've always been a great cheerleader."

That made me laugh out loud. "I was never a cheerleader. But I refuse to watch people I love talk themselves out of what they really want. So stop it, okay?"

He uncapped his highlighter and resumed reading, and I slid off the chair. My talk with Braden could wait. I might have settled Ben's mind a little, but mine was plenty mixed up. I wanted some sisterly advice. Someone to help me digest this mix of giddy uncertainty and hope. I pushed through the brewpub's door and out into the Florida sunshine, pausing to dial Brenna's number on my phone.

The phone rang twice before Brenna's warm voice answered. "Hey, sis. Aren't you supposed to be working?"

"I am. Sort of." I leaned against the railing outside the brewpub, watching a group of guests meander toward the beach. "Are you free for lunch? I could really use a sounding board right now."

There was a brief pause, then a shuffle of papers. "For you? Always. Everything okay?"

"Yes. No. Maybe? That's why I need the sounding board." I sighed, running a hand through my hair.

"Say no more." I could hear the smile in her voice. "Island Breeze in thirty minutes?"

"That works. You're the best, Bren."

"So I've been told. See you soon."

As I marched through the resort toward my car, my

phone buzzed in my pocket. I pulled it out and squinted at the screen against the glare to see a message from Eli.

> Eli: Hey sis! I've heard on good authority that you've been working too hard. Need a stress reliever?

A smile touched my lips despite my racing thoughts. Trust Eli to know when I needed a distraction, even if he didn't know the half of *why* I was stressed.

> Harper: You have no idea. What did you have in mind? More unsolicited advice about my love life?

> Eli: Ouch. And here I thought we bonded over parrotfish costumes. But I was thinking something more… immersive.

> Harper: ???

> Eli: Diving! Jules and I were planning on hitting the reef Saturday afternoon after my classes were finished. Figured maybe you and Mr. Architect Fancy Pants might want to join us?

My breath caught. Diving. With Eli and Jules… and Chase. The idea sent a jolt of mingled excitement through me. Being out on the water, away from work, just the four of us… it sounded idyllic. A picture of easy coupledom that felt dangerously appealing, especially when my own feelings were accelerating at warp speed.

The image of the clear blue water, the peaceful quiet beneath the surface, the thought of sharing something *I* loved with *Chase*… it was undeniably tempting. A chance to see him in a different element. A chance, maybe, to just *be* together without the weight of the resort pressing down. Taking a deep breath, I typed back, choosing hope over fear.

> Harper: That sounds amazing. Assuming Mr. Architect Fancy Pants is free, count us in. What time Saturday?

> Eli: Perfect! Meet at the dive shop around two? We'll take Sunset Diver. Prepare for maximum relaxation… and probably some terrible jokes.

> Harper: Wouldn't expect anything less. See you then. Thanks, Eli. 🩶

I slid the phone back into my pocket, my heart doing a nervous flutter kick. A double date dive, where I was dating my brother's best friend. What could possibly go wrong? Everything, probably. But as I walked toward the restaurant to meet Brenna, a tiny spark of exhilaration ignited within the anxiety.

***

Island Breeze Bistro buzzed with the lunch rush as I slid into the vinyl booth across from Brenna. She looked up from her iced tea, her auburn hair catching the sunlight streaming through the window, and one look at my face told her everything she needed to know.

"That bad, huh?" She pushed a menu toward me, though we both knew I'd order the same thing I always did. The red vinyl booth squeaked as I settled in.

"Yes and no. I just left Ben looking like he was about ready to use his anatomy textbook for kindling."

Brenna laughed softly. "EMT classes getting to him?"

"Understatement of the year. But I think I talked him off the ledge." I flagged down Marge, the waitress who'd been serving us since we were kids, her gray hair pulled back in the same tight bun she'd worn for twenty years.

"Fish and chips with extra tartar?" Marge didn't even pull out her notepad.

I nodded. "And—"

"Lemonade, minimal ice." She winked. "I've got you, honey."

As Marge bustled away, I pressed my fingertips against my temples, trying to ward off the headache that Ben's stress—and my own swirling thoughts about Chase—had triggered. The checkered floor, the familiar scent of frying fish, and the low hum of local gossip were usually grounding. Today, they were just loud.

"Okay." Brenna set her iced tea down, her warm eyes, so like Ben's but infinitely kinder, fixed on me. "Ben might be struggling with anatomy, but something tells me your stress headache isn't solely related to sibling support."

"No." I took a deep breath. The words I'd been holding back, the confession I hadn't even fully admitted to myself until this moment, felt ready to burst. "I'm falling for Chase. Hard and fast and totally out of control." The admission felt both frightening and freeing, like jumping from a cliff and finding out mid-fall that I was enjoying the sensation.

"Oh, Harper." Her voice held no surprise, just gentle understanding. "I can see how that would be scary for you."

"It's happening so fast, Bren. One minute, he's just Eli's friend. The next, he's… everywhere. In my thoughts, in my dreams." I paused as Marge delivered my lemonade and left. "In my bed every chance we get."

Brenna's eyebrows shot up, a small smile playing at her lips. "And this is a problem because…?"

"Because I have Finn to think about. Because the last man I trusted walked away without a backward glance. Because Chase is Eli's best friend, which is weird, and now he's our business partner. Plus, if this all goes sideways, it's not only my heart on the line." The words tumbled out, gaining momentum. "It's Finn's heart, the resort's future, our family's stability."

Brenna reached across the table, her hand covering mine. "Breathe, Harper."

I tried, pulling air into lungs that suddenly felt too small. The diner continued its dance around us—a couple arguing in hushed tones in the corner, a family with sunburned cheeks laughing over milkshakes, tourists poring over maps and brochures—all oblivious to my internal crisis.

"Finn adores him," I continued, softer now. "He always has. Chase treats him like he matters, like his opinions are important. If this doesn't work out…" My voice cracked, and I cleared my throat. "Finn has never had a father figure. What if he gets attached and then loses Chase?"

Marge arrived with our food, the smell of fried fish momentarily distracting me. I picked at a French fry, not really hungry despite having skipped breakfast.

"And then there's the resort partnership," I continued once Marge left. "What happens if we break up? Chase has invested so much money and energy in the redesign. Will he walk away from that? Will he stay and make things awkward? Will Eli be caught in the middle?" The questions had been circling my mind like hungry sharks.

"Not to mention," I added, stabbing a piece of fish, "the whole island will have an opinion. You know how Dove Key is—nothing stays private."

"All valid points." Brenna nodded, taking a thoughtful bite of her chicken sandwich. "And underneath all that, what's really scaring you, Harper?"

The question hit me squarely in the chest. I set down my fork and looked out the window at Main Street with its vivid hanging flower baskets, watching tourists window-shop at Brenna's currently closed-for-lunch bookstore down the street. When I turned back, I couldn't meet her eyes.

"I'm terrified of how much I want this." My voice was barely audible. "How much I want him. It's like he's unlocked something I've kept buried since Jarod left. And that makes me feel vulnerable. Exposed."

Brenna was quiet for a moment, sipping her tea. The distant clatter of dishes from the kitchen filled the silence.

"You have every right to be scared, Harper." Her voice was steady, anchoring. "You've got a hell of a lot on your plate, more than most people realize."

My eyes stung with unexpected tears. Validation was sometimes all you needed to feel a little less overwhelmed.

"But I've watched you with Finn all these years," she continued. "The way you've put his needs first, how you've balanced being both mother and father, how you've kept the resort running even when it was held together with duct tape and sheer force of will. You're the strongest person I know."

I snorted softly. "I don't feel very strong right now."

"That's because love isn't about strength. It's about vulnerability." Brenna's eyes grew distant, and I knew she was thinking about Hunter. "Remember how everyone reacted when Hunter and I got together? All our brothers threatened bodily harm. The entire island had opinions about a Coleridge and a Markham crossing battle lines. And especially about Hunter himself."

I smiled despite myself. The Coleridge-Markham feud had been legendary in Dove Key, until Hunter and Brenna had shocked everyone by falling in love and ending it forever.

"Mom eventually came around with Hunter, didn't she?" Brenna continued. "Sometimes you have to trust that love, real love, is worth the risk and the fight."

I pushed a fry through a pool of ketchup, considering her words. "But Hunter didn't have a child to consider. He didn't have your family's livelihood tied up in his business decisions."

"No," Brenna acknowledged. "But he had his own demons. His own fears. And we faced them together." She leaned forward, her expression earnest. "That's what I'm trying to tell you, Harper. Have you actually talked to Chase about any of this?"

I shook my head, embarrassed. "Not really. We've been so caught up in… everything. And Chase has always been quiet. He doesn't really talk about what's going on in that head of his."

"In other words, he's a man." Brenna pushed her plate aside. "Look, I can't tell you what to do. But I can tell you that bottling up these fears isn't going to make them go away. Chase deserves to know what you're worried about, especially regarding Finn."

I nodded slowly, knowing she was right. The noise of the diner seemed to recede as I considered her advice.

"And, Harper?" Brenna's voice softened. "For what it's worth, I've seen the way Chase looks at you. Like you're the sun and he's just grateful to be in your orbit. He's looked at you like that for a while now. Longer than the renovation."

A flutter of something—hope, maybe—stirred in my

chest. "But what if it's not enough? What if I'm not enough?"

"That's the risk we all take." She shrugged, her simple honesty cutting through my tangled thoughts. "But maybe Chase, with his steadiness and quiet strength, is exactly what you need right now. A balance to all the chaos."

I thought about those thoughtful hazel eyes, the way his hand always found the small of my back in a crowd, how he listened like every word I said mattered. The way he'd built a relationship with Finn based on respect and genuine interest, not obligation or strategy.

The bustling diner continued around us, but for a moment, everything felt clearer. The fears were still there, lurking beneath the surface, but they seemed less over-whelming than they had an hour ago.

"Talk to him," Brenna urged gently. "Not about complications with the resort or Eli, but about what you think. What you fear. What you hope for. Then take it one step at a time."

I nodded, feeling steadier now. "One step at a time. Maybe I just need to get used to being part of a couple. Actually, Eli invited us to go diving on Saturday. Just the four of us—Chase, me, him, and Jules."

Brenna's eyes lit up. "Perfect! Away from work, away from everything. A chance to just be together."

"I could see how it goes, then talk to Chase alone after-ward," I muttered, picking at a piece of fish.

"Don't rush things, but don't be afraid to talk to him, either," Brenna said.

Marge brought the check, and I insisted on paying despite Brenna's protests. As we slid out of the booth, the vinyl squeaking beneath us, I felt both lighter and heavier —lighter for having shared my burden, heavier with the knowledge of what I needed to do.

Outside the diner, the Florida sun beat down, immediately wrapping us in its humid embrace. Brenna hugged me tightly.

"Harper?" she called as I turned to leave. "You deserve to be happy. Remember that."

I smiled, raising a hand in acknowledgment as I walked toward my car. The path ahead with Chase was still fraught with challenges—family opinions, business complications, the ever-present fear of having my heart broken again. But perhaps it wasn't entirely impossible.

After all, a Coleridge and a Markham had found their way to each other against all odds. Maybe Chase and I could too.

One conversation at a time.

Chapter Fifteen

CHASE

FIFTEEN FEET BELOW THE SURFACE, I hovered in the water as the timer on my dive computer ticked down the final minute of our safety stop. My breathing created a steady rhythm through the regulator. Inhale, exhale, each breath a contained universe of compressed air.

Below us, the reef pulsed with life, a living painting that no artist could capture. I hadn't realized how much I'd missed this—the weightlessness, the muffled silence, the absolute presence required by the underwater world. Launching Latitudes and diving into the resort renovations had consumed every waking moment for months, but here, suspended in blue, I remembered why I made time for this.

A shimmering school of yellow-tailed snappers swept past, their movements so synchronized they seemed to share a single mind. Their vibrant colors caught the filtered sunlight, flashing gold against the backdrop of coral formations and swaying sea fans. The massive coral below us hosted a busy community of cleaner wrasses darting in and out of its folds, while purple sea fans waved gently in the current.

I adjusted my buoyancy with a small exhale, trying to maintain neutrality without rising or sinking. It had been too long since my last dive, and my muscle memory felt rusty. The slightest breath changed my position in the water, a reminder of how diving demanded complete awareness of your body.

I glanced over at Harper, floating effortlessly through the water. Seeing her like this, unburdened and graceful, struck something deep inside me. Even behind her mask, the wonder in her eyes was clear. She felt the way I did here, free and *alive*. A moment of pure intimacy in a world all our own.

Something shifted in my chest as I watched her. Sharing this silent, weightless world felt unexpectedly intimate, as if we'd discovered a secret language. Up on the surface, we balanced work discussions about the resort renovations with careful steps into a relationship neither of us had planned. But down here, where words couldn't intrude, the connection was both simpler and more profound.

I let the feeling sink in. I'd been consumed with the launch of Latitudes and the resort project, buried in stress and deadlines. I hadn't realized how much I'd needed this—the escape, the reset, the connection. Harper hovered nearby, her movements fluid and confident.

A movement to my right caught my eye. Eli's distinctive neon yellow fins with *Follow Me* written in permanent ink on the tips flicked as he gave me an exaggerated okay sign, his eyes conveying the unspoken critique of my wobbly buoyancy. Twenty-plus years of friendship meant he never missed a chance to needle me about my rusty dive skills. I responded with an equally exaggerated okay, adding an eye roll behind my mask.

Next to Eli, Jules floated serenely, her trim black wetsuit and streamlined position making her look like she belonged here more than any of us. With her dark hair swept into a neat ponytail and her movements precise and economical, she reminded me of a sleek reef shark—elegant, composed, slightly intimidating. Despite being a relatively new diver, Julianne Verne approached underwater skills with the same meticulous attention she brought to the resort's financials.

After signaling the dive was finished, Eli lifted his thumb and we rose slowly, the surface shimmering above us. The meditative calm shifted with each foot we climbed, anticipation building until we broke through. Bright sunlight blinded me momentarily, *Sunset Diver* rocking gently from where it was moored nearby.

"Woo!" Harper pulled her regulator free, her face split with a grin as she pulled her mask down. Water droplets caught in her eyelashes, making them sparkle in the afternoon sun. "That was fabulous!"

"Not bad for a resort master scheduler," Eli said, floating effortlessly beside her. "You're starting to look like you belong down there, sis."

"The visibility was exceptional today," Jules said, still peering into the blue water. "I counted two species of butterflyfish I hadn't seen before."

"Ooh, somebody's been studying her fish ID books," Eli said, smiling at her with obvious approval.

We swam the short distance to *Sunset Diver*, its white hull gleaming in the sunshine. Eli reached the ladder first and climbed aboard with the practiced ease of someone who did this multiple times daily. He leaned over to offer Jules a hand, which she accepted with a small nod.

"Need a boost, old man?" Eli called down to me, grinning. "Those custom homes aren't keeping you in diving shape."

"No, but the running does, asshole," I replied mildly, waiting for Harper to go ahead of me.

She was already moving up the rungs, water streaming from her. I definitely didn't watch the way it clung to her curves as she climbed. And I absolutely wasn't caught staring when I hauled myself onto the deck after her.

"Like what you see, Ashworth?" she asked quietly, a teasing glint in her eye as she reached for a towel.

"Can't complain about the view."

The routine kicked in. Tanks were secured, masks stowed, wetsuits peeled off in the humid afternoon air. Harper and I reached for the freshwater hose at the same time, our hands brushing.

She stepped back, her eyes playful, handing me the hose with a grin. "You go first. Looks like you need it."

Eli shook his head, passing out towels. "Or maybe you two should shower together. Save water."

I caught the look in his eye, a mix of amusement and something else—scrutiny. The boat deck settled into a post-dive rhythm. Eli pulled cold beers and sodas from the cooler, passing them around along with a bag of chips and a container of cookies.

"Refreshments for the successful divers," he announced. "Jules brought some cookies too, because she's secretly the best person on this boat."

"Don't tell anyone," Jules said dryly as she grabbed a can of soda. "I have a cultivated reputation for heartlessness to maintain."

Harper and I sat close on a bench seat, sharing a towel, her wet hair brushing my shoulder. The casual intimacy felt natural, but I was acutely aware of Eli's watchful presence.

"So," Eli said, cracking open a beer, "how was the view from down under? You both looked cozy."

"I managed my air pretty well, I think," I shot back. "Good thing you didn't charge us by the minute. I'd have to trade you the SUV to settle up."

"We could work out a payment plan." Eli turned to Harper. "Seriously, though, you did great. No panic, no flailing. Almost like you knew what you were doing."

"Thanks to you," she said, her eyes warm. "And you didn't even need to rename the dive boat."

Jules leaned in and grabbed a cookie. "That sounds like a story."

Harper laughed, a sound I didn't hear nearly enough from her. "Eli called it the *HMS Flail* during a refresher session I had a few years ago. Nice, right?"

Our interaction caused a sense of belonging to wash over me. Eli's jokes, Jules's steady presence, Harper fitting so well into the group—it felt solid. But beneath the surface-level ease, Eli's attention wasn't casual. He had a way of looking that saw everything, especially the things you tried to hide.

"That reef never gets old." Harper leaned back, her shoulder brushing mine. "Every time I think I've seen it all, there's something new. Those little blue fish darting in and out of the staghorn coral today? I could have watched them for hours."

"They're a type of chromis," Eli said. "I still want to take you night diving. Whole different world down there after dark. The parrotfish wrap themselves in mucus cocoons to sleep."

"That's… disgusting and fascinating," Harper said.

"Just like your brother," Jules added, earning an appreciative laugh from all of us.

Jules passed around the fresh fruit plate while Eli launched into the story of a moray eel encounter I'd heard more than once.

"So there I was, face-to-face with this green moray," Eli said, gesturing expansively. "Must have been seven feet long if it was an inch. I'm showing the guests the proper viewing distance when this absolute unit of an eel decides today's the day to inspect every inch of my mask."

"Funny how that eel grows a foot longer every time you tell this story," Harper said, reaching for a cookie.

"Artistic license," Eli replied, unfazed. "Jules, back me up here. You've seen that moray at Blue Dropoff. It's enormous, right?"

Jules looked up from where she was drying her dive computer with a microfiber cloth. "I've seen it, yes." Her lips curved in the slightest hint of a smile. "Though I don't recall it attempting to remove your mask with its teeth like you claimed last time."

"Details." Eli waved dismissively. "Chase, tell them about that tiger shark that buzzed you last year."

"It was a nurse shark, and it was sleeping under a ledge until you decided to wake it up," I corrected, grinning at the memory. "Which is very different from your version, where it was circling me like I was chum."

Harper laughed, the sound carrying across the water. "Did anyone spot that massive grouper lurking under the coral overhang? I swear it was watching us like we were the exhibit and it was the tourist."

"Good eye." Eli nodded approvingly. "That's Old Grumpy. He's been hanging around that spot for at least three years. Territorial as hell but makes for a great landmark."

The conversation flowed, shifting to the resort's renovations.

"What's the timeline for the bungalows?" Eli asked, leaning back with his elbows resting on the tank holders.

Harper took a sip of her drink. "Painting the interiors this month. The renderings look incredible. Chase's design keeps the classic Keys feel but with all the contemporary amenities our guests expect. The indoor-outdoor showers are going to be a major selling point."

"Thanks to Austin's input, the bungalows are coming along very nicely," I added. "And the pool cabanas are on schedule to be finished soon."

"Those bungalows are going to look great," Jules said, reaching for some fresh fruit. Her tone shifted, more serious. "But just looking ahead… cash flow for the Q3 draw on the loan, when we hit the heavy interior finishes for the bungalows, is going to require really tight management of the operational budget. We planned for this quarter's negative, obviously, but there's less wiggle room than I'd like moving into the next phase."

The words hung in the air, sinking into me like stones. I nodded, trying to keep my response level. "Appreciate the heads-up, Jules. We're tracking the change orders closely. Hopefully, we don't hit any major delays."

My post-dive relaxation was quickly replaced by the tight knot of financial pressure. We'd planned for this—everything charted, every risk calculated—but hearing it out loud shook me. Latitudes needed the project to stay on course. The other projects I'd landed, like the Franson guesthouse, would help the bottom line, but Siesta Sunset would either make or break me.

Eli and Jules shifted, momentarily distracted. Eli pointed out a distant boat, and Jules turned around to look.

It created a brief window of privacy, just enough for Harper and me to face each other more directly.

Her eyes found mine, her expression softening. Even with her hair wet and tangled, she looked beautiful, relaxed in a way I rarely saw her at the resort. She traced a finger along the edge of the bench between us.

"God, I've missed this," she said quietly. "Being out on the water. Diving. It's like… coming home to a place you forgot you needed. Are you enjoying yourself?"

I held her gaze, enjoying the rocking of the boat beneath us, the salt drying on my skin, the warmth of her beside me. "There's nowhere else I'd rather be. Not just the diving. Being here. With you."

Her smile lit up her face, but there was something vulnerable in her eyes. She placed her hand on my arm, her touch warm against my cooled skin. "Can I admit something?"

She had my full attention, her words cutting through the complicated mix of anxiety and connection. "Of course."

"This, us… it feels really good. Maybe too good." Her breath was shaky. "I could fall pretty hard for you. And honestly? I'm still not sure that's a good thing." She swallowed hard but held my gaze.

Her directness surprised me, but more than that, empathy surged within me. I reached for her hand, holding it tightly, my voice low. "Hey. I get it. This is a lot. For both of us."

Her eyes searched mine, looking for something solid to hold onto.

"I've got a hell of a lot riding on this project too, personally and professionally. It's intense." I squeezed her hand, making sure she felt the strength behind my words. "But, Harper, we knew it wouldn't be simple. We'll figure it out. Okay? We take it one step, one dive, one budget report at a time. Together."

"I like the sound of that."

She leaned in and brushed a quick kiss over my mouth. The connection felt raw and powerful, the reassurance settling in. It didn't erase the fear, but it softened the edges, made it something we could face instead of something that would consume us.

I reached out to smooth her wet hair. "And for what it's worth, I could fall pretty hard too."

The admission wasn't one I'd planned to make, but sitting there with the taste of her on my lips and the gentle rock of the boat beneath us, it was the most honest thing I could offer. I avoided close relationships specifically because they made me feel off-kilter. Unsure of myself, without a strong foundation. And of all the times to fall for a woman, this might be the worst. Yet as I stared into Harper's eyes, I couldn't deny the ever-deepening attraction. My business concerns hadn't vanished—if anything, they loomed larger than ever—but somehow sharing this connection with Harper made them feel less isolating.

Eli called out, breaking the moment. "All right, lovebirds. You guys ready to head back?"

I nodded, exchanging a final, meaningful look with Harper. I felt both the burden and the buoyancy as Eli turned the boat toward shore, the ocean stretching out infinitely around us. But Harper's vulnerability and my own reassurance made it feel shared, less isolating. Grounded and adrift at the same time, I let the sea take us back.

Chapter Sixteen

HARPER

I DRUMMED my fingers on one of the several renovation binders, and Jules's latest budget projections stared back at me accusingly. The resort's transformation was moving forward, but the numbers always made my stomach clench. I checked my calendar and made a mental note to pick Finn up from the resort Kids Club by five, to tell Mom about Chase, and to confirm when the first round of room furniture would arrive. I was just wrangling several stray locks of hair into some sort of order when Mom knocked on my doorframe.

"There you are," she said. She wore a fitted shirt and capris, and her silver-streaked brown hair was loosely held with a silver clip. "I was afraid I'd have to hunt you down."

"Ah, you're here to interrogate the suspect in her natural habitat?" I gestured to the chaos.

Her expression was serious. "Yes. She appears overworked."

I smiled. "You sound like Brenna. Is this going to be a family-wide thing?"

Mom came the rest of the way in, closing the door gently. "Maybe it should be. Did you get that timeline update?"

"Timelines, I have. Delivery dates, I don't. I was about to start grilling Joe."

She glanced over the binders on my desk. "All in due time."

I raised an eyebrow. "You're uncharacteristically patient."

"A habit I've learned is handy to acquire." With a smile, she took a seat in one of the armchairs. "Are we ready to tackle the updated financials?"

I nodded, pulling the printed budget spreadsheet from a drawer and handing it to her. Though Mom was stepping back from day-to-day operations, she still liked to be somewhat in the loop. She perused the document.

"All looks good to me." Her sandals barely made a sound on the carpet as she got up to hand the paperwork back.

"Wow." I accepted the spreadsheet before stacking it neatly. "You really have gone soft. You're sure you didn't swap my mom for a different model? Less scolding, more complimenting?"

She laughed, the same sharp but affectionate sound as always. "You know me better than that. Just wait until you're my age. You'll be ganging up on poor Finn before you know it."

My chest tightened as she pushed to her feet. I took a deep breath, hesitating, then leaped. "Mom—there's something else we need to discuss."

She turned and sat again. A glint of curiosity showed in her eyes, or maybe even expectation. "Oh?"

I swallowed, realizing how much I'd built this up in my mind. How many different ways I'd imagined this moment playing out. "It's about Chase. We're seeing each other, and it could become serious."

It already is serious.

I braced for the blow. An explosive *What are you doing?* Maybe a more subtle variant—a thinly veiled lecture. But I got none of that.

She was quiet, and then a knowing, almost amused smile touched her lips. "Well, I have to admit, I've been wondering when one of you would finally acknowledge it. It's been rather obvious for a while now."

My jaw dropped. "Wait, what? Obvious?"

She sat back in the chair, crossing her legs and looking entirely too satisfied with herself. "Yes, obvious. To everyone except, apparently, you two."

"We've been careful," I insisted, confused and trying to retrace every supposedly subtle step.

"Not careful enough to fool a mother," she said. "I had my suspicions about the way you two played off each other when the renovations started. That impression has only strengthened since."

"Huh?" I felt like I'd stepped into a different universe, one where everything I believed was true had inverted. "You're not mad?"

"No. I'm happy for you both." Then she laughed. "After what happened with Eli and Jules, I can hardly protest."

I let out the breath I'd been holding, relief washing over me. "So, you're okay with this?"

"Okay, yes. But you know my feelings about mixing resort business with personal relationships." Her tone softened, but her gaze was steady. "Chase being a partner adds another layer entirely."

I nodded, the weight of her caution settling in my chest but buoyed by the unexpected blessing. "I know, Mom. I can't deny that this whole thing is a bit of a ticking clock."

She rose again and glanced at the pictures of Finn on my desk. "Just promise me you'll be careful."

"Absolutely. Careful is my middle name. Right next to martyr."

"Just know I'm here if you need advice. Romantic or otherwise."

"Thanks. You've always been there."

Mom reached for the door handle, then paused to turn back. "Why don't you invite Chase over for Sunday dinner?"

I burst into laughter, the sound escaping before I could stop it. "Wow, Mom. Zero to sixty much? You're literally throwing him into the deep end of the Coleridge pool."

Mischief danced in her eyes. "From what I've seen, that young man can swim quite well. He managed to win you over, after all."

"That's…" I shook my head, unable to argue with her assessment. "Okay. I'll ask him, but don't blame me if he runs screaming in the opposite direction."

"He won't," she said with unnerving confidence. "See you at dinner, sweetheart."

With that, she slipped out the door.

I FLIPPED the parrotfish over with a sigh. We had spent weeks refining the costume. Finn needed it perfect—realistic, he'd told me in all seriousness—and I'd sent him to the official kindergarten dress rehearsal with the glue-encrusted creation I thought he'd love.

Now it was home, shedding glitter like a miniature

parade, one pectoral fin bending in the wrong direction. I gave it a worried look as Chase knocked and let himself in. The scent of chicken tenders hung in the air. "Wow, something smells amazing," he said, wrapping me in a casual hug. "Am I too late to get a plate before the private rehearsal?"

"Your punctuality needs work, buddy," I teased, pulling back to check for Finn-induced glue damage as I moved the wayward fin. "If you're brave enough to eat chicken tenders with ranch, have at it. You have about five minutes until the star makes his entrance."

He set a bottle of wine on the table and peered over my shoulder at the rogue fish. "What's flopping around?"

"His pectoral fin," I confirmed, moving the costume to the couch and clearing a spot for us. Toys were tidied but still present, their containment always short-lived. "Finn's deeply concerned about the realism."

"As he should be," Chase said, feigning gravity as he picked up the leftover chicken tenders and ate one in a single bite. "Parrotfish are famously authentic creatures."

He lounged back against the counter and wiped a second piece of chicken in a leftover smear of ranch dressing, the comfortable intimacy of his posture mirroring how it felt between us now. All the awkwardness and tension that defined our every move, every interaction, only weeks ago, had evaporated. In their place was an easy familiarity that could be either relief or terror, depending on how deeply I thought about it.

He picked up the wine bottle again, a question in his eyes.

"Yes, please." He pulled two glasses from the cabinet as I thought about the upcoming Sunday dinner conversation. "I might need extra fortification tonight."

"What do you mean? We're about to receive a scintillating reef fish performance." He was handing me my glass when Finn charged in, a six-year-old bundle of anticipation.

"Chase!" Finn came to an abrupt halt. "I need to practice for the show! Are you gonna watch me?"

"You kidding? I've got front-row seats." Chase set down the glass and pointed to the green and blue pile of sequins and felt. "Is this your famous costume? The one with the realistic fins?"

Finn nodded so enthusiastically I was afraid he'd decapitate himself. He quickly pulled on the costume. I held my breath, but it stayed together. I bent to adjust his fishy cap, and Chase pinned the floppy fin so it had more structural integrity. Finn wiggled his face into something that might have been intimidating, had he not been so blatantly pleased. "I'm gonna be so good. I'm learning my lines really fast."

"You must have your mom's brain," Chase said, looking at me as he settled back into the couch. I sat next to him, and he draped an arm over my shoulders.

"She's helping me. We practiced ten times yesterday, didn't we, Mom?" Finn climbed onto the ottoman, puffed up his chest, and did a wild arm flourish. "I'm a parrotfish. Please don't step on me because I live on the reef, which is super fragile. But that's not all..." He stopped and blinked at us as if expecting a cue.

"Keep going, buddy," Chase said. "What else do you do?"

"I poop sand!" Finn shouted with such unrestrained glee it sounded more like a superpower than a biological fact. "Lots and lots of sand. That's why we have beaches. And I'm here to tell you..." He glanced around as his eyes grew wider and wider, clearly searching for more lines.

"Save the reef!" I whispered.

"Right! Save the reef!" Finn burbled, triumphant, thrusting his fin-clad arms to the sky. "You don't want me to poof out of existence!" He bounded across the room, the words flying faster and faster, the force of his felt feet echoing through the cottage. "Please don't get rid of me or all the sand you love so much will go away!" Finn turned back and bowed. "Was it good?"

Chase applauded with appropriate enthusiasm. "Very strong first act. Great movement, lots of intensity. If you really want to impress the grown-ups, add a few 'blub blubs.' And remember the extra emphasis on sand-pooping."

Finn grinned, dashing to hug me. "I've got more lines, but I'm still learning those." He turned to Chase, eyes wide and sparkling with a kind of childlike urgency I'd never seen directed at anyone but me or one of his overindulgent aunt and uncles. "Chase! You have to see the real play! It's next month! Will you come? Please?"

The question hit him, surprise registering before anything else. The glass of wine remained on the table, forgotten. The entire house seemed to pause. He looked at me, a moment of searching, then slowly back at Finn. The smile on his face was the kind I'd waited a lifetime to see on someone who didn't feel obligated to care.

"Wow, buddy," he said, voice warm and even. "Getting a personal invitation from the star parrotfish? I wouldn't miss it for the world. You let me know when and where, okay?"

"Okay! Mom, isn't that great?"

I swallowed the lump in my throat. "The best, sweetie. You better start practicing your autograph."

Finn giggled and parrot-finned his way into his room, confident in his new favorite fan.

Chase turned to me. "That was some serious drama. Think he'll need an agent after this?"

"Probably. I hear Spielberg is recruiting heavily from the ten-and-under crowd."

He grinned, then checked his phone. "What's the running time on this thing?"

"About twenty minutes," I said. "Four and a half hours if you count backstage negotiations over costume details."

"Perfect. Plenty of time to help him memorize before bed." He got up, stretching. "I'm guessing that's my job, since someone else did all the hard work. I suppose it won't kill me to have an official title."

"I can think of a few that fit." As I studied his tall form heading down the hallway, shoulders broad and relaxed, my worries trailed him like a shadow I couldn't seem to shake. He and Finn were already so close!

I joined them, getting Finn out of his costume without any wardrobe malfunctions and into pajamas.

"And remember, my character is essential to the reef. So I'll need to really shout out my finale."

"That sounds very strategic," Chase said, leaning against the wall as I shepherded Finn into bed.

"You want to call it a night, Mr. Famous Actor?" I tucked Finn in.

"Good night, Mom. Good night, Chase."

Chase leaned over, eyes slightly cautious but filled with something else that tugged at my heart. A hug request was issued, approved, and returned. I exhaled as we left the room, Harper and Chase again, just the two of us.

I poured wine into two glasses. "He's going to be crushed if you can't make it," I said, voice light but tight, floating somewhere between a tease and a confession.

"I'll be there." He raised an eyebrow.

"I know you will. Thank you." After taking a huge swig of wine, I inhaled a breath. "I told Mom about us today."

Chase's shoulders tensed beneath his shirt. He set down his glass and faced me. "And?"

"And… she wasn't that surprised." I ran my finger around the rim of my wineglass. "Said it was kind of obvious."

"Obvious?" His eyebrows shot up. "How?"

"Apparently, we've been broadcasting on all frequencies." I laughed softly.

"That's kind of… unsettling." His shoulders relaxed, but his eyes remained watchful. "What else did she say?"

I took another fortifying sip of wine. "She trusts my judgment."

"Well, it's a relief to be all official now, I guess."

"One more thing." I resisted the urge to take another gulp of wine. "She asked me to invite you to Sunday dinner this week."

His eyes widened, and then he smirked. "Sunday dinner? With the whole clan? Do I get hazard pay?"

"Not the whole clan. It's always a mixture, depending on who can make it. Think of it as a test. To see if you can survive mashed potatoes and interrogation."

He laughed, a warm sound that made me feel like maybe, somehow, this could all work out. "Will I need Kevlar?"

"Probably," I said, but I couldn't keep the hope from my voice.

He took my hand and squeezed it gently. "Okay. Sunday dinner, so I'll be all dressed up. Ready to face the music… or at least the mashed potatoes."

Chapter Seventeen

CHASE

I FOLLOWED Harper up the path to Helen's house, feeling like I was crossing some invisible line. She was wearing a flowered dress that hugged her hips and a teasing smile that suggested she was aware of my nerves.

She paused by the porch swing, a bright look in her eye. "Relax, Chase. It's a family dinner, not an execution."

Easy for her to say, when it wasn't her future being weighed and measured with every glance and comment. My collar suddenly felt too tight. I adjusted my tie as I stepped into the warmth of the Coleridge world.

Helen's house smelled like roast chicken and fresh bread. A line of family photos led into the living room, creating a breadcrumb trail of Coleridge history. I brushed a hand over my freshly shaved jaw, already imagining Helen's curious gaze sizing me up as more than just Eli's friend or the resort partner. Eli sent me a text earlier stating he had to fill in tonight leading a night dive. Should

I have been relieved or disappointed that he and Jules wouldn't be here as buffers? Probably both.

As we entered the kitchen, Helen smiled at us. "I hope you brought your appetite." She took the wine I'd brought and gave me a once-over that felt like both approval and a silent evaluation.

"It smells incredible," I replied with a smile.

When we walked into the back family room, Harper stayed close, her hand lightly brushing my arm in a way that steadied me more than I wanted to admit. I surveyed the room—worn furniture that spoke of years of use, soft light, and the kind of warmth that was simultaneously welcoming and muffling.

Ben was there, more cleaned up than usual and wearing a shirt that didn't have paint or grease stains. "Chase. Harper," he said with a nod, his tone almost amused. "Good to see you both here."

I nodded back. "Glad to be here."

Austin was by the sliding door to the back patio, a beer in hand. He wore a fresh T-shirt that clung to his frame, his dark hair still damp from a recent shower. But his stance was classic Austin, quiet and watchful. He acknowledged us with a lift of his beer, his expression somewhere between friendly and skeptical.

Before I could attempt conversation, Finn barreled through the room and launched himself at me. "Chase! You're here!" He was beaming, his face a mix of joy and mild sunburn.

He pulled me over to the couch, talking a mile a minute about a drawing he'd done of a dinosaur. Lying on the coffee table, it was a glorious tangle of crayon lines and enthusiasm. "What do you think?"

"I think it's the most awesome dinosaur I've ever seen," I replied, and a bit of the tension melted away under the force of his excitement. Finn's uncomplicated joy had a way of doing that.

I glanced back at Harper, who gave me a reassuring smile as if to say I was doing fine.

Ben cracked a beer and handed one to Harper. Then his green eyes lifted to meet mine as he held out a can to me.

"Sure," I replied and took the offered beverage. "Thanks."

"Welcome," he said with humor lurking in his eyes. "We'll try not to rake you over the coals too much tonight."

That made me laugh. "Got to admit, tonight feels a little different than past Sunday dinners."

I drifted over to Austin, standing just out of the main current of Coleridge activity. "Catch any big ones lately?"

"Not as much as usual," he replied as he studied the leaves of the trees outside the slider. "Wind's been kicking up. Maybe it'll die down next week."

I nodded, glancing at Ben and Harper's conversation, aware of the small but significant ways these people were already fitting me into their lives. It was strangely comforting and worrisome all at once. I took a sip of my beer and glanced at Austin again. "Maybe I'll take you up on that trip sometime."

Austin's eyes glinted with interest, and I couldn't help but feel like I'd passed some minor test. "Offer still stands. Just let me know when."

The dive trip with Eli and Jules had been a strong reminder of how much I loved being on the water—on it or under it. And Austin was regarded as one of the best fishing guides in the area. Too bad we were entering several critical phases of the resort reno. "It might be a while, though. After the dust settles a little here. Literally." We shared a laugh, and my shoulders loosened more.

Harper ducked out to help Helen with dinner. When the two women came back with steaming dishes, I immediately jumped in to help. I was the new guy, long-time presence in this family or not, and wanted to make damn sure I made a decent impression. And the difference tonight was profound, like seeing everything in high definition, the colors more vivid, the details sharper. I was here as Harper's… boyfriend? At our ages, the word practically made me cringe. But I sure wasn't here as Eli's friend.

We sat around the large dining table, the spread a feast of roast chicken, roasted potatoes, and vegetables fresh from Helen's garden. The plates of food went around like clockwork, a rhythm to the meal that felt practiced and intimate. I tried to take part in the easy flow of conversation, hyper-aware of my own presence and the new role I occupied. Finn sat beside me, asking endless questions about my new office and if we could build a treehouse there.

"Depends," I said, sharing a smile with Harper as I filled her water glass from a pitcher on the table. "What's the zoning like for treehouses, do you think?"

"Huh," Finn replied seriously. "Not sure. You can figure out that part. But we'll need blueprints and a crew."

"Do you have those too?" Ben teased as he loaded his plate.

"I'm pretty sure I know someone," Harper said with a soft laugh.

Despite the lightness, I was constantly aware of Helen, of the careful way she included me, never excluding but never letting me off the hook, either. As the platter of chicken made its way around again, she caught my eye. "Things seem to be moving along quickly at the resort,

Chase. I admit I wasn't thrilled about taking on that loan, but you've been managing the expenses diligently." She paused, taking a sip of her wine, her gaze steady over the rim of the glass. "Keeping everything balanced with a project this size, especially with the partnership structure… that takes real skill."

The compliment landed with surprising weight, and a flush crept up my neck. "Thank you, Helen. I appreciate the support. It's definitely a complex project, but we're tracking everything closely." I decided to offer a bit more, sensing this was more than just polite dinner chat. "I made sure to build a healthy contingency fund into the budget right from the start, and it should cover most typical overruns, which is important since we made the strategic decision to phase the work on Room Block One to manage upfront costs. That's a risk when working on old buildings. But as long as nothing completely unforeseen pops up, I'm confident we can keep things on track financially."

Helen nodded slowly, seemingly satisfied with the answer, though a flicker of that inherent Coleridge caution remained in her eyes. "Good to hear. We're all counting on this renovation paying off."

The *we* hung in the air, encompassing family, legacy, and the future tied up in those resort walls.

"We've had plenty of hiccups and none have derailed us or the budget," Harper added. "Jules warned us that the upcoming quarter is tight, but by then the biggest expenditures should be finished."

I shot her a smile, staying quiet about the fact that I'd been on plenty of jobs where something blindsided us last minute. Usually, the skeletons in the closet were uncovered during the demo phase, but there were plenty of exceptions to that rule. I resisted the urge to cross my fingers and took a sip of wine instead.

"You must be so busy with the new firm," Helen said as she passed a bowl of potatoes to Austin. "I'm impressed you have time for a distraction like this meal."

"I'll make time," I replied as I filled her wineglass. "It's been a while since I've been to dinner here. Besides, a man's gotta eat."

"He skips way too many meals," Harper said, not missing a beat, and I wasn't sure if that was a vote of confidence or just her amusement at my floundering.

"Commitment is so important when you're starting out. It must be a challenge to keep focused." Helen's eyes were warm, but I sensed a depth to her words.

"He's always been a pretty focused guy," Ben added, amused, but I noticed a hint of camaraderie in his tone.

I couldn't help wondering if her subtle question was a probe as to how well my new venture was going. "I've taken on several new projects besides the resort remodel, but I'm used to juggling. If it gets to be too much, I'll just hire Finn to help out."

A round of laughter went around the table as he high-fived me.

Ben smirked at us. "Did Eli put you through the ringer before giving you his blessing? Sounds like him."

Harper laughed. "I hardly heard a peep from him about it. Chase wasn't quite so lucky, but he pulled through just fine."

I shrugged, pretending not to care. "I think he's just mad he's not here to harass me tonight."

"His loss is our gain," Helen said with a warm smile that made me hope the interrogation phase of dinner was over.

Indeed, the conversation moved on, and we discussed Ben's classes and how things were looking up. "Got pretty good grades on my midterms," he said and made eye contact with both Harper and me. "I wanted to thank both of you for the help."

"Happy to do it," Harper said, glancing at me.

"It was nothing," I added. "You're doing all the hard work."

The Coleridge brothers were all hard workers. It was obvious in their hands and their shoulders and their stubborn attitudes.

Austin talked about a canceled charter due to a storm, and Finn piped in about how he saw the biggest wave ever at the beach. I listened and contributed, trying not to come off as overly cautious.

Dinner wound down, and Harper leaned in close, whispering, "You okay? You look like you're holding your breath."

"I'm good." Despite the intensity, I felt grounded. Like I was already part of something important. "I was a little tense when we first arrived, but nobody's eaten me alive yet."

We moved to the patio for coffee. Outdoors, it was cooler, a breeze rustling through the trees. Harper talked with Ben, both of them laughing over some shared joke about an old boat they used to own. I liked seeing her like this, at home and at ease with her family. It was all so different from what I'd known growing up. But I could see the appeal, even with the expectations and uncertainties that came along for the ride.

Helen refilled my coffee, her hand resting on my shoulder for an extra moment. "It was nice seeing you here tonight."

"I'll have to stop by more often," I said, though it came out more as a question than a promise. "Think I might explode from eating that much, though."

"I wouldn't accept anything less," she said. "And we're

not so bad once you get to know us. Then again, you already do."

I grinned. "Tonight hasn't quite been the same."

She patted my shoulder before letting go. "Maybe it's just a new chapter of the same book."

I let one hand rest on Harper's arm as I sipped my rich coffee. It was easy to imagine this becoming routine, but the thought of it came with a thousand what-ifs. What if Harper decided I was too much of a distraction? What if I let Finn down? What if I was in over my head with a family this tight-knit? And most importantly, what if I didn't have a clue how to navigate any of this?

Harper caught my eye. The look she gave me was full of confidence, both in me and in us, and I knew then that this wasn't just some temporary detour in our lives. It was bigger than that.

She poked me in the side. "Survived, did you?"

I quickly patted myself for injuries. "Pretty sure everything's still there."

"And what do you think?"

I considered her question, the way it felt to be part of this. The easy camaraderie. The scrutiny. The high stakes if I messed up. "I'd say tonight was a good start."

"More than that." Her voice was light, but I knew she understood the layers beneath my answer.

I wrapped my arm around her shoulders and pulled her close, feeling more connected to this family and to Harper than I ever thought I could. "We'll see."

Harper rested her head against me, and her warmth, her trust, the steadiness that came with having her in my life engulfed me. It felt like home or at least what home should be like. The kind of home I'd never known.

The night wrapped around us, stars scattered across the sky like a blueprint I couldn't quite understand yet.

Finn had fallen asleep on the couch, and soon we'd have to wake him and take him home. But for now, this moment of quiet felt sacred.

I'd spent my whole career planning for the future. Blueprints, timelines, projections—all of it focused on what was coming next. And here I was, finally feeling like I belonged somewhere, with someone, and I couldn't stop wondering if this was a future I was ready for.

Chapter Eighteen

HARPER

I LOGGED the final approval for the new poolside loungers into our renovation tracker, a satisfied smile tugging at my lips. The spreadsheet before me was showing more green check marks than red flags for once. My gaze drifted to the small stack of paint swatches on the corner of my desk, each labeled in Chase's precise handwriting. I ran my finger across the top one, the soft blue-gray that would transform our tired guest rooms into something fresh and inviting. Just like he had transformed so many quiet evenings into something I looked forward to.

A knock sounded at my open door. Jules leaned against the doorframe, her dark hair pulled back in its customary bun.

"You're smiling at a spreadsheet." One beautifully arched eyebrow lifted. "Should I be concerned?"

"I'm smiling because, for once, we're not hemorrhaging money or time." I turned my laptop toward her.

"Room Block One is on schedule, and the pool remodel is actually ahead."

"Don't jinx it." Jules stepped into my office, her eyes scanning the renovation tracker with the same intensity she applied to our financial statements. "That is a very reassuring progress report. Speaking of which, I've finished the quarterly projections. Want to review them tomorrow morning? I've got dinner plans tonight."

"Oh? You and Eli having a date night?"

"We are." A smile softened Jules's features. "We're heading to that new seafood place on Big Pine Key."

"Have fun." I saved my work and began shutting down my computer. "I've got plans too."

"More construction meetings with our architect?"

I laughed but didn't rise to her bait. I didn't need to. Jules knew more than most about the intricacies of becoming involved with someone you worked with. "Chase is bringing over the flooring samples for Room Block One tonight. We need to finalize the selection before the installer schedules the job."

What I didn't mention was the pizza waiting in my fridge or the way my skin tingled with anticipation at the thought of Chase's hands on me later, after Finn was asleep.

The past two weeks had flown by in a blur of renovation meetings interspersed with moments that felt like sunshine breaking through clouds I hadn't even realized were there. Little things, casual interactions that somehow filled spaces inside me I'd forgotten were empty.

Like Tuesday last week, when we'd stolen away for lunch during a chaotic day. We'd ended up at a tiny sandwich shop, crammed at a corner table, blueprints spread between our turkey clubs.

"This is seriously the best sandwich I've ever had,"

Chase had declared, somehow making the statement sound both utterly sincere and slightly ridiculous.

"You said that about the Cuban at Tropical Hops last Thursday," I'd countered, wiping a bit of mayo from the corner of his mouth with my thumb, the casual intimacy of the gesture making our eyes lock for a long beat.

His eyes had darkened as he caught my hand, pressing a quick kiss to my palm—quick but deliberate enough to make my breath catch. "I'm a man of varied and excellent tastes."

There had been dozens of other stolen moments—text messages that threatened to make me laugh out loud during tedious staff meetings, the way he'd started carrying my coffee order in his head as easily as ceiling heights and square footage calculations.

And then there were the nights. After Finn was tucked in, those late-evening conversations on my porch swing or curled up on my couch meandered from resort business to philosophical debates about the best movie trilogies. Conversations that inevitably led to more.

The physical part. God, the physical part was unlike anything I'd experienced before. Not just the intensity, though there was certainly that. It was the attentiveness, the way Chase approached my body like an architect approaches a challenging but inspiring project—with curiosity, enthusiasm, and a determination to understand what made it sing.

Last Sunday night, he'd walked me backward toward my bedroom, his lips never leaving mine as he whispered, "Tell me what you like, Harper. I want to know everything you like."

And for once in my life, I had.

But there was more than just the physical connection. There was the way he'd sat at my kitchen table three nights ago, patiently helping Finn with a kindergarten alphabet project, his big hands guiding my son's much smaller ones as they traced letters onto construction paper.

I hadn't meant to let myself hope. I really hadn't. Six years of being Finn's only parent had taught me the value of self-sufficiency, the danger of expectations. But watching them together, seeing Chase fold himself into our little world with such natural ease, I couldn't help the tender shoot of possibility that had taken root inside me.

My phone buzzed with a text notification, pulling me back to my office and the present moment. I smiled as Chase's name flashed on the screen.

> Chase: Flooring samples secured. ETA your place 6:30. Pizza and professional opinions to follow. Maybe other things too…

I bit my lip, warmth spreading through me as I typed back a quick response.

Jules appeared in my doorway again, purse in hand. "I'm heading out. Don't stay too late."

"I'm on my way too. Have fun with Eli."

The late afternoon sun cast golden light over the resort, highlighting the areas of busy activity. The visible progress. Landscaping was taking shape, and the freshly painted building gleamed like a promise waiting to be fulfilled. Everything was buzzing with potential, and I felt like I was, too.

I let myself enjoy the sensation. I'd spent too long denying it.

I headed home, where Finn met me at the front door. He glanced up at me, his face shining with expectation. "Is Chase here yet?"

"Not yet, sweetheart. But soon." I kissed the top of his head. "Think you'll have room for pizza?"

He nodded, a sticky smile spreading across his face. "Uh-huh. We got pepperoni, right?"

"And extra cheese," I confirmed.

Muffled sounds drew my attention to the kitchen, where my mother emerged. Her hair was pulled back in a loose braid, and she had that familiar look of satisfied relief that came from quality time with her grandson, now over.

"Well, I've got all the dishes in the dishwasher, and there's fresh lemonade in the fridge," Mom said, coming over to kiss my cheek. "You guys have a good night."

"Thanks for watching him, Mom." I squeezed her hand, grateful as always for her unwavering support. "I hope he wasn't too much of a tornado today."

She laughed, ruffling Finn's hair. "Wouldn't be the same if he wasn't. Good thing he's an angel too." With a wave, she shut the front door behind her.

Finn bounced ahead of me into the living room, full of questions about when Chase would arrive. I watched him, imagining nights like this stretching far into the future.

I set down my things and glanced around the cozy space, envisioning where we'd sit, eat, and plan. In my mind, I saw the three of us curled on the couch, Chase with an arm around me, Finn asleep against his chest. The image made me feel like I was floating, like the old anchor of fear had loosened its hold at last.

I straightened the coasters on the table, aligning them precisely with the corners. "Why don't you put your toys away? Chase and I need to look at floor samples."

"Can I keep the LEGOs out? Chase said we might finish the spaceship tonight." Finn's eyes were wide and hopeful, a miniature negotiator in training.

"Fine. Just the spaceship pieces, though, not your entire collection."

"Yes!" Finn pumped his fist in the air and raced to his bedroom.

I smiled after him, then moved to the kitchen to check on dinner preparations. The pizza was ready to heat, salad prepped in the fridge, and I'd even picked up a tiramisu from Sweet Dreams—Chase's favorite. Nothing fancy but thoughtful. A comfortable family evening that felt both significant and perfectly ordinary.

My phone buzzed on the counter. Chase's name appeared on the screen, and I smiled as I answered.

"Hey. Are you on your way?" I nestled the phone between my ear and shoulder as I arranged three plates on the counter.

"Harper." Something in his tone made me stop. "A situation just came up."

The plate in my hand stilled. "What kind of situation?"

"The Franson project." He sighed, the sound heavy with frustration. "The county inspector came by this afternoon for the pre-drywall check on the guest suite addition, and we failed. Badly."

"Oh." I set the plate down. "That doesn't sound good."

"It's not. There are issues with the electrical installation. If we don't get this fixed immediately, it pushes back drywall, which pushes back everything else, and the Fransons are hosting a family reunion in two weeks."

I leaned against the counter, a cold feeling settling in my stomach. "That sounds stressful."

"It's a nightmare." His voice was tight with tension. "Marilyn tried handling it—she's been on the phone with the electrical contractor all afternoon—but I need to be on site for this. I'm there now."

The cold feeling spread. "So you're canceling."

A beat of silence. "I'm really sorry, Harper. I have to

stay here until this is resolved, and I'll probably need to be here first thing tomorrow too, to make sure everything's ready for the re-inspection."

"Well, we need to get together soon. What about the flooring samples? We have to choose something by Friday to keep the Room Block One schedule on track."

"I know." The strain in his voice was evident. "I was thinking maybe we could meet for lunch tomorrow to go over them. Or I could drop them off in the morning for you to look at, and then we can discuss by phone?"

Neither option would be as effective as going through them together tonight as planned, with proper time and attention. I glanced at the cleared coffee table, the space I'd made for our work together.

"It's fine," I said, though it wasn't. "We'll figure something out."

"I'm really sorry about dinner too. I was looking forward to it. And I know Finn was excited about the LEGOs." Chase paused. "This project, the Franson addition, is a big deal for Latitudes. They're connected to half the property owners in their luxury beach development. If I mess this up…"

"I get it." And I did, intellectually. But all I saw was Jarod's face when I told him I was pregnant. "Your business needs you there."

"Harper." His tone took on an edge. "I can't predict when something goes sideways on a site. It happens, and it's my job to fix it. Look, I'll make it up to you both. I promise. This is just—"

"An emergency. I understand." I cut him off, unable to bear another word when disappointment was swelling inside me. "Really, it's fine. We're fine."

"Are you sure? You sound—"

"I'm sure." I forced conviction into my voice. "Go fix your client's electrical issues. We'll reschedule."

Another pause. "I'll call you later? Once I've got things under control here?"

"Sure." The word came out clipped. "Let me know when you can reschedule the flooring review."

"Harper…"

"I need to go tell Finn. Go handle what you need to handle, Chase." I ended the call before he could respond, before my voice could betray the irrational hurt building inside me.

I stood motionless in the kitchen, staring at the three plates I'd arranged. Three plates. When had I started thinking of us as a given? When had I started expecting Chase Ashworth to be there at our table as if he belonged?

I wanted to understand. I wanted to be understanding. But the old habit of protecting myself was powerful, a shield that came up as fast as this disappointment had hit me. I tried to squash it, but I could feel my heart hardening again, cooling in a way that terrified me.

I thought of the pizza sitting in the fridge, of Finn's hopeful smile. My throat tightened, a sign of past betrayals affecting the present in ways I didn't want to admit. My response to Chase had been stark and cold, like something an ice queen would say. But it was all I could manage in the moment. All the warmth, all the hope—gone.

Finn was in the living room, placing his toy cars in a wicker basket. He looked up, expectation shining in his eyes. I hesitated, struggling for the right words. The ones that would make it sting less.

"Sweetheart," I started, my voice too cheerful, too bright. "Chase had an emergency at work. He can't come for pizza tonight."

The light in his eyes dimmed, the corners of his mouth

turning down. "Oh. But we were gonna build LEGOs after…"

I kneeled beside him, smoothing a hand over his hair. "I know. I'm sorry. He feels bad, too."

Finn nodded, a brave little nod that only made my heart ache more. He turned back to his cars, the air heavy with his quiet disappointment.

I watched him, my own hurt amplified. Especially after Finn carefully placed the half-finished LEGO spaceship on top and carried the basket to his room.

I dropped onto the couch and opened my laptop, the bright screen blurring before my eyes. It took me a moment to realize I was staring at the renovation schedule, the tasks and deadlines so neat compared to my personal chaos. Now this one phone call, this one cancellation, over-shadowed all the progress. I wanted to be angry, but all I felt was hurt and scared about where things stood.

I took a shaky breath and picked up my phone, debating whether to send Chase a message. Something softer, less brittle. But what if he didn't reply until tomor-row? What if this was the start of a pattern, like last time? The thought twisted in my chest, and I set the phone down, unable to face it.

Finn returned to the living room. "When is dinner?"

I stood and pulled him to me. "Let's get that pizza in the oven right now, sweetie."

We walked to the kitchen, our disappointment shared but somehow lighter together. I pulled him close to me, focusing on the warmth of his small body against mine. But even with Finn here, the sense of connection I'd started to believe in felt impossibly far away.

Chapter Nineteen

CHASE

"I DON'T GIVE a damn who did it, Marcus." I kept my voice even despite the pressure building behind my temples. "It's wrong. The inspector cited multiple code violations on this wall alone."

Marcus, my project manager, nodded tightly and avoided meeting my angry glare. "I've already called Walsh Electric. They're sending someone first thing tomorrow."

The Franson electrical inspection had failed in spectacular fashion. Standing under the harsh work lights, I stared at the exposed north wall wiring like it was a personal betrayal. Every single outlet had been flagged—wrong gauge, improper grounding, the works. What had started as a routine inspection this afternoon had morphed into a full-blown crisis threatening to sink a cornerstone project for my fledgling firm. And somewhere across town, Harper and Finn were probably finishing pizza without me.

"Tomorrow's not good enough." I crouched down to examine the junction box. "Mr. Franson wants this guest suite finished by the end of next week. We need someone here tonight."

"Chase, it's almost eight—"

"Then call Tommy directly. If he gives you some crap about needing to pay the emergency rate, tell him I'll use another contractor from now on." I straightened up, dust clinging to my jeans. "And call the drywall guy too. They were lined up to start first thing tomorrow." Because I'd assumed the electrical would pass.

Around us, the half-finished guest suite stood in limbo, an unlikely marriage of luxury and construction chaos. Imported Italian tile worth more than my first car sat stacked near an exposed wall cavity. Custom brass fixtures waited in their protective wrapping while fine sawdust coated every surface. The contrast was almost comical— high-end finishes meeting construction disaster.

But I wasn't laughing. Not even a little.

Marcus stepped away to make the calls while I pulled up the original plans on my tablet. The Franson project wasn't just another job. William Franson was a retired real estate developer with connections throughout South Flor-ida, and his home was one of many in this exclusive, high-end residential development. This guest suite addition to his waterfront home represented the kind of high-end resi-dential work that could put Latitudes Design on the map— or sink us if we screwed it up.

If I screwed it up.

My phone buzzed. Marcus had sent the inspector's full report. Fifteen violations, each one requiring rework. I scrolled through the list, mentally calculating costs and delays. This would damn near destroy my profit margin.

"Walsh can have someone here by nine," Marcus said, returning with a grim expression.

"Fine. The drywall guy?"

"They're on standby."

I rubbed my eyes. I saw a night of minimal sleep ahead. "Call the inspector on his cell and get him back here tomorrow. We need to get that drywall started as soon as possible."

"Okay. Chase." Marcus lowered his voice. "Franson called while you were checking the bathroom. He's... not happy."

"I'm sure he's not." I forced a tight smile.

As Marcus stepped away, my mind drifted to Harper. To the way her voice had changed when I called to cancel our plans. Our routine meeting about the resort flooring renovation had somehow evolved into dinner plans with her and Finn. Pizza and a movie—nothing fancy, but something I'd been looking forward to.

I pulled out my phone, checking for texts. Nothing from Harper since our call earlier. My stomach twisted with something that felt uncomfortably like guilt. The memory of our conversation played back in my head. Her tone had been professionally polite—the exact same voice she used with difficult resort guests. Then it had transitioned to icy, bordering on glacial. Not the warm, teasing Harper I'd grown accustomed to.

Despite her words that she understood, her clipped responses told me it wasn't fine. And the thought of Finn's disappointment made my chest ache. The kid had been excited about us building his LEGO creation together. And dammit, so had I.

For the next hour, I coordinated with suppliers, arranged for rush deliveries, and worked through contingencies with Marcus. The project was salvageable, but it would take precise execution and a lot of overtime.

When my phone rang with Franson's name on the

display, I stepped outside to take the call. "William," I answered, injecting confidence into my voice.

"Chase." Franson's tone held the distinctive note of a wealthy man unaccustomed to inconvenience. "I understand there are… issues."

I laid out the problems and our solutions succinctly, emphasizing our immediate response and the quality control measures we'd implement going forward.

"This will not affect your finish date," I assured him. "My team will work through the night if necessary."

"I expect nothing less," Franson replied. "My wife has her heart set on her parents staying in that space next weekend."

After promising updates by morning, I ended the call and leaned against the side of the house, exhaustion settling into my bones. The evening stretched ahead— hours of supervising emergency repairs when I should have been enjoying myself with Harper and Finn.

Harper.

My thumb hovered over her contact. What would I even say? Sorry I bailed on you and your son for a construction emergency? Sorry my business has to come first right now? The truth was, I wanted to be in both places at once, and the impossibility of that made me irrationally frustrated with the entire situation. I started typing.

> Chase: Thinking of you. Hope you and Finn
> had a good night despite…

I deleted it. Too casual, like I hadn't just disappointed them. Another attempt followed.

> Chase: I'm really sorry about tonight. The
> inspection failure could have…

Delete. Now I was making excuses.

Finally, I pocketed my phone without sending anything. Harper's silence felt weighted, significant in a way I wasn't ready to examine too closely. When had the thought of disappointing her become as dismal as the prospect of a failed project?

The electrician arrived just after nine, a grizzled man named Ray, who greeted the disaster with a low whistle and a shake of his head. "Whoever wired this place should be banned from touching anything more complicated than a flashlight." He leaned forward to examine the junction box.

"Agreed. Can you fix it tonight?" I asked.

Ray sized up the work, calculating. "I can get the north wall done. The rest will have to wait till morning."

"Do what you can. I'll be here until you finish tonight."

While Ray worked, I used the time to review the resort renovation plans I'd meant to discuss with Harper. The flooring samples would need to be decided on by the end of the week to keep on schedule. Another deadline looming, another pressure point.

Marcus approached me around 10:30, fatigue evident in the slump of his shoulders. "Inspector confirmed for eleven in the morning, and drywall to start after lunch. Tile guy says he can still make Thursday if we get the bathroom finished by Wednesday night."

"Good. You should head home. I'll stay with Ray until he finishes."

"You sure? You look wrecked."

A wave of fatigue washed over me that I pushed back with everything in me. "Nothing coffee won't fix. I'll need to be back here at five anyway."

After Marcus left, the site grew quieter. Just the sounds of Ray working and my own thoughts circling back to Harper. A part of me wanted her to understand that sometimes business emergencies happened. Another part acknowledged the guilt swirling through me at her obvious disappointment.

Just past midnight, Ray finished with the north wall. "The rest has to wait. I'll be back with the crew by six a.m."

After he left, I did a final walk-through of the space. The reworked section looked good, up to code and properly done. One crisis partially averted. In my car, I set a watch alarm for 4:30 a.m., ensuring I'd be back before the crew arrived. I rested my head against the steering wheel for a moment, allowing myself five seconds of pure exhaustion before straightening up and starting the car. Three or four hours of sleep, then back to this site before heading to Sunset Siesta to face Harper. Whatever her reaction tomorrow—cold professionalism or warm understanding—I knew one thing for certain. Her opinion mattered more than I wanted it to.

And that scared me almost as much as the prospect of Latitudes Design failing before it truly began.

I squinted against the morning light as I ended the call with Marcus, the brightness amplifying my headache from too little sleep. "Just walk the inspector through everything we fixed. The documentation's all there. Then call me when he signs off." My voice sounded like I'd been gargling gravel, matching how I felt after less than three hours of sleep. The peaceful morning scene at Sunset Siesta—palm fronds swaying, early guests strolling toward breakfast—felt disconnected from my internal chaos. I needed coffee, a shower, and about twelve more hours of sleep. Instead, I was here to face Harper.

I slipped my phone into my pocket and took a deep breath. My reflection in the resort lobby's glass doors confirmed what I already knew. I looked like hell. Dark circles underlined bloodshot eyes, and yesterday's stubble had evolved into the beginning of an unintentional beard. My button-down shirt was already looking rumpled, even though it was straight from my closet. Not exactly the polished architect image I typically maintained, but right now I didn't care about appearances.

The lobby was quiet, with only a young couple checking out and a staff member polishing the wooden coffee table. I nodded at the familiar face as I passed, making my way toward the hall where Harper's office was located.

Her door stood partially open, a strip of warm light spilling into the hallway. I paused just outside, hearing the soft click of her keyboard as she worked. Normally, I'd knock, crack a joke, watch her face light up with that smile that had become increasingly important to me. I pushed the door open and stepped inside without announcement, deliberately closing it behind me. The soft click of the latch engaging felt significant, creating a private space for whatever conversation would follow.

Harper glanced up, my sudden entrance startling her. Her expression shifted quickly from surprise to wariness, her posture stiffening as she registered both my presence and my disheveled appearance.

"Chase," she said in a carefully neutral tone.

I crossed the room in a few strides and stopped in front of her desk, not bothering with small talk. "Harper, about yesterday. I want to apologize again. Properly."

She turned away from her keyboard to give me her full attention. The careful blankness of her expression made my chest tighten as she folded her hands on her scribbled desk calendar.

"I look like I crawled out from under a construction site because I basically did," I continued, resisting the urge to fidget. "The Franson project inspection failed catastrophically yesterday afternoon."

Her expression softened somewhat, concern replacing some of the guardedness. "That sounds tough."

"This wasn't just some minor setback," I explained, leaning forward with my palms on her desk. "William Franson is connected to half the high-end property developers in South Florida. If word got out that Latitudes Design couldn't handle a fairly simple guest suite addition…" I shook my head. "It wasn't a choice between clients. It was a potential catastrophe for my company. If I didn't fix it immediately, the penalties and the damage to my reputation could have sunk me before I even got started."

I straightened up and met her eyes directly. "But that doesn't change the fact that I bailed on you. On Finn. Hearing how… polite you were on the phone yesterday? That told me just how pissed off you really were."

The professional mask she wore cracked slightly, a glimmer of hurt crossing her features before she could suppress it. "Finn asked about you," she said quietly. "Multiple times."

The words landed like a physical blow. I closed my eyes briefly, the image of his disappointment making me feel even worse.

"I told him sometimes grown-ups have to work unexpectedly," she continued. "He understands that concept pretty well, living at a resort."

"Still. I should have—"

"What, Chase?" For the first time, a hint of frustration

colored her voice. "Abandoned your client during a crisis? Let your business suffer? That's not realistic."

I paced a few steps, the restless energy of exhaustion and emotion making it impossible to stand still. "Honestly? Trying to manage that Franson mess last night, knowing I'd blown off our meeting and dinner... it sucked."

I gestured vaguely around the room, trying to articulate feelings I was still processing myself. "This whole thing—launching the firm, the massive scope of the resort project, trying to figure out us..." I motioned between Harper and me, the unspoken complexity of our relationship hanging in the air. "It's a lot, okay?"

"I know it is." She rose to her feet, watching me with unreadable eyes.

Moving to the window, I stared out at the manicured resort grounds without really seeing them. "Some moments, like yesterday, feel like I'm juggling knives, like I'm spread so thin I'm going to drop everything. I'm terrified of failing, Harper." The confession emerged almost against my will. "Failing with Latitudes, failing this renovation... failing you."

When I turned back to her, the professional mask had disappeared. Harper's expression had softened into something more vulnerable, her eyes fixed on me. "I get it, better than most people would. Running a business while trying to maintain a personal life isn't easy. Especially with a new venture."

I nodded, relief washing through me at her understanding.

"But..." She hesitated, her fingers tracing a pattern on her desk calendar. Then her eyes met mine, direct and honest. "When you feel like you're failing or like it's too much... Is this"—she gestured between us—"part of the problem? Are we making it harder?" She paused, shoulders tensing. "Do you need to take a step back?"

The question hung in the air, heavy with implications. My immediate instinct was to deny it, to reassure her without hesitation.

But something stopped me, perhaps the bone-deep exhaustion or the memory of my conflicted feelings last night. For a second, I considered it. Would halting this passionate but increasingly complicated relationship make things simpler? Would it allow me to focus on the business without the added emotional investment?

It was only a moment of consideration, barely a heartbeat, but Harper saw it. Her face registered the hesitation, her eyes filling with hurt before her expression composed itself again.

"No." The word came out firmly from my mouth, leaving no room for doubt. I crossed back to her desk in two quick strides. "Absolutely not. Taking a step back from you is the last thing I want, Harper. Our relationship isn't the complication making things harder. It's the reason the hard stuff feels worth tackling."

She watched me, measuring my sincerity against the hesitation she'd witnessed.

"But finding the balance between everything…" I continued. "I'm still figuring that out, and I'll get better at juggling. But, baby, I need a little help here too. I'm in a field where shit goes sideways on a regular basis. We need to find a way to deal with that. And we will."

The tension in her shoulders eased a touch, and a small smile—the first since I'd entered her office—curved her lips. "I knew even last night I wasn't being fair to you. I was disappointed, sure, but I've seen enough construction to know how these things go. I shouldn't have gone cold on you."

"You're allowed to be disappointed," I countered.

"Maybe." She rose from her chair and rounded the desk, closing the distance between us. "But I also know what it's like to have a million responsibilities pulling you in different directions. I deal with that every day between Finn, my family, and this place. I was hardly acting like a supportive partner last night. So, I'm sorry too."

Up close, I could see the shadows under her eyes, carefully concealed with makeup. Had she slept poorly too? The thought both comforted and troubled me.

"Finn still wants you to help him with his LEGO spaceship," she said, more upbeat now. "He's very proud of it. Says it's an *architectural masterpiece* that you'll appreciate."

I laughed, genuine warmth replacing some of the tension in my chest. "A budding designer, huh? I'd love to see it."

"Maybe dinner tomorrow? If your crisis is resolved by then?"

"I'll make it work," I promised, then winced. "That sounded like—"

"Like something I'd say when I'm overcommitting?" Harper raised an eyebrow, a hint of her usual playfulness returning. "Welcome to my world."

We both laughed, the sound breaking the last of the heavy atmosphere.

I reached for her hand and brought it to my lips. "For what it's worth, I really am sorry about yesterday."

"I know. So am I, and I'm glad we cleared the air. And for what it's worth, I believe you when you say you don't want to step back."

Her belief settled something vital inside me, a shaky foundation finding solid ground. But the tightness in her posture still told me she'd seen that moment of hesitation, that fleeting consideration of an easier path. I'd offered reassurance, and she'd accepted it, but I knew the memory of my uncertainty lingered between us. I needed to show her, not just tell her. I stepped closer, releasing her hand only to cup her cheek, my thumb brushing softly against her skin.

"Good," I murmured. "Because stepping back isn't an option."

I leaned down, intending a simple, sealing kiss. But the moment her yielding lips met mine, something sparked—a release of the tension we'd both been holding, a flare of the connection we'd almost let slip. Her hands came up to grip my shirt, pulling me closer as if she needed the physical proof that I wasn't pulling away. The kiss deepened instantly, moving from tender reassurance to something raw and demanding.

I groaned against her mouth, backing her gently against the edge of her sturdy desk. My hands slid down her back, learning the curve of her waist again, pulling her hips flush against mine. The friction ignited a fire low in my abdomen. I was hard in an instant, pressing against her, needing her to feel the undeniable truth of how much I wanted this, wanted *her*.

Harper let out a low, wrenching moan against my lips as I ground against her, a sound of pure need. Her fingers gripped my hair, holding me fast as the kiss plunged deeper, tongues tangling, panting breath mingling. The deadlines and disasters receded into a dull roar behind the rush of blood in my ears. We were lost in it, the raw urgency overriding doubt, reclaiming the space between us with desperate intensity.

An insistent text tone against my thigh shattered the moment. We wrenched apart, breathing heavily, eyes wide.

I cursed under my breath, fumbling for my phone as

Harper smoothed down her shirt, color high on her cheeks, her lips swollen and kiss-bruised.

I scrubbed a hand over my face as I glanced at the caller ID. Marcus. The Franson job. Reality slammed back in. "Shit. I've got to go."

Harper let out a shaky laugh, glancing pointedly at the desk we were pressed against, then back at me. "Well, at least your phone saved us from another potential desk escapade. My back barely survived the last one."

A wry grin touched my lips despite the interruption. "My desk misses you. At least we're not in a closet this time." The reality of the call pulled me back.

"Hey, it's okay." Harper's voice had regained its steadiness, though her eyes still held the echo of our interrupted passion.

I pocketed my phone again and stroked a hand down her arm. "I can get tunnel vision when I'm knee deep in a project. It's maybe not my most attractive quality… but it's part of what makes me good at what I do."

Her smile steadied. "And I can get a little impatient when I'm overwhelmed. We both have our less attractive sides. And you're very good at what you do. I see the evidence of that every day. And night."

I barked a laugh, more relieved now. "We're good together."

"Yes, we are." She gave me a brisk pat on my chest before releasing me. "Go handle what you need to handle."

The echo of her words from yesterday wasn't lost on me, but this time they carried a different tone—supportive, with maybe a touch of shared exasperation at the timing.

"I'll see you tomorrow," I promised as I stepped forward. "Six?"

She nodded, but that gleam stayed in her eye. "Don't

be late—Finn gets cranky if he has to wait too long for dinner."

"I'll be there," I said with conviction and leaned down to give her a quick but thorough kiss. "Even if I have to walk away from a burning building."

Her laugh followed me into the hallway, a warm sound that eased some of the lingering tension in my lower back. We'd found our way back to solid ground, or at least the appearance of it. But as I returned Marcus's call, I couldn't shake the feeling that something had shifted between us—a new awareness of just how complicated the path forward might be. Had that kiss been me trying to convince her or myself?

The immediate crisis had passed, vulnerability offered, accepted, and sealed with fire. Yet Harper had seen my doubt, and I knew that kiss, however powerful, couldn't erase it completely. The fragility of what we were building remained, requiring more than just passion to sustain it.

As I strode through the lobby toward the resort entrance, one thought crystallized with absolute clarity—I didn't want to back away from Harper Coleridge. That kiss proved it more than any apology could. But wanting something and managing to keep it were two very different challenges, and I'd never been good at failing gracefully.

Chapter Twenty

HARPER

THE BONFIRE CRACKLED MERRILY, spitting embers that danced like rogue fireflies against the black sky. Laughter drifted on the breeze, mingling with the scent of woodsmoke, and the salty tang carried in from the darkening sea. I leaned back against the smooth driftwood log, the warmth of the fire pleasant on my face, the rough fabric of Chase's flannel shirt—loaned when the evening air turned cool—a comforting weight around my shoulders.

Beside me, Chase stretched out his long legs, looking utterly relaxed. He caught my eye and offered a slow, easy smile. Things felt… good. Almost normal, if anything about falling for my brother's best friend, our business partner, could be considered normal.

The past few days since our charged conversation in my office had been surprisingly smooth. He'd thrown himself back into work, resolving the Franson crisis with focused efficiency, but he'd also made a point of checking in and communicating clearly about schedules. He'd come over for a spaghetti dinner as he'd agreed and yesterday, he'd even managed a short visit to witness Finn's latest rehearsal. Now that the play was quickly approaching, Finn practiced every chance he got, including muttering about parrotfish to his cereal. Chase was *showing* me he could juggle it all, that he was reliable. And I wanted desperately to let go of the breath I'd been holding since… well, since Jarod.

But deep down, beneath the surface of this newfound comfort, a tiny sliver of sharp doubt remained. I couldn't quite shake the memory of that fractional hesitation before he'd reassured me he didn't want to cool things between us. He'd denied it, yes, his words firm, his lips and hands even more so. Yet, that split second of uncertainty I'd perceived had lodged itself in my mind, a tiny burr under the saddle of my cautious hope.

He said what I wanted to hear… but did he really mean it?

I pushed the thought away, focusing instead on the scene around me. Eli and Jules were huddled together on a blanket nearby, Eli whispering something that made Jules laugh and swat his arm playfully. They looked so effortlessly content, their earlier relationship drama resolved into a comfortable, established partnership. Brenna and Hunter were sharing a bag of popcorn, Hunter's large frame a protective presence beside my sister, their easy affection a quiet counterpoint to Eli's more outgoing charm. Braden was enthusiastically explaining the nuances of hop varieties to a slightly glazed-looking Chase. It was… relaxing. My family, starting to feel like *our* family.

"Prepare for galactic domination!"

Finn's excited call cut through the general murmur. He burst into the firelight circle, proudly holding aloft the LEGO spaceship he and Chase had painstakingly assembled. It was ridiculously complex, all gray bricks and transparent blue engine parts, far beyond anything I could have managed.

"Whoa, check it out!" Eli abandoned Jules momentarily to admire the creation. "Does it have hyperdrive?"

Finn puffed out his chest. "Yep! And laser cannons! Chase showed me how to make the wings fold back for atmospheric entry." He turned expectantly to Chase, who had stopped listening to Braden mid-sentence about pilsners.

"It's a masterpiece, Finn," Chase said with pride. He pointed to a small lever. "Show them the secret escape pod."

Finn giggled, demonstrating the feature with a flourish. "It's for emergencies!"

I watched Chase interact with my son, my heart doing that familiar ache-and-swell thing. He didn't talk down to Finn—he engaged with him, respected his imagination, celebrated his enthusiasm. He kneeled beside Finn now, pointing out different parts of the ship, listening intently as Finn explained the function of each imaginary component. Seeing them like this, heads close together in the flickering firelight, Chase's usual focused intensity softened by easy affection… it was the exact picture of the future I secretly craved, the one I was terrified to fully believe in.

Later, after the LEGO ship had been sufficiently admired and s'mores had been distributed—Eli predictably burning his marshmallow to a blackened crisp, Chase achieving perfect golden-brown toastiness—Finn snuggled beside me on the log. He leaned his head against my arm, smelling faintly of smoke and graham crackers as he drowsily watched the flames dance. Chase had moved to another log, drawn into a conversation with Hunter, something about local building regulations, leaving me and

Finn in a small bubble of quiet amidst the surrounding chatter.

The fire popped, sending a shower of sparks toward the starry sky. Finn reached for the LEGO spaceship at his feet, his small fingers finding the tiny lever that activated the retractable wings. With careful precision, he pushed the mechanism, making the wings fold back with a satisfying click. The blue transparent pieces caught the firelight, glowing almost magically.

"This is my favorite part," he murmured, more to himself than to me. "Chase says real spaceships need to change shape for different kinds of flying."

I smiled, smoothing his hair. "I imagine he would know."

Finn shifted, turning his face up toward mine, his blue eyes serious in the dim light. He burrowed into my side and whispered so only I could hear, "Mommy?"

"Hmm?" I murmured, smoothing his already messy hair.

"When Chase finishes all the new buildings…" He paused, his brow furrowed in thought. "Will he be my dad then? For real?"

The air rushed out of my lungs. The crackling fire roared in my ears, drowning out all other sounds. Finn's innocent question, spoken so matter-of-factly, landed like a punch, striking that precise point where my deepest hopes met my most profound fears.

Finn sees it. He expects it. He's building a future in his head based on sandcastles and LEGO spaceships.

Cold panic clawed its way up my throat. I pulled my son closer instinctively, needing his solid warmth against me to counteract the sudden chill spreading through my veins. I glanced frantically toward Chase. He was still deep in conversation with Hunter, oblivious to the emotional earthquake that had just occurred beside the firepit. Thank God.

"Oh, sweetie," I managed, forcing my voice to sound light, casual, even as my heart hammered against my ribs. "Chase is… Chase is our very special friend. He cares about us very much."

"I have a friend at school, Jason. His mom had a special friend and now he's Jason's dad," Finn persisted, his logic crushing me further. "And Chase builds stuff like dads do."

"We'll see what happens, honey," I murmured against his hair, hating the vague non-answer but unable to offer more. "Right now, isn't it nice that he helps you build such amazing LEGO spaceships?"

"Yeah, that's awesome." Apparently satisfied for the moment, Finn snuggled back against me and returned his attention to the mesmerizing flames. But his question echoed in my mind, amplifying the doubt sown by Chase's hesitation in my office.

He admitted feeling overwhelmed. And I didn't imagine that pause before he said he was all in.

Finn's innocent assumption of permanence felt like a dangerous counterpoint to Chase's admitted fear. Was I leading my son toward heartbreak by allowing this connection to deepen, by letting myself hope this time was different? The weight of responsibility crushed me.

The bonfire gathering began to wind down naturally after that. Eli and Jules were the first to leave, Eli dramatically yawning while Jules gave me a quick hug. From across the fire, Brenna caught my eye with a questioning look I pretended not to see. Braden headed back toward Tidal Hops, likely to check on his fermenters.

Finn dozed as he slumped against me.

Chase stretched, rolling his shoulders. "Well, much as I

hate to leave the party, I should probably head home. I need to look over the Franson schedule to make sure we finish on time."

"We should get going too," Hunter said as he grasped Brenna's hands in his and gently pulled her to her feet.

But I barely noticed them. Tonight, I needed space. I needed to process Finn's question, to wrestle with the implications away from Chase's perceptive gaze.

"Of course." I forced a smile that felt brittle.

He stood up, and I gently disengaged Finn before standing beside him. He tilted his head down, his expression sharpening in the dim firelight. "You okay? You got quiet there for a bit."

"Just tired," I lied, avoiding his eyes. "Long week."

He didn't push, just leaned down and gave me a kiss. It was warm, lingering, tasting faintly of smoke and beer and the promise of something I was terrified of losing. It felt different against my lips now, tainted by the fear Finn's question had reignited. When he pulled back, his eyes searched mine for a moment. I hoped my own fear wasn't broadcasting itself like a faulty radio signal.

He ruffled Finn's hair. "Night, buddy. See you soon."

"Night, Chase," Finn mumbled sleepily.

Then Chase walked away down the beach path, his tall frame disappearing into the shadows. Finn shifted position, sleepily staring into the hissing remains of the doused fire.

Will he be my dad then?

The question pulsed in my mind, in time with my heartbeat. I needed to talk to Brenna. Just as she and Hunter reached the edge of the beach path, I called out, my voice a bit shaky. "Brenna? Wait up!"

She turned, Hunter pausing beside her. Brenna walked back toward me, concern etched on her face in the dim light. "Everything all right?"

"Can I... can I talk to you tomorrow? Swing by the shop?" I asked, trying to keep my voice steady.

Brenna glanced back toward where Chase had disappeared, then looked closely at my face. "Of course. Is this...?" She gestured vaguely after Chase.

I nodded, unable to form words.

"Okay," she said softly, giving my arm a reassuring squeeze. "How about at lunchtime?"

"Yes. Thanks, Brenna."

"You three looked really happy tonight, you know," Brenna added gently, her eyes kind.

The comment, meant to comfort, felt like twisting a knife. "Yeah," I managed, forcing another weak smile. "That's... that's what I need to talk to you about."

Brenna gave me one last worried look before rejoining Hunter. I watched them go, then glanced down at Finn, now fast asleep as he slumped on the log, his face peaceful and trusting. The contrast between his innocent assumption and my own paralyzing fear was stark. I lifted him into my arms and hugged him tight, the scent of woodsmoke clinging to his hair, and wondered how on earth I was going to navigate this.

SEEKING refuge from the relentless Florida sun and the even more relentless churn of my own thoughts, I pushed open the familiar door to Bookshop in Paradise. The immediate cool quiet was a balm, the air thick with the comforting, dusty scent of paper and ink, a world away from resort budgets and bonfire anxieties. Sunlight streamed through the large front window, illuminating intricate patterns in the worn area rug near the entrance. Brenna raised her head from a nearby display, where she was meticulously arranging a display of author spotlights. One glance at my face, and the welcoming smile she offered shifted instantly to quiet concern.

"How are you holding up, big sister?" Her question was soft, filled with concern.

"Just another day in paradise." I gave her a weak smile. "Is now still okay to talk?"

"Always." She moved away from the display, wiping her hands on her apron. "Let's go in the back. I just put on a fresh pot of coffee."

After she flipped the front door sign to *Closed*, I followed her through a doorway into the small, cluttered back office. It was crammed with boxes of books, shipping supplies, a small desk overflowing with invoices, and two surprisingly comfortable, mismatched armchairs tucked into a corner. Brenna waved me toward one while she poured coffee into two thick pottery mugs.

"Okay." She handed me a mug and settled into the opposite chair. "Spill it. What happened last night?"

I wrapped my hands around the warm mug, letting the heat seep into my chilled fingers. After taking a deep breath, the words tumbled out, fueled by lack of sleep and pent-up anxiety. "Finn. He, uh… he asked me something."

She waited patiently, her gaze steady and encouraging.

"Brenna, he asked if Chase was going to be his dad."

The words hung in the quiet office, feeling even more leaden now than they had last night. I stared at my sister, my vision blurring. "Finn wants it. He sees Chase as… permanent. And it terrified me."

"Oh, wow." Brenna reached out, her hand covering mine where it rested on the arm of the chair. Her touch was firm, grounding. "Honey, of course it terrified you. That's a huge question from a six-year-old."

"But it's not just the question," I insisted, needing her

to understand the layers of fear Finn's innocent words had unearthed. "It's… it's Chase. Remember I told you how he canceled our plans last week? How he came over the next day and admitted he was feeling overwhelmed? How he hesitated before he said he wanted to stay together?"

Brenna nodded slowly, her brow furrowed in concentration.

"That hesitation…" The memory made my stomach clench again. "I tried to ignore it. He's been great since then, really present, reliable. But when Finn asked that… all I could think was, what if Chase wasn't just reassuring me? What if he really is overwhelmed and scared? What if Finn builds all these hopes, lets Chase become this central figure in his life, and then Chase realizes it is too much and walks away? I can't put Finn through that, Brenna. I just can't." The last words were choked, thick with the fear I'd carried since Jarod left.

"And," I added, dropping my gaze back to my mug, the next admission feeling even more dangerous, "it's not just Finn I'm worried about. I'm… I'm in love with him. And that makes the thought of him leaving unbearable."

Brenna was silent for a long moment, letting my words settle in the small space. She took a slow sip of her coffee, her expression thoughtful. I braced myself for platitudes, for reassurances that everything would be fine.

"Okay." She set her mug down. "First off, your fear is completely valid. Given your history with Jarod, and knowing Chase admitted to feeling overwhelmed, and then having Finn drop that specific question? Anyone would be reeling. You are absolutely right to be scared."

Her validation unlocked a pressure valve. Tears pricked my eyes. "So I'm not making too much of all this?"

"Not even remotely." Brenna offered a small, sad smile. "You're a mother protecting her child and a woman protecting her own heart after it was shattered. That's not overreacting, Harper. That's survival."

She leaned forward, her gaze intent. "But fear can be a tricky thing. It kept you safe for a long time after Jarod. It made you cautious, independent, strong. But now it might be blinding you a little."

I frowned. "What do you mean?"

"Think about Chase. Think about *his* perspective. You said he admitted feeling overwhelmed, that he hesitated. Why do you automatically assume that hesitation means he's going to leave?"

"Because…" I started, then faltered. "Because that's what happens? Because it gets hard, and people bail?"

"Jarod bailed," Brenna corrected softly but firmly. "That doesn't mean Chase will. Harper, you told me yourself that Chase has fears too. Fears about commitment, fears about failing with his new business, failing our renovation project, failing *you*. When you asked him if he needed to step back, you probably hit *his* deepest insecurity square on. Maybe that hesitation wasn't him thinking 'Yes, I need an out.' Maybe it was him thinking, 'Shit, she sees right through me, she knows I'm terrified I'll screw this up.'"

I stared at her, absorbing the alternative interpretation. Chase, scared? It seemed counterintuitive. He was always so confident, so capable.

"His fear doesn't cancel out his feelings for you, Harper," Brenna continued, her voice earnest. "Sometimes, the more someone cares, the *more* terrified they are of messing it up. He didn't want to break up, did he? He hesitated, felt the fear, and then recommitted. Doesn't that count for something?"

My mind raced, replaying that conversation in my office. His exhaustion, his raw honesty about the pressure, the flicker of uncertainty in his eyes, followed by the firm denial. The passion. Had I misinterpreted his fear as doubt? Had I projected my own history onto his momentary struggle?

"He's been *showing* you he's trying, hasn't he?" Brenna pressed gently.

I nodded slowly, thinking of the past week. The easy companionship, the shared laughter, the way he looked at Finn with such genuine warmth. He *had* been trying.

"So maybe," Brenna suggested, her voice kind but firm, "instead of focusing on the possibility of him leaving, you need to focus on the reality of him staying, even when he's scared. Maybe this isn't about waiting for him to prove he won't leave. Maybe it's about you both learning how to navigate your fears *together*."

The idea washed over me, both frightening and strangely liberating. Talking about the fear itself, not just dancing around it. Acknowledging *his* potential vulnerability alongside my own.

"You need to hash this out with him, Harper," Brenna said. "Not just about Finn getting attached, but also talk about Chase's hesitation. Ask him what he was afraid of in that moment. Share your fear triggered by Finn's words. Put it all out there."

"That sounds..." I swallowed hard. "Utterly terrifying."

"Probably." Brenna smiled wryly. "Building real trust usually is. Believe me, I know. But look at the alternative. You keep holding your breath, analyzing every glance, every pause, driving yourself up the wall and probably pushing him away with suspicion he hasn't earned. Don't let Jarod's ghost and Chase's fear have that much power over something that feels this real."

She reached across and squeezed my hand again. "You

found the courage to face down Mom about the renovations, to face down our brothers about being with Chase. Find the courage to face Chase himself. With all of it. See what happens when you both stop protecting yourselves and start protecting each other."

I looked down at our joined hands, then met Brenna's steady gaze. She was right. It felt like standing on the edge of that cliff again, the wind whipping around me, the potential for a devastating fall immense. But maybe the potential for flight was worth the risk.

I took another shaky breath, the scent of old books and possibility filling my lungs. "Okay. I'll talk to him."

As I left the quiet sanctuary of the bookstore and stepped back out onto the sun-drenched, noisy reality of Main Street, the conversation ahead with Chase loomed large and frightening. But for the first time, I wondered if maybe I wasn't the only one bringing fear to the table. And if sharing those fears might be the only way for us to move past them.

Chapter Twenty-One

CHASE

THE FLOOR-TO-CEILING WINDOWS framed a breathtaking view, their edges gleaming against the backdrop of glittering ocean. The lavish Italian porcelain tile, designed to resemble bleached driftwood, reflected the room's elegant ambiance with its polished surface, exuding an air of understated opulence. The newly completed Franson guest suite smelled of fresh paint, new grout, and money. Lots of money. It was sleek, modern, and precisely the kind of high-end coastal luxury William Franson had demanded. Standing here now and seeing it finished, professional pride surged within me, momentarily eclipsing the exhaustion that still clung from the near disaster not so long ago.

"Magnificent, Chase. Absolutely magnificent." William Franson beamed, running a satisfied hand over the seamless edge of the custom concrete countertop in the kitchenette area. He was a man accustomed to getting what he wanted, and right now, he looked like he'd just unwrapped the Hope Diamond. "Better than I envisioned. That workspace integration"—he gestured toward the cleverly concealed desk area built into the custom cabinetry—"is genius. It doubles as a private work area for me and a guest living suite."

"The goal was a seamless blend of relaxation and functionality. I'm glad it meets your approval, William."

His wife, Claire, who had been quietly inspecting the intricate tile work in the massive walk-in shower, emerged with a soft smile. "It's more than approval. It's perfection. You've truly captured that indoor-outdoor feeling we wanted." She glanced toward the sliding glass doors that opened onto a private patio.

"Thank you, Claire. The custom sliders were key to that."

Marilyn, my unflappable office manager and miracle worker, materialized beside me, holding out the final completion certificates and warranty documents arranged neatly in a modern leather portfolio. Her presence was calming, her efficiency an example of the smooth operation I was trying to build with Latitudes Design.

"Just a few signatures needed here, Mr. Franson," Marilyn said, her voice calm and pleasant as she presented the portfolio on the built-in dining nook table.

Franson waved a dismissive hand, already reaching for the offered pen. "Whatever you need. Chase delivered what he promised. On time, too, despite that little electrical hiccup."

Little electrical hiccup.

Right. The one that had required ripping out newly installed wire, calling in emergency electricians, and working Marcus, not to mention myself, nearly into the ground for seventy-two straight hours. The one that had utterly torched my profit margin on this supposedly lucrative project.

I kept my smile fixed, nodding agreeably. "We strive for client satisfaction above all." Which sometimes meant eating costs that weren't technically my fault but reflected poorly on my firm's oversight if not handled swiftly.

While Franson signed off with a flourish, I let my gaze wander over the finished space. The cool gray walls, the warm wood accents, the subtle textures of the linens on the king-sized bed, the way the light played across the floors in the main area. It *was* good work. Damn good work. It was the kind of project that belonged in architectural digests, the kind that could launch Latitudes Design into the next tier.

But my internal ledger kept running its own ruthless calculations. The original healthy profit margin had dwindled to something barely above break-even. It was a vivid reminder of how precarious this solo venture still was, how much pressure rested on every project, every budget line, every client relationship.

Especially the Sunset Siesta renovation.

"A pleasure doing business with you," Franson declared with a nod at me as he capped the pen. He handed the paperwork back to Marilyn. "I'll certainly be recommending Latitudes Design to my neighbors. Expect calls."

"Thank you, William. We appreciate the confidence."

Marilyn kept up a seamless stream of conversation as she walked out with them, leaving me alone in the pristine, sun-filled guest suite. The silence was abrupt after Franson's booming enthusiasm. I walked over to the large window overlooking the water and traced the edge of the frame. It was done. A success, by the client's measure. But the financial reality left a bitter taste. I needed more wins like this, *profitable* wins, to keep Latitudes afloat, especially with the massive undertaking at Sunset Siesta consuming so much of my time and resources.

Back in my own office at Latitudes Design later that afternoon, I stared at the Sunset Siesta master plan on my secondary monitor, the intricate lines and phases representing months, potentially years, of work—and financial interdependence. Today, my partnership stake felt less like an opportunity and more like an anchor tied to my ankles while I tried to tread water.

An email notification pinged softly, pulling my attention to the main screen. The subject line made my breath catch: *Project Bid Update—Thorne Residence*. This was a high-end renovation project on Little Torch Key I'd poured weeks into developing a proposal for, the one I'd been counting on to provide a much-needed financial buffer alongside Sunset Siesta.

My fingers hesitated over the trackpad. I took a slow breath, bracing myself. "Please be good news."

I clicked it open.

DEAR MR. ASHWORTH,

Thank you for your detailed proposal for our residence renovation. We received several highly competitive bids, and after careful consideration...

MY EYES SCANNED DOWN, skipping the pleasantries, searching for the verdict.

... WE HAVE DECIDED to proceed with Marino Architects for this project. While your design concepts were innovative and impressive, we

*felt Marino's extensive portfolio of similar large-scale historical reno-
vations in the Upper Keys provided a stronger assurance…*

THE REST BLURRED, but that didn't matter. I lost to a
bigger, more established firm.

"Goddamn."

I slumped in my chair. The professional pride from the
Franson walk-through evaporated, replaced by a cold wave
of anxiety. The Thorne contract would have provided
stability, breathing room, proof that Latitudes could
compete and win against the big players. Now everything
balanced precariously on the Sunset Siesta project, on the
Coleridge family, on my ability to deliver flawlessly there
despite corroded pipes, hidden foundations, and the
increasingly potent distraction of Harper herself.

Could I handle it all? The question echoed inside my
head.

A soft knock sounded at my door before it opened.
Marilyn stood there, holding two coffee mugs and a small,
familiar pink box from Sweet Dreams Bakery on Main
Street. She placed one mug—my usual black, strong—and
a classic glazed donut on the corner of my desk, pushing
aside a stack of material samples to make room. Her presence was quiet, unobtrusive, but deeply supportive.

"I saw the email," she said simply, her voice calm and
pragmatic. She'd been copied on the bid reply. She took a
sip from her own mug, her gaze sympathetic but not
pitying.

"Thanks." I managed a weak smile as I reached for the
coffee. Its warmth felt good in my hands. "Yeah. Marino
got it. Longer track record."

Marilyn nodded, settling into the visitor chair. "Their

loss, Chase. Your proposal was better." She wasn't just saying it. Marilyn didn't give false platitudes, and I knew my design was top notch. "We're still landing more contracts than we're losing. That's huge for a firm that's only been open six months. The Franson recommendation today? That's worth more than you think. Word gets around fast in their circle."

I took a bite of the donut. The sugary sweetness was a small comfort, a reminder of simple pleasures amidst complex anxieties. "I know. It just… this one would have helped. A lot."

"It would have, but we adjust. We keep building momentum. You knew starting your own firm wouldn't be easy."

"I know. I'm just frustrated." I took another, larger bite of the donut.

She stood and headed for the door, both hands wrapped around her mug. "You're already miles ahead of where most new firms are at this stage. Focus on Sunset Siesta, knock that out of the park, and the next Thorne-level client will be calling *us*."

Her pragmatic confidence was what I needed to hear, even if I wasn't entirely feeling it myself. "Thanks, Marilyn. I needed that."

"Anytime." She gave me one last encouraging look. "Now finish your donut. Sugar helps."

She left, closing the door softly behind her. My gaze returned to the Sunset Siesta plans, the weight of the project pressing down with renewed force. Marilyn was right—we were doing well, technically. But the margins were thin, the pressure immense.

Failure wasn't an option. Not with Latitudes Design. And certainly not with Harper. I finished the donut and wiped my hands clean. Picking up my coffee, I forced myself to focus on the guest room lighting schematics.

"One problem at a time," I said softly. "That's how you build something lasting. Right?"

———

THE FLUORESCENT LIGHTS of the home improvement store hummed overhead, casting a flat, unforgiving glare on endless aisles stacked high. Lumber, plumbing fixtures, garden supplies—each section smelled distinctly different, a strange olfactory map of domestic ambition and weekend projects. This wasn't my usual environment. My world was typically one of curated samples, precise CAD drawings, and client consultations in tastefully appointed offices. But after the day I'd had, I needed the distraction.

I pushed the oversized shopping cart, its wheels rumbling unevenly on the concrete floor, searching for the specific marine-grade sealant Harper had mentioned needing for a minor repair near the pool pump house. A practical problem with a practical solution. Unlike the tangled mess currently occupying my thoughts.

Losing the Thorne bid stung like hell. And Harper was tangled inextricably with that professional anxiety. Harper, whose presence in my life was both essential and fundamentally destabilizing to the ordered world I'd always inhabited.

It took a while, but I located the sealants in aisle nine. I scanned the labels, my focus blurring from lack of sleep and too much caffeine, and found what I needed near the bottom. Given Siesta Sunset's oceanfront location, I grabbed an entire case. My eyes drifted past the caulking guns to the endcap display. Bright primary colors snagged my attention. A child-sized tool belt, complete with a miniature hammer, wrench, and screwdriver clipped neatly into loops.

I moved the cart toward the display.

My hand reached out, almost of its own accord, and picked up the tool belt. The red canvas fabric was sturdy yet lightweight. The tiny hammer head was blunt and safe, but pretty well made. It was exactly the sort of thing Finn would adore.

A faint smile raised my lips as a vivid image flashed in my mind—Finn, his face screwed up in concentration, wearing this very tool belt as he "helped" me measure a two-by-four on the worksite. Or maybe using the little hammer as we built a birdhouse for the backyard. Or standing beside me at my drafting table back home, his small hand reaching for one of my specialized pencils, wanting to draw buildings too.

Before I could analyze it, before logic could intervene, I tossed the tool belt into my cart alongside the marine sealant. It landed with a soft clatter next to the sensible, necessary item I'd actually come here for.

I pushed the cart toward the checkout lanes, feeling slightly dazed. After checking out, I walked out into the bright, humid glare of the parking lot, the automatic doors sliding shut behind me. Inside the quiet sanctuary of my SUV, I placed the box of sealant onto the floor but placed the child's tool belt deliberately on the passenger seat beside me.

I stared at it. At the cheerful red belt, the tools designed to build interest without smashing fingers. It looked out of place against my sleek black leather upholstery. A gaudy, innocent anomaly in my controlled environment.

And I knew, with a certainty that made my breath freeze in my lungs, *why* I'd bought it. It wasn't a random impulse. It wasn't because Finn might like it. It was because when I saw it, I hadn't just thought of Finn. I'd thought of *us*. Me, Harper, Finn. Building something, and not just sandcastles. Something real.

A family.

The realization hit me with the force of a physical impact. My hands closed over the leather-wrapped steering wheel, my knuckles pale and ghostly. This feeling for Harper wasn't just intense attraction or deepening affection anymore. It had expanded, shifted, and grown roots that now intrinsically included her son. I wasn't falling only for the competent, beautiful, frustratingly guarded woman who challenged and captivated me. I was also falling for the idea of a life with her, a life that included bedtime stories and scraped knees, and coaching little league, maybe. A life filled with the kind of messy, unpredictable, warm chaos I'd witnessed in her cottage, so different from the cool, ordered quiet of my own upbringing. Or my present life.

Panic, icy and razor sharp, immediately followed the revelation.

A family? Me?

The concept was enormous, terrifying. My parents' marriage had been a masterclass in emotional distance, a polite arrangement devoid of warmth or genuine connection. I'd spent my adult life prioritizing control, precision, professional success—things I understood, things I could manage. I could calculate wind shear and load-bearing capacity, but the physics of falling in love were entirely beyond my expertise.

The pressures I was already juggling magnified exponentially. Latitudes Design, teetering financially after the Franson near-disaster and the lost Thorne bid. The massive, complex Sunset Siesta renovation, where my professional reputation and personal investment were deeply intertwined with Harper and her family.

What if I failed?

What if I failed *them?*

I needed control. I needed stability. I needed to focus on the tangible, the solvable—the architectural plans, the budget spreadsheets, the construction schedules. That was my territory. That was where I felt competent. I needed to get a grip on these emotions. I wanted Harper and Finn in my life. But in order to feel secure with that, I had to get the business on firmer footing.

I started the SUV, the engine humming smoothly, a familiar sound of controlled power. I relaxed my clenched hands and shook them out. The child's tool belt sat on the passenger seat, a bright red symbol of both the future I impulsively reached for and the overwhelming vulnerability it represented. I pulled out of the parking space, heading back toward the resort, toward Harper. Not with a plan, not with any clear answers, just with the terrifying, sinking realization that I was out of my depth, drowning in these uncharted waters of actually giving a damn.

And I had absolutely no idea how to swim.

Chapter Twenty-Two

HARPER

IF CHAOS HAD A SCENT, mine was a mix of clean laundry, glitter glue, and whatever last-minute dinner Finn had rejected half an hour ago. The kitchen counter was a battlefield of lunchboxes, scattered construction paper, and the lone, precious parrotfish tail we'd nearly lost to the trash. Somewhere under all that, my clipboard lurked, a reminder that I was both general manager and reluctant seamstress, all while hoping one didn't show up in the shoes of the other.

Finn, cheeks faintly blue from face paint, darted through the tangle of chairs and discarded markers, arms tucked in like bright green fins. He landed in front of me with a flourish, shoving his chin out. "Look, Mom. Watch my 'eating coral face.'"

His jaw dropped, lips stretched wide and ridiculous, one eye squeezed shut. He looked less like a tropical reef species and more like a fish in urgent need of dental care.

"Convincing. I feel the spirit of the parrotfish alive and

well in this kitchen." I reached for the elastic band on his tail, fingers snagging on Velcro. "Did we lose your dorsal fin again or is it hiding with the missing socks?"

He twisted around, suddenly frantic, tugging the waistband around as though it held the meaning of life. I caught sight of the fin in the great room, half-stuffed beneath a couch cushion and wedged next to the remote and an empty juice box.

There was a sharp knock at the door. The sound cut through Finn's dramatics and the low thrum of my nerves. I brushed a stray curl from my forehead, flicked my gaze to the hallway mirror—pale, clean blouse, necklace readjusted, eyes a little more tired than yesterday—and forced a steadying breath.

Chase's silhouette hovered in the glass for a split second before he stepped in, keys dangling from his fingers. He took in the mess with a quick scan—no judgment, just that quiet, subtle smile he saved for Finn. Still, the tightness was there at the corners of his mouth, just out of reach from anything Finn or I might fix. I'd first noticed it a few days ago, right after he'd lost out on the home remodel he was hoping to land. If anything, the lines in his brow had only deepened since, the relentless pressure of putting out a million small fires.

"Hey, buddy," Chase greeted Finn, making his way over without hesitation. "Is that a real parrotfish or an extra from *Sharknado 5*?"

Finn bounced from foot to foot. "It's me! Watch this." He darted over, mouth already forming his next line, posture practically vibrating. "You know parrotfish help save the reef, Chase? I've been working on my speech. Wanna hear?"

"Definitely," Chase said, offering a high five that Finn slapped with the unbridled confidence of a six-year-old convinced he was changing the world one monologue at a time. Because after a series of costume revisions that rivaled Sunset Siesta's and endless rehearsals, tonight was the big kindergarten play.

The two of them fell into the familiar pattern with Chase kneeling down to Finn's height. Finn launched into his best theater voice, mangling *coral bleaching* and *algae* with all the right seriousness, flapping the half-secured fin so hard I worried for both costume and furniture.

While he performed, I wrapped myself in logistics— find Finn's shoes, double-check my purse, make sure there was enough time to make it across Dove Key before the curtain went up. I caught Chase glancing at his phone, thumb sliding across the screen like a reflex he was barely aware of, face hardening for an instant before Finn drew him back in.

He was good at this. At showing up, at smiling, at being the sunniest version of himself for a boy who adored him. But it didn't erase the line between us that had been growing sharper, two people who worked too hard and weren't good at navigating the complexities that caused. He'd asked me for understanding, for help. And I'd done my best to be quietly supportive and whatever the opposite of clingy was.

But Brenna's voice echoed in my head. That we needed to talk this over. That I needed to come clean with my fears and get him to admit his, which had sounded so easy while we were sitting in her office. I fiddled with the hem of my sleeve, trying to gather my own resolve with the same practical efficiency I'd bring to resort staff schedules.

Because what if I asked for honesty and didn't like the answer?

I balled my hand into a fist and tapped it on the counter. No more evading. There would never be the perfect time, and I could at least get the ball rolling. Finn trotted off to hunt for socks, tail flapping, and the thud of his feet disappeared down the hall. I watched Chase watching him, his shoulders rising and falling in an endless breath he probably didn't realize was audible. Before the space between us could fill up with small talk or excuses, I edged closer.

"Hey. Got a second?"

He didn't jump. But he did look over a beat too slowly, wariness flashing over his face before he managed the careful version of a smile. I hated that I recognized it.

I leaned back against the edge of the kitchen island, fingers lacing together to keep myself from fussing with the stack of mail. "I've been thinking about what you said. About work and feeling stretched thin. I can see it, Chase. Even when you're trying to hide it. The way you come in smiling for Finn, but your shoulders are up near your ears."

He hesitated, staring past my shoulder at the lamp, or maybe just through it. "I know. I'm sorry. I'm in a really precarious spot right now, but things will settle down. We're good—you and me. Really." His voice was practiced, low, and meant to soothe, but with a razor-sharp edge. He rubbed the back of his neck, eyes darting to the digital clock on the oven.

I didn't step away. "Are we? Sometimes it feels like maybe all of this is just…"

Too much? Too heavy? The cost of caring? The words trailed off, refusing to fit neatly together.

Chase ran a hand through his hair, making it stick up a little at the crown—boyish and impossibly tired. "Work's been utterly over the top," he said, voice flattening. "That Franson thing took a lot out of me. The budget numbers Jules sent over weren't great, but it's nothing I can't handle." Another pause. He wouldn't meet my gaze for long. "We're starting the other part of the first floor of Room Block One tomorrow, and I'm just trying to make sure it goes smoothly. Just be a little patient with me, okay? We're fine."

"I know we're starting the other side tomorrow." Despite my best efforts, my voice took on a sharp edge. "I'm the general manager, remember? I don't sit around all day, either."

"No, you sure don't. I can hardly keep up with you." After a lopsided smile, he glanced pointedly toward the hall, then at the clock. "We should probably get going, right? Don't want Finn to be late for his big debut."

He was right, technically. But the words landed with the weight of a slammed door. It wasn't that he didn't care. I knew that. He just couldn't or *wouldn't* walk through the opening I'd offered. That familiar frustration pressed against my chest, a coil of disappointment that almost burned.

Chase was already scooping up Finn's discarded hoodie and laying it on the arm of the couch, defaulting to logistics as if the question hadn't been asked. "I'll make sure we've got everything. The head too. Can't let our parrotfish go topless."

I swallowed, pressing my hands to my thighs to keep from wringing them in front of him. My voice was too bright when it came out. "Right. The play. Wouldn't want to miss the"—I couldn't help it—"dramatic fin-flapping."

Finn skidded in, one foot already halfway into a shoe, the sock on backward. "Mom, can you do the Velcro? My flipper's stuck."

I kneeled down, tugging his sock around and working the stubborn fin over his shoe while he fidgeted. "I hope you're not going to upstage everyone with that coral-eating face."

Finn grinned at me, arms thrown out for balance, entirely untroubled by any tension in the room. "Chase says I'm the best parrotfish. Right?"

Chase ruffled his hair. "Best in the Lower Keys, minimum. I'd put money on it."

We marshaled our way through headpieces, stray scales, and the obligatory last bathroom stop. I locked the door behind us and caught Chase's gaze for just a second on the way to the car. He gave me the kind of half-smile that was all apology and none of the answers I wanted.

I dropped Finn off backstage, his nerves manifesting in little vertical jumps to see how much his dorsal fin flapped. Telling him to break a leg would only tempt fate, so I gave him a huge hug. The school cafeteria still smelled faintly of hot dogs and floor cleaner, though tonight it had been transformed—at least in theory—by rows of folding chairs and a burst of glittery banners taped above the makeshift stage. Voices rose and fell in happy, nervous waves as parents scanned the program for their kid's name. I found seats near the front, and Chase landed in the seat beside me.

I spotted Eli leaning against the wall near the doors, laughing at something Jules whispered in his ear, and waved them over. Mom, resplendent in breezy linen and a colorful turquoise necklace, sat on my other side.

Chase pulled out his phone, thumb hovering as a litany of work notifications scrolled past the lock screen. I reached for a breath, wished it tasted less like worry and more like optimism.

The house lights dimmed, such as they were, two fluorescents flickering overhead and the glow of iPhones snapping last-minute photos. The principal hustled up, microphone in hand, to tell us how grateful she was for parent volunteers, for the community, for everyone's patience during the last program when the projector melted.

The curtain shimmied open, and the ocean paraded out: starfish in orange onesies, a clownfish with swimming goggles, the world's most solemn-looking jellyfish, and my own son in an explosion of neon blue and lime green, flapping his handmade fins like a soldier marching to war.

Finn beamed when he spotted us. My heart did an awkward thump that only seemed to deepen when Chase's face softened, the weariness retreating entirely for that single, shining moment. He clapped and laughed when Finn delivered his first line, all clear enunciation and gleeful finger-wagging about helping keep the reef healthy.

The crowd melted into the background. There was just Finn, owning the stage with his coral-eating face and his unrestrained joy, and Chase, grinning wide, so obviously proud you'd think Finn had invented the parrotfish.

Finn's big scene was a speech about coral bleaching, that he had rehearsed approximately five million times. "When it gets too hot, the coral gets stressed, and then we all have to work together to help." He flapped his fins so hard he nearly upended the backdrop. The audience giggled. He closed with a flourish, "The reef needs us all!"

And there it was. That ache in my chest—pride so fierce it almost stung, tangled with longing and something else sharper and lonelier. I looked sideways at Chase again. His eyes were locked on Finn, and for a second, he wasn't the architect with endless deadlines or the man I kept missing even when he stood beside me. He was just there, wholly present and all in, for the kid in blue sequins.

It made my heart hurt for everything we still hadn't said.

For the finale, Finn and the other fish swayed to a tune called "Swim, Little Fishies, Swim." Half the class belted gleefully off-key. Chase snapped a quick photo when Finn struck his final pose—one arm up, mouth open in the world's most ambitious coral chomp.

The curtain wobbled closed, applause filling the little space. Eli gave a loud whistle, and Mom covered her ears and winced at him, smiling all the while. I whooped, clapping until my hands stung, and Chase did the same. For one reckless moment, I wanted to grab his hand and pretend nothing had changed.

Instead, I drew my arms in, that thin layer of awkwardness resettling.

People began shifting, stretching, milling for cookies at the back. Mom turned in her seat, caught my eye, and smiled wide. "He was spectacular, Harper. He was loving every second."

I took her hand for a second. "Thanks, Mom. I'm just glad he didn't trip over the jellyfish."

We shuffled out of the cafeteria to wait for the victorious kindergartners to appear. Chase stood stiffly at my side, our arms almost brushing yet a million miles apart. Eli sidled over, Jules at his side, both sporting fresh programs and that slightly smug post-family-performance glow. Eli looked me over with exaggerated seriousness. "I can honestly say I've never seen a parrotfish sell it that hard. Broadway could use that level of fin action."

Jules flashed a quick grin. "Who did his makeup? Because those scales were popping."

The warmth of their teasing nearly covered the subtle, searching glance Eli sent back and forth between me and Chase. I caught it and then made a show of fixing Finn's backpack I had slung over my elbow. The intuition in Eli's eyes unsettled me—he saw more than he'd ever say, and he was smart enough not to say it here.

"Finn did a good job," Chase said quietly to me, folding his arms as the last group filtered out.

"Yeah," I answered, wishing my tone were lighter. "He really gave it everything."

For a second, I thought we might manage a conversation with real feeling. But the distance yawned wide again, and we stood in the echoing space.

The door at the side of the stage banged open, and Finn catapulted out. He spotted Chase first and made a beeline, nearly colliding with a parent and a kid still half in costume.

"Chase! Did you see my big swim? Was I fast?" Finn's face was alight with pure hope, cheeks flushed, costume tail swinging dangerously.

Chase bent down, putting all of himself into it for Finn. "Light speed, buddy. Nobody even came close. You crushed it."

Finn preened, bouncing on his toes. "Did you see me do the flip?" He tried to demonstrate in the narrow aisle, tripping over a folding chair and righting himself with a laugh.

"I saw the flip."

"The whole room saw the flip," Eli added.

Finn's eyes danced. "So now we can get cheeseburgers, right? You and Mom and me." His face—so open, so bright with trust—made my throat ache.

There it was.

A silence even louder than applause, and my ache turned to a raw wound.

Chase's eyes flicked to me, apology already baked in. The veneer of grown-up busywork, of obligations settled onto his shoulders. The spell of the play had snapped, reality shoving its way in. "Buddy, I wish I could. We've got some inspections at the resort first thing in the morning. I've got to make sure we're ready. But I'm sure glad I was here tonight."

Finn's hope was a live wire in my hands. "Finn, honey, Chase has lots of big projects, remember?" My smile was sugar and splinters. "But you and I can still grab those burgers on the way home, and you can tell me how you remembered all your lines."

Finn's smile wavered. He managed a valiant nod, the corners of his mouth folding down, then back up. "Oh. Okay." He looked at Chase anyway. "But maybe you can come next time?"

Chase reached out, smoothing one of Finn's wayward scales. "Definitely. Next time, for sure. You were great tonight. I mean that."

Finn's arms locked around Chase's waist in a sudden, desperate squeeze. Chase hugged him back. Then he stood, already stepping away, voice rough. "I'll see you soon, okay?" He pressed a quick kiss to Finn's forehead, then offered me a look—half-plea, half-sorry.

"Drive safe," I said, the words hollowed out.

He disappeared into the crowd. I pulled Finn into my side, biting down on my own disappointment. I could feel Mom watching and Eli's quiet scrutiny. I made myself bright, glittery, parade-perfect for Finn—smiling, joking about bun-patty ratios, and carrying us both out into the sticky night.

But inside, all I could feel was that public sting, the jagged edge of not enough, the certainty that none of the conversations we needed most could happen in a cafeteria, under the lights, with everyone watching. And if I couldn't fix it for Finn, I'd at least make sure he felt loved, holding his small hand tightly in mine as we stepped out into the night.

Chapter Twenty-Three

CHASE

DRYWALL DUST DRIFTED in lazy currents through the bare corridor, turning the sunlight slicing in from half-hung windows into hazy streaks. The echo of a hammer three doors down synced with my heartbeat—a steady, reassuring thud that cut through the tension webbing my chest. Sometimes I thought the noise of construction was better therapy than any deep-breathing exercise. You could drown in it, let the grind of machines and the bark of a foreman replace whatever the hell you were avoiding.

Like Harper Coleridge.

The first floor of Room Block One was a half-skinned beast this morning—wires exposed, patched over in blue tape, scraps of old insulation sticking to unfinished studs. Every footstep sounded like it echoed straight into the Gulf. The new drywall on the east hall glared against the yellowing, water-stained plaster that had been peeled away in the other rooms. It smelled like rain on concrete, sweat, and the faint tang of salt.

The crew moved with that peculiar dance of practiced urgency of hauling, measuring, bantering with saws and the occasional dirty joke. Foreman Joe stood out—stocky, back permanently bent like the pressure of the entire building settled between his shoulders, a blue bandanna stuffed under a battered ballcap.

As he moved ahead, I lingered, tablet open to yesterday's punch list, one hand sliding along the smooth curve of fresh copper pipe in Room 1113. Pipes. It seemed everything involved frustrating issues with water lately. Tension tightened my jaw. It wasn't just the lingering frustration from the play three days ago—that feeling of failing Harper and Finn despite my best intentions. It was compounded by last night. I'd shown up with pasta in a tangible attempt to fix things, to close the distance that had crept between us. But just as we sat down, I'd gotten a call about a possible leak under the pool deck that had to be dealt with immediately. I'd wasted three hours chasing shadows while they ate without me. Another attempt derailed. Another night where work took precedence, leaving the strain between Harper and me unaddressed.

Again.

This gnawing frustration wasn't just about the relentless crises or the feeling of constantly being two steps behind. It was about *us*. I was acutely aware of the words I hadn't said, the vulnerability I hadn't shown, the chasm that each thwarted attempt at connection seemed to widen. It wasn't that I was deliberately avoiding the hard conversation. Hell, I'd replayed a dozen versions in my head of how to tell her how overwhelmed I felt, how much this all meant, how terrified I was of failing her.

And God, I missed her.

I *knew* I needed to lay it bare. But every time I even got close to finding a quiet moment, the universe, or at least the Sunset Siesta renovation schedule, seemed to conspire against us with another urgent demand. Now the silence felt like my own damn fault, another unaddressed failure in a growing list. And the thought of her thinking I was just avoiding *her* was another weight on my already overloaded shoulders.

Joe's voice boomed from down the hall. Not the usual worksite holler, but sharp, taut. Urgent. "Chase! You're gonna want to see this. Now."

I crossed to where three guys had gathered in the north corridor outside Room 1115. Their shoulders closed off a patch of newly exposed wall. Sawdust and splintered wood littered the floor in a haphazard drift, too pale and fine for fresh demo.

Frowning deeply, Joe stepped back so I could see. The paneling—ancient, floral print, now in splintered chunks— had just been peeled from the main load-bearing wall to reveal the bones of the building.

Only these bones looked rotten as old driftwood.

The vertical beams were laced with hollowed-out tunnels, brittle and punky to the touch. Dark tracks meandered along the grain, some of them gaping open enough to fit a finger through.

Time stopped.

My heart stopped.

When I tapped one of the studs with my knuckle, it didn't even *thunk*—it gave off a powdery sigh, a puff of dust drifting down to the sill. I pressed a bit harder. Wood collapsed under my thumb, leaving a soft hole the size of a marble.

All of it—the original framing, the joinery, the sill plate near the floor—looked like it had survived a war fought by termites and slow rot. The exterior cladding might as well have been a bandage on a bullet wound. My chest went cold as my gaze inevitably drifted upward.

Joe didn't hide the quiver in his voice. "Holy hell, Chase. Look at this. This whole section… it's damn near sawdust inside."

Years of training flared to life, triage protocol beating in time with my now racing pulse. Load path, redundancy, shear, how much mass could even one compromised stud carry before the dominoes fell. This wall ran dead center, the main support for everything above, second floor and roof line.

All of it.

The damage here, hidden by decades of surface-level repairs, meant any remaining contingency we'd written into the budget was about to go up in smoke.

I crouched low, pressing fingers into the swollen edge where the sill plate met the concrete foundation. The wood crumbled, layers peeling away in damp, stringy ribbons. I glanced up—every joist pocket above looked similarly suspect, the fasteners mottled with rust, new insulation jammed into spaces that should've been dry. Someone had repaired the outer skin half a dozen times but never bothered to probe the heart.

"Jesus." The dread inside me didn't flare, exactly—it crept. Cold and hard and inevitable. My responsibility as architect and, hell, as a partner in this place, was suddenly crushing. Finishes were cosmetic. This was existential. I tilted my head up and followed the imaginary path of first floor, to second floor, to attic, to roof. If the load path failed here, everything above would sag, maybe collapse. Best-case scenario was shutting down half the building, emergency shoring, specialized crews, engineer on speed dial.

Worst case? I wasn't ready to name it.

I pushed to my feet. "Joe, no more demo on this line until I've got a structural engineer on site. Set up temporary shoring on both sides. Brace the ceiling joists. And get photos. Lots. I want every inch of damage documented."

"You got it, boss." Joe squatted next to a sickly beam, whistling low, thumb gouging the spongy edge with visible unease.

I thumbed my phone, scrolling to the structural engineer's contact—Dr. Elena Alvarez, our mercifully on-call specialist from Key West. Her phone went straight to voicemail. I kept it brief, voice as steady as I could. "Elena, it's Chase Ashworth. We have major termite damage on a load-bearing wall in Room Block One at Sunset Siesta. North corridor, Room 1115. I need an urgent assessment for immediate shoring and full replacement protocol. Call me back ASAP."

Every instinct wanted to keep it contained, not raise an alarm until I had specifics, but my hands shook a little anyway. If the rest of this wall line was similarly rotted, the safety of the whole building was in question.

I dialed Harper. She answered on the second ring, voice breathless but businesslike. "Hey, Chase. I'm—"

"Harper, you need to get over to Room Block One. Right now. It's serious." My words were measured but came out more brittle than I liked.

A pause. "How serious?"

"The kind where I'm halting all work, and I need you here in person. Bring your phone and don't say anything to the staff until you've seen it."

She didn't ask for details. Just a soft exhale, then, "On my way." There was something grounding in her directness. If the world started to fall, she'd meet it standing.

I ended the call, stepped back into the corridor, and looked over the crowd of workers now standing with tools dropped, boots shuffling on old boards. Every single person on this site had probably seen disaster, but there's a special hush that comes when someone realizes the thing they're working on might be unsalvageable.

In a single morning, the ground beneath our feet had shifted. Some days, the hardest part of the job wasn't building something new. It was deciding whether there was anything left worth saving.

And somewhere beyond the dust and caution tape, Harper was on her way, and everything would hinge on the next few hours.

THE OLD, flickering fluorescent lights in Sunset Siesta's conference room always seemed calibrated to highlight exhaustion, not productivity. I sat sandwiched between a stack of structural prints and an even taller stack of bad news, trying to pretend the clock on the wall didn't sound like a countdown to impact. Harper anchored the head of the table, back straight, voice steady. Jules sat across from me, typing steadily on her laptop. Joe sat on my other side with dirt-streaked hands and anxious eyes. Only the steady voice of the engineer on the speakerphone reminded me that, technically, this was still just another Tuesday afternoon at Sunset Siesta.

If your idea of Tuesday involved shoring up the heart of a sinking ship with nothing but coffee and adrenaline.

Harper had set up this emergency meeting after seeing the termite damage. From her blanched face, I probably hadn't needed to give her the thorough explanation I did. The conference room was on the list of things to be remodeled in the next phase. For now, a weak thread of resort music bled through the door, something tropical and too cheerful by half. The old oak table was a sea of clutter —blueprints unrolled, marked in red and highlighter, half a dozen notebooks, and my laptop open to engineering standards I hadn't had to quote since college.

"We opened up the north corridor wall behind 1115," Joe said to the speakerphone, jaw set like a block of concrete. "Looks solid outside, but the studs behind… you could scrape the inside with your thumbnail. Termite tunnels everywhere, big as a pencil. Whole sill plate's shot. Most of the joist pockets at the base are black, mushy."

Harper absorbed it, lips thinning. She didn't flinch— just nodded, eyes flicking down her notes and then over to me.

The engineer's voice buzzed through the speaker, cool and detached. "Joe, I need you to get me detailed photos of every connection point—beam to joist, sill to founda-tion. Use a ruler for scale and include a coin for reference if possible."

Joe nodded. "Chase already had me do that. I'll send the files to you ASAP."

"Good," Elena replied in that calming, professional voice. "No additional demo until we understand the load transfer. Shoring goes in at six-foot intervals, each side. Do not touch any electrical until we clear the zone for safe access."

I scribbled furiously, mentally mapping the next dozen moves. Every answer Elena gave doubled my mental work-load, the kind of math you only do when something's gone truly sideways.

Jules spoke up, "We need at least a rough shoring esti-mate by the end of the day, Chase. Labor hours, tempo-rary supports, any specialty hardware—we've got maybe thirty grand left in the contingency and only half that isn't already spoken for. I need a timeline hit, worst-case scenario, for the lender package. Does this impact the planned reopening of Room Block One?"

I eased out a heavy sigh. "Depends on how much retrofitting we end up needing to do. My gut instinct is yes. There will be a delay. But we won't know for sure until we get Elena's report."

Joe raised a brow. "I can get the shoring started as soon as we get the green light. But if any more of that wall crumbles, it could mean the whole block needs to go cold until it's rebuilt."

Silence hung. Full, unblinking. The fluorescent buzz and the muted rattle of a passing cleaning cart in the hallway were the only things that dared interrupt.

The engineer's voice was sharp. "Chase, your crew has eyes on the ceiling cavity too, yes?"

"Yes. We'll send a camera up as soon as the first shoring's in. If we see more beam loss, you'll have photos within the hour."

Jules piped up again, "Chase, is this isolated, or do you see signs in adjacent rooms?"

"None yet." I'd been over every inch of the first floor in the hours since the discovery. "We'll know more once we map the full line. But if the rot runs all the way through…"

I trailed off, not wanting to elaborate on the consequences. Costs would skyrocket, timelines would sink, and all our pretty projections would land in the shredder.

Harper met my gaze. "Chase, I'll trust you to take point on this. All demo halts on Block One north until Elena has signed off. You'll update us on the budget and timeline for Jules by the end of the day. Copy?"

I swallowed, impressed as hell with her despite the circumstances. "Understood. Already working on the draft. Will loop Joe and Jules in."

Jules sounded tired, her usual poise on edge. "Any additional costs that'll hit the loan, I need flagged immediately. If this impacts our occupancy rate for more than two weeks, it changes everything about our operating capital for next quarter." She placed both palms against her eyes, then dropped them as if aware of what she was doing. "I don't see how this doesn't blow the budget completely apart, and I'm not sure the bank will give us more money."

I scrawled a list, my handwriting degenerating the further my mind ran ahead. Lumber prices, custom supports, engineer fees—it was an avalanche, and we didn't even know if the peak had broken yet.

Elena's tone softened, maybe hearing the strain. "My junior associate is already on the way for an emergency assessment. I'll be along soon. Let's not panic just yet, okay?"

Harper leaned in, palms pressed to the edge of the table, eyes moving down her checklist. "Anything else we need right now?"

Nobody spoke. It felt like there should be a bell or a buzzer to signal the moment a place crosses from manageable chaos into open crisis.

"Meeting adjourned," Harper said, softer this time.

Joe gathered his things, legal pad under arm, mouth pressed flat. The look he shot me was absolute, wordless commiseration. He clapped my shoulder, hard enough that I felt it even after he left the room.

Jules lingered, or maybe just hesitated. "Harper, Chase, keep me in the loop. Anything, even a hunch, I need it."

"You'll have it," Harper replied. "Thanks, Jules."

Then the accountant left too. Suddenly, the room felt twice as large, twice as empty. Harper rubbed at the crease between her brows, shoulders slumping for the first time all day.

My laptop screen reflected the overhead glare. In the glass, I caught the lines carved deeper than usual at the corners of Harper's mouth, the telltale tightness of someone holding it together for everyone else. The way she fielded questions, never let a detail fall, never once let panic into her voice. Even now, with our history crackling in the air and half the future of the Coleridge legacy shaking overhead, she held the line.

Damn, she was good.

There were moments I envied it, her ability to dig in and manage disaster after disaster, the way she radiated command and reassurance even when I knew—when I could feel—it was costing her something. I thought of myself, spinning between site visits and late nights, always a half-step from unraveling. With Harper, there was no unraveling. Just motion. Always forward. Even now, crisis mode slipping away, she looked almost luminous. Tired, but absolutely in her element.

"Never a dull moment." I straightened my chaos of papers into some semblance of order. "We should start charging extra for the thrill factor."

She laughed, a bright sound that finally cracked the tension in the room. "Maybe we can call it an adventure package."

I smiled, and the weight shifted just enough to breathe again. She caught my eye and held it, something soft and familiar warming the space between us.

"It's going to be okay," she said.

Her confidence nudged at the knot in my chest. "I know. It's just… a lot."

She nodded, moving closer. There was something reassuring in the way she stood so close, like all those walls weren't crumbling. "You're doing everything you can, Chase. We'll get through this."

"I hope you still feel that way when we're replacing half the building."

She swallowed audibly and raised her chin as if readying herself for bad news. "Do you blame me?"

I cocked my head, dumbfounded. "Why would I blame you for termite damage?"

She laughed, but it came out shaky. "Well, if not blame, then you owe me a 'I told you so'. This is exactly what you warned me about when we agreed to do the room block floor by floor."

I mustered a smile and couldn't resist running a knuckle down the smooth skin of her arm. "You just said it. We agreed. Blame never even entered my mind, so put it out of yours, okay?"

"I am sorry, though."

"So am I. These things happen. Now we have to figure out where to go from here."

I reached for a scattered folder just as she did. Our hands met atop the faded architectural rendering, fingers brushing in a potent tangle of intent and accident.

We both froze.

Time caught its breath.

Her eyes, dark as wet earth, met mine. Something hungry, raw, and familiar flared up in the space between us. The conference room vanished, and there was only the shock of her skin on mine and a cascade of memories I couldn't bury. The soft exhale of her breath, the faint tremble in my own hand. For half a heartbeat, the rest of it—shoring, schedules, the imminent doom—fell away. I dropped my eyes to her mouth and saw, crystal clear, the way her lips tasted, how her lips always curled up at the corners when she wasn't on guard.

The pull was tidal. I leaned in before I even registered

it. Her hand turned up under mine, just barely, in an unspoken question I ached to answer.

Then everything snapped back, hard. I blinked, mind slamming on the brakes so sharply it almost hurt. The resort was falling apart. Literally. My new business was riding the edge of a landslide.

What the hell am I doing?

I jerked my hand away, too quickly. Cleared my throat, the sound coming out rough and awkward, echoing off the glass and fake wood. "I need to get the shoring estimate to Joe. I'll text the framing crew, too."

She didn't chase me with her eyes. Didn't smile. Just pulled the structural drawing toward herself, looking suddenly as tired as I felt. "Yeah, there are a billion things to do. At least. Thank you, Chase."

I scooped up my laptop and the sheaf of half-ruined plans and headed for the door, the strain in my shoulders radiating all the way down my spine. Halfway out, I turned for one last look at her—alone at the table, surrounded by the detritus of another day saved, but not won.

God, I wanted to work things out with her. But how could we when I couldn't straighten out the thoughts in my own head? When the roof was literally threatening to collapse above us?

The light outside the conference room looked different than when I'd come in, dark and murky by comparison. Somehow, everything I wanted was another cracked beam. Still standing, just barely, beneath the weight of what might come next.

Chapter Twenty-Four

HARPER

IT ONLY TOOK forty-eight hours for the conference room to take on the ambience of a fallout shelter after too many days underground. Half-empty coffee cups, mountains of plans and receipts, wrinkled Post-its clinging to every surface like paper barnacles—my version of structural triage. Somewhere under the layers, the faint scent of panic lingered, edged with mildew and that sharpness old AC units get. I wasn't sure which was fraying faster, the walls or my mental state.

A knot of tension sat at the base of my skull, threatening to bloom into a headache. Every surface, my laptop screen included, was crusted with a thin layer of stress. In this fluorescent, flavorless light, Chase had become the storm's eye. His blueprints shouldered the biggest piece of real estate on the table, diagrams annotated with block letters and, now and then, a snatch of profanity if you looked close enough. He was hunched over the plans, fingers braced against the edge as if holding back a flood.

We'd just finished another triage meeting, more dire warnings from Jules and tense updates from Joe.

Chase tapped out something on his phone—probably tracking down a materials supplier or asking for updates from Elena. He didn't look up. Didn't look at me. Hadn't looked at me, really, since that flash of connection we'd had in this very room two days ago.

The almost kiss.

And that hurt. I rolled my shoulders, considering his reaction. Right now, staring grimly at that structural report, Chase looked less like a confident architect and more like someone bracing for impact. He wasn't talking about our future, but he wasn't running away either.

He was still *here*, trying to hold the damn roof up.

Did I need to have more faith? It was obvious in every single way that Chase wasn't Jarod. But that didn't mean he and I wanted the same things.

I shook my head and got back to the current crisis. "Jules, the contingency isn't going to cover this. We need to be realistic. The new projections Chase sent over this morning are… astronomical. Is there any chance the bank will extend our credit line? Even a short-term bridge loan?"

Across the table, Jules sighed, pushing escaped wisps of hair from her forehead. She'd been putting in the extra hours too, and it showed. "I already spoke with Dan Gillespie at the bank this morning. He was sympathetic, but the answer was a firm no. Given the existing loan size and the… unforeseen nature of these structural repairs, they're not willing to extend further credit at this time. We're maxed out."

The words landed like lead weights. Maxed out. No more wiggle room.

Chase's eyes flicked to the spreadsheet on his laptop,

then to Jules. His hair, always artfully controlled, looked one run-through short of wild. His stubbled jaw clenched.

I folded my hands on the table. "So what are our options? Pause the Room Block One reno indefinitely?"

"Delaying will hurt our projected revenue significantly," Jules countered. "We were counting on that income to service the current loan. Pushing it back means we're just kicking the can down the road and potentially digging a deeper hole."

Even Joe, in a sweat-stained Latitudes Design T-shirt, shifted uncomfortably as he pushed to his feet. "Not to interrupt the war council, but those guys with the shoring are coming at three. I'll get started on prepping the space now."

"Thanks, Joe. Just text me if you need anything." I mustered my management smile, knowing how unconvincing it sounded. He gave Chase a wary glance, then slipped out, boots thudding heavily as he went.

I returned to Elena's structural report. The verdict was that the damage didn't extend all the way through the first floor, but everything affected would have to be replaced. Fully one-quarter of the first floor.

It was a financial and structural disaster. We were staring at a six-figure repair bill with no clear way to pay for it without compromising the entire renovation vision or the resort's immediate financial health.

"What if we scale back the finishes in Room Block One and the bungalows?" Jules suggested. "Go with a more basic tile, standard fixtures instead of the custom ones?"

Chase finally looked up, his gaze direct and pained. "We could, but that undermines the entire premium experience we're selling. It's a short-term fix that devalues the long-term investment. And it still wouldn't cover the full structural cost."

"We may need to delay the next phase, then," I added softly. "I know how much you like the new lobby design."

The silence in the room was heavy, thick with unspoken fears. No one had a magic bullet.

As I stared at the report, willing solutions to present themselves, Chase fielded three more calls in five minutes —contractors, a hardware supply, then Marilyn from Latitudes. With every interruption, his responses got shorter, the edge in his voice more pronounced. He rubbed the bridge of his nose, staring at the report again.

"Thanks for the update. I'll wait to hear from Marcus," he said, ending the last call. The silence he left behind was deafening. For a beat, the only sounds were my typing and the hum of the air handler.

Finally, Chase closed his laptop with a defined *click*. The exhaustion was plain on his face, but beneath it, a new resolve was hardening his expression.

"Okay." His voice was low but firm, cutting through the despair that had settled in the room. He stared at me, then at Jules. "There are no good options on the table right now. Gutting the project isn't one I'm willing to consider, and neither is bankrupting the resort." He paused, taking a deep breath, and met my eyes squarely. "Give me a day or two. I need to run some numbers, make some calls. I'll come up with something. We're not sunk yet."

Jules looked skeptical but also tired enough to grasp at any offer of a solution. "Chase, if there were an easy answer, we would have found it."

"I know." He met her gaze. "This won't be easy. But I'll find an answer. We'll make it work."

"Let's hope so." Jules gathered her things and headed out the door. "Let me know what the magic answer is when you find it."

He pushed out a sigh, folding his arms across his chest.

The fatigue etched in the lines around his eyes looked like it was weighing him down from the inside out. I glanced at his hands—strong, steady, but tight at the knuckles.

I wanted to say something. To do something that didn't involve shuffling another stack of invoices or untangling the resort's spaghetti knot of budget disasters. It felt wrong, watching him hollow out right in front of me, knowing how much pride he took in never letting the seams show.

I thought about Finn, about how I'd learned to sense his meltdowns half a mile before they happened, the subtle warning signs in his posture or voice. Chase, on the other hand, had armor honed from years of never letting anyone in deeper than surface-level warmth.

My phone vibrated—a low buzz against the pile of folders. I ignored it. Instead, I reached for the French press someone had abandoned and refilled Chase's mug and my own with the dregs. The brew was tepid and harsh on the tongue. Still, it filled the silence.

"I haven't seen you eat today," I tried, sliding the mug within reach of his elbow. "If you don't start taking care of yourself, the termites are going to win by default."

That got a ghost of a smile from him, gone before I could take hope in it. My reward was three solid seconds of him almost relaxing, his eyes slipping closed as the caffeine hit.

"Thanks," he murmured.

Small victories.

I let the silence stretch, not wanting to scare him off. He'd talk when he was ready. Or maybe he wouldn't, and I'd have to go first. Again. Eventually, the tension pressed too hard on my chest. I shifted, leaning forward, voice softer.

"Chase, I know things are wild right now, but are you okay?" I gestured to his wrinkled clothes—the same ones he had on yesterday. "You look like you haven't slept. Can I get you anything?"

He raked a hand through his hair. His face was frustrated, harried, maybe even a little panicked. For the briefest second, his eyes met mine, that complicated hazel laced with gold, before flicking away toward the structural report. "I'm fine, Harper. Just…" He stopped, collecting himself. "Just focused on solving this before the entire block collapses."

I tried again, gentler this time, reaching for the spot between us that was supposed to be safe. "You don't have to handle all this pressure alone, you know. I'm here. You can lean on me."

His mouth flattened, expression shifting to something tight and closed. There was a flash of pain—almost, then gone—before he leaned back in his chair. "I appreciate that. You're always such a rock. I should take lessons from you. You're right, and we'll get together soon, okay? Please, Harper. Right now, I need to focus on fixing this. I will find a solution. Just give me some time."

I tried to nod like it was fine, like that didn't hurt, but my throat threatened mutiny. The part of me that knew how to book entertainment and soothe tantrums insisted I push again, press past his walls. The woman in me—the one who remembered how to want and ache and hope— wanted to take his face in my hands and make him look at me, make him see how hard I was trying.

His phone rang, jarring in the overworked quiet. He snatched it up, glancing at the screen. His face tightened a notch further. "Yeah, Marcus? What's going on?" The minute he heard the reply, his whole bearing changed— crisp, focused, that professional confidence kicking back in. "Okay, I'm on my way."

He clicked the phone off, standing so fast his chair

rolled back. He gathered a handful of papers, grabbing his keys and the plan tube he'd brought in two hours ago. "Sorry, I need to run. Another fire to put out on a different job. We'll sync up later." His hand brushed mine as he walked by, a light tangling of fingers that was all he could give.

It was deliberate, a gesture that he understood what still lay between us.

A gesture that he was doing the best he could.

For a moment, I stayed where I was, staring at the crater left by his absence. The crisis hadn't changed—the money was still short, the beams still gnawed, the future still sharp-edged and uncertain. But the thing I feared most wasn't the collapse of a wall or a building. It was this, the way he could withdraw so completely, the way he made me feel like my support was something he couldn't afford.

He chose to carry all of it alone. The structural load and the emotional one. He chose not to trust me with the weight, even though I'd all but begged him to let me help shoulder it. And wasn't that what I'd told myself I wanted? Partnership. Someone who could meet me in the hard places and say, *Let's do this together.*

I looked down at the mug I'd brought him. Still three-quarters full, cooling fast. Was this what it would be, loving a man who turned inward when things got tough? Because I couldn't even lie to myself anymore.

I was in love with Chase Ashworth, and there was no going back.

The door clicked shut behind him, and with that simple hush of wood against frame, every last scrap of composure I'd been clinging to evaporated. I stood in the center of the mess and waited for the next breath to feel less impossible.

It didn't.

The relief of no eyes on me was almost as sharp as the ache in my throat. I pressed my palms to my eyes, felt the hot, gritty pressure building, my nose stinging in that prelude-to-ugly-cry way I hadn't allowed in years, never at work, not with anyone but Finn safely asleep in the next room.

The conference table was cold and unyielding under my hands as I braced myself, sucking in one useless breath, then another. My vision blurred. I sagged into the nearest chair, folded forward, elbows on knees, and let my face fall into my hands. A sob slipped out, ugly and relieved and raw. The sound didn't bounce off these walls the way laughter did. It seemed to sink straight into the carpet, private as a wound.

I sat there and let it go—frustration at the resort's fragility, anger at Chase for shutting me out, the old, stubborn pain that whispered maybe I was always destined to carry things alone. Somewhere between breaths, I wiped my nose on the inside of my wrist, suddenly aware of a sticky ring of dried coffee on the table beside my elbow. I focused on that, weirdly grateful for its existence, a reminder that I was still in the realm of the physical, the solvable. If only the human heart wiped clean as easily as old coffee.

The door opened with the soft creak of hinges, and I didn't even have time to hide the evidence before Eli slipped in. No sunglasses, no bright-lipped joke ready, just his own tired shadow painted by the door. He paused to take in the carnage—documents, plans, Harper-shaped misery.

"Hey." The word was small. Genuine.

I sniffed, straightened as best I could, and swiped under both eyes, trying to reassemble my manager face. "Hi. It's just... stress. The termite beam situation..." My voice warbled and collapsed. I was mortified and too wrung out to fake it.

He crossed the room in those lazy-long strides of his, not stopping until he leaned his hip against the table beside me. He didn't try a joke. Didn't even smile. "This looks like more than termite stress."

I tried to pull myself back together. Swallowed and pressed my lips in a line. But the tears slipped out anyway, more stubborn than I was. "He won't let me in, Eli! He says he's fine, but he's clearly drowning, and then he just… leaves. On to the next crisis." It felt childish and dangerous to say it, like wishing for something I couldn't have.

Eli found a half-crumpled napkin in his pocket and offered it. I took it, the little ordinary gesture gutting me more than the situation itself.

"I don't get it," I said, staring at the floor. "I know we're all tired. I know he's under more pressure than anyone, but he keeps shutting me out. Like every time I try to help, it's just another brick in whatever wall he's building between us."

Eli dropped into a chair next to me to meet my eye, his own concern in full view. "I get why you're upset. It sucks feeling shut out." He draped his arm over my shoulders, steadying, and I leaned in. My big brother. "Chase has always had this weird default setting. Whenever things get overwhelming—especially the emotional kind—he retreats into his architect cave. You know, like a turtle pulling its head into its shell." He paused, the corners of his mouth twitching. "It's a terrible look. Honestly, he kind of resembles a constipated turtle."

That broke something inside me, but not in a bad way. The sound that came out was a laugh chopped in half by tears. I swiped at my eyes again, a fresh burst of gratitude and pain all tangled up.

Eli leaned in. "But here's the thing about Chase, the thing I've known since we were both dumb enough to think pizza rolls were a food group. He always sticks his head back out. He needs time to process. Maybe kicks a few metaphorical wastebaskets in private, curses at the world a bit, draws an angry floor plan no one'll ever see. But he doesn't run. He just... turtles." He gave my shoulder a squeeze. "Give him a minute. He'll be back."

I wanted so badly to believe it. "You really think so?"

Eli nodded, no hesitation now. "Yeah. He's an idiot sometimes, but he's a loyal idiot. He cares about you, Harper. You two will figure it out."

His certainty was balm—clumsy, homemade, dangerously reassuring. I leaned into him for a second, just letting myself be someone's little sister instead of the manager, the mom, the everything-holder. "Thanks."

After Eli gave my shoulder a solid, comforting squeeze, I straightened. He stood, stretching with exaggerated slowness, clearly trying to lighten the moment. "If you need anything else, I do offer distraction services—bad impressions, interpretive dance, whatever gets you through to happy hour."

A smile tugged at my lips. "Maybe hold off on the dance. For now."

"Suit yourself." He grinned, ruffling my hair just enough to be annoying and comforting at the same time. "I'm around. Yell if you need anything. Or if you want to burn the termite beam in effigy, I'll bring marshmallows."

I rose to my feet, and he pulled me into a hug, tall and solid, like an anchor. He was warm, his chin brushing the top of my head. "You got this, Harper."

I hugged him tightly. "You give pretty good pep talks. Who knew?"

A few seconds passed before he let go, backing toward

the door with a wink. "Don't cry too long. It's bad for your complexion."

"Get out of here," I said, not bothering to hide the affection in my smile. "Thanks, Eli."

The door closed behind him, leaving me alone with the mess and the hurt but also with a sliver of hope I hadn't had before. Eli knew Chase better than anyone. I sat there for a few minutes more, letting my brother's words sink in and loosen something knotted inside me.

Maybe Chase was turtling. Maybe he needed time to work through whatever storm was raging beneath that controlled exterior. And maybe—hopefully—he would come back once he'd done it, and we could work things out.

Eli's words hadn't magically fixed the crumbling walls or the budget, but they'd cracked open a window in my self-made fallout shelter and let in a ray of light. The mountain ahead was still immense. But as I wiped my face and picked up my clipboard, the climb looked a little less like a desperate scrabble in the dark and more like ascending toward a distant, possible dawn.

Chapter Twenty-Five

CHASE

I STOOD in the center of my great room, the space I'd meticulously carved from the bones of a neglected conch house. Restored wood floors gleamed softly under the recessed lighting, reflecting the clean lines of the custom shelving and the carefully curated art and furniture. This room, a fusion of the original formal living room and parlor to make a seamless yet much larger space, represented years of painstaking work, late nights sketching, and the satisfaction of bringing a vision to life. The house itself had won awards, graced magazines, and earned me plenty of offers. Tonight, it just felt quiet. And the silence amplified the low-grade buzz in my skull, the exhaustion that came from being out of ideas.

My laptop lay on the mahogany table in the corner—a piece I'd restored myself—displaying a spreadsheet that showed a number that still didn't look real, even after hours of recalculations. Of considering every possible solution and alternative. I'd spent the last hours since leaving work staring at spreadsheets, trying to find a way to leverage my own savings, maybe a personal loan, but the numbers were too vast. Nothing touched the black hole the termites had chewed through the budget.

Essential repairs only, and the cost might as well have had its own line item for soul. There was no trimming this into something palatable. Every possible solution tasted like sawdust and compromise.

And failure.

Sunset Siesta's bungalows were mudded and painted, ready for flooring I might need to downscale drastically. The pool project—seventy percent done—was on hold, the contractors already scenting a stall. If I paused construction altogether, the whole vision I'd sold Harper and her family would fall apart, piece by piece, in slow motion. That prospect itched at every perfectionist bone in my body. Still, the math didn't care what I thought.

I ran a hand over the cool stone of the fireplace surround, remembering the satisfaction of refinishing it, getting the joints just right. This house was my fortress, my statement—proof of control, precision, aesthetic mastery. Everything in its place. Unlike the chaotic mess currently consuming my thoughts and threatening the future I was only just beginning to believe in.

To complicate things even more, Eli was on his way over. I'd been incredulous when he suggested coming over for a drink tonight so I could blow off some steam. He knew how buried I was. Frowning, I pulled out my phone to read our text exchange from earlier.

Chase: Too damn busy, man.

He'd texted back quick, persistent.

> Eli: Dude. Can't pour from an empty pitcher
> and all that.

Then immediately after:

> Eli: I'll be at your place at 7 p.m. I'm not
> asking.

That last one hit differently. Eli only played the *best friend imperative* card when something was on fire, real or emotional. I couldn't hide my own shadows from the guy who knew my tells better than my mother ever had. And now his sister was involved too, all jumbled into a big, ugly mess.

This wasn't like the night when we'd casually shared bourbon on the deck and I'd haltingly confessed what had happened between me and Harper. Tonight was different. I had the sinking feeling he wasn't coming over to shoot the breeze or admire the architectural details of my house.

The doorbell chimed, sharp and distinct in the quiet house. I took a breath, squared my shoulders, and opened the door. Eli stood on the porch, but the usual lazy grin was absent, replaced with a steadiness that put me on notice immediately. He stepped inside, his gaze sweeping the expansive room—the soaring ceilings, the strategically placed lighting highlighting the blend of historic texture and modern design.

He looked me up and down, unwavering. "Rough day?" His voice was low as he followed me toward the seating area. "You look like something the tide dragged in, refused, and then threw back again."

If I'd had any energy, I might have smiled. Instead, the

words scraped raw. I gestured toward the bourbon on the sideboard. "Pour yourself one. Try no sleep for nearly forty-eight hours thanks to termites eating the damn resort from the inside out." I didn't bother to hide the snap. "Then tell me how photogenic you look."

Eli poured two fingers into a heavy crystal tumbler, then turned, leaning back against the sideboard, studying me, all traces of the wiseass invisible. "Yeah, I know it's bad, man." He hesitated, running a hand through his hair in that way he did when he was flustered. "I'm guessing it's no surprise that I'm not here for a glass of your bourbon, good as it is."

I poured myself a healthy measure, fortification for having my suspicions confirmed. "I figured. So out with it."

"I found Harper sobbing in the conference room this afternoon. Alone. She didn't even hear me come in. She tried to hide it, but"—he stopped, winced as if replaying it—"I've never seen her like that, Chase. Not even when Mom almost lost the house back in the day."

The words registered slowly, thickly. The image of her, warm, tough, always-holding-it-together Harper, sitting alone and crying because of something I'd said—or hadn't said—felt like a physical blow. I sank onto the edge of the tailored linen sofa, staring at the intricate pattern of the antique Persian rug beneath my feet.

That was on me.

The guilt from earlier, the impatient conversations and the cold distance I'd created, came slamming home. I'd been too buried in blueprints and bank statements to see what it was costing her.

"She… she say anything?" Useless question, but the only one I could manage.

Eli came over and sat in the armchair opposite me,

setting his drink down deliberately. "She said you were shutting her out. That you looked right through her at the meeting this afternoon. And maybe I shouldn't say this, but to hell with it. I'm her big brother. I'm pretty sure she's scared you're about to bail—just like her last guy did, only this time it would be the whole resort walking out on her too." He leaned forward and forced eye contact between us. "You got her hoping for more, Chase. Real future, not just next month. That's scary shit. Especially when the person you're counting on suddenly goes all cave dweller."

I wanted to argue, to insist I was just protecting her, trying to shield her from how bad it really was. How inadequate *I* felt. But the words tasted cheap and hollow. Instead, I picked up my glass, the cool weight of it familiar, and took a long swallow. The bourbon burned but barely scratched the surface of the knot in my chest.

Eli let the silence hang. The quiet hum of the house, the sound of high-end climate control and isolation, filled the space. He finally spoke, gentle but relentless. "I'm not throwing stones, Chase. Jules has seen me sink plenty of times. Stress gets heavy, and we get stubborn. Sometimes it's just easier to build the walls than talk it out. Thing is… when Jules drags me back, it helps. Makes the load lighter, not heavier. I had a pretty ugly dive rescue last week. It all came out okay, but there were some moments that were very dicey. When I dragged my ass home, she didn't try to fix anything. Just handed me a beer, rubbed my shoulders, and sat with me as I talked it out. It mattered. And it wasn't weakness. It was being real."

Something about the way he said it, casual but not, impacted deeply. I kept looking at my hands, idly shaking the ice in my glass. "It's not… It's not that I don't want to talk to her. Or lean on her." My gaze drifted around the room, taking in the precise placement of every object, the controlled beauty I'd fought so hard to create. "I look around this place, at all this effort to make something perfect, ordered. And then I look at the resort numbers, at Harper… It feels like if I say it all out loud, admit how precarious everything is, it's too much. Like if she sees how bad it really is, how close to the edge *I* am, she'll realize what a bad bet this all was. I can't—" The burn in my throat threatened to close off the rest.

Eli nodded, not rushing me. Just sat, hands clasped around his own glass, a study in patience.

So I tried to lay it all out, the words stumbling at first, then gaining momentum. "Since the termite thing, it's like everything's fallen off a cliff. The budget we fought for, gone. I'm supposed to have all the answers. I sold everyone this dream. All of *this*"—I gestured vaguely, encompassing the resort, Harper, Finn, maybe even this damn house— "and now I might have to cut out half the stuff that makes the place unique, that makes it worth saving. Every choice feels like a lose-lose. And all I can think is, if I screw up… If I mess this up for Harper, for Finn, and your whole family, it proves every voice in my head that says I'm not cut out for this. That the real me, the one who built *this* house as a shield, the one who always picks the safe play, was right all along."

My hands trembled slightly. I forced them to still, finally meeting his dark blue eyes. "I'm not scared of the work. Or the numbers. I'm scared of letting them down, Eli. I bought Finn a new tool belt at the home improvement store, but I haven't given it to him. Because I'm scared shitless. Scared of how easy it was to pick up something just for him, how much I already need them both. That's the part that gets to me. Needing someone, needing a family… and not knowing if I can keep them whole."

The silence thickened, broken only by the faint tick of the antique clock in the wall.

"I don't know how to do this," I said. "I've always felt like my parents screwed me up. I don't know how to be all of it—the guy who saves the business, makes her feel safe, who never leaves, who's always got the next plan. Right now, it feels like I'm failing on every front."

Eli took a long pull from his bourbon, just looking at me over the rim. "All right. That's the realest I've ever heard you talk." He let the words settle, almost smiling, but gentler. "Can I be practical for a second?"

I shrugged, feeling hollowed out but lighter for saying it.

Eli steepled his hands. "Look, I get it. Relationship stuff is heavy. So let's break it down. Right now, what's the biggest fire? The one you have to put out to even start thinking straight again?"

I snorted, but it was as close as I'd come to laughter in two days. "It's the money. We need serious cash, fast, just to cover the structural work. If we can't pay for that, none of the rest matters. I'll have to gut the renovations, pause everything, maybe even tell everyone we've got to start over in a year. And picturing Harper's face when I say that…" I broke off, the image enough to gut me.

Eli leaned forward, sharper now. "Okay. How much are we talking? And is there any way to get it without running up the resort's debt or bankrupting yourself? Sell the fishing boat, hawk Eli's Greatest Hits on CD?"

That did get a laugh out of me—short, dry, but real.

"No boat or mixtape is covering this, man. We're talking… low six figures, bare minimum." I found myself scanning his face for judgment.

But there wasn't any. "Okay. So any solutions you haven't thought of yet?"

"None." I raked a hand through my hair, mimicking his gesture. "Not without a new loan in my name, but I'm not sure I could get approved for how much we need. And we need a lot of cash, pronto. I don't know…"

My words trailed off as the gears, at last, started to turn again. Not the panicked thrashing from before. More like the click of something new locking in place.

My gaze swept across the room again—the hand-plastered walls, the restored Dade County pine floors, the view out to the lushly landscaped garden. Assets. Just not ones I liked to think about liquidating.

"My house," I said, the words feeling foreign in this space I'd poured my soul into. "It's worth a fortune. Historical designation, great location, and with the magazine spreads… Hell, I've had a client, Arthur Albright, who's told me more than once if I ever decided to sell, to call him first. Name my price."

Eli's jaw practically hit the floor, his glass halfway to his lips. He gestured around the stunning room. "You'd sell *this* place? You've spent years on it. This house is… you."

"Yeah, but…"

The idea of sacrificing this monument to my past self was like pulling a tooth with my bare hands. Painful. But under it, a sudden charge. Resolve. As the image of Harper's exhausted face, Finn's trusting grin, and the chaotic warmth of their cottage superimposed itself over my flawless living room, a different kind of certainty clicked into place.

This perfect house was a shell.

Harper and Finn were where life was, where *home* was for me now. I ran a hand along the smooth, cool arm of the sofa. "This place is what I used to want. Ordered, impeccable, detached. But it's never felt like a home. I can always restore another house. Another Harper…? Not so much. If I blow this with her…"

Eli smiled, crooked and proud. "You're further gone than I thought."

I grinned for the first time in what felt like days, the decision solidifying, chasing away some of the exhaustion. "Maybe so. I've never been in love before." I froze for a moment, hardly able to believe I'd admitted that out loud. Already, the urgency was waking me up from the inside out. My body still ached, but it felt like momentum now.

His smile softened at the corners. "Yeah, this whole being in love thing is new to me too. But I'm catching on."

"Well, keep your big mouth shut about what I just said. That's the first time I've said it out loud, and your ugly mug wasn't who I had in mind to say it to."

"Don't worry about that." Eli's grin faded. "Are you sure about selling the house, man? That's a massive move."

"I'm sure." I nodded. The rightness of it, a strange mix of relief and wildness, coursed through me. "It's not just about Harper. I'm a partner in this damn thing now. My ass is on the line too."

Eli sat back, shaking his head like he'd just watched a stuntman land a jump. "I should have known you'd go big or go home. And apparently, home is optional."

"It is when you've got something better."

I pulled my phone out, already scrolling through my contacts until I found Albright's number—the one who'd walked this very house with me after the magazine spread, eyes lit up, promising obscene cash if I ever called.

Eli raised his glass. "For what it's worth, I think you're making the right call."

"Hope so." My thumb hovered over the screen. This house represented years of work, a gratifying kind of

success. But it didn't hold a candle to the messy, complicated, terrifyingly wonderful future I saw with Harper.

There was only one way to find out if I could secure it.

I hit call. The phone began to ring, loud in my ear,
softly echoing in the perfect acoustics of the room I was
about to let go of.

Maybe this time, doing the hardest thing was exactly
what love looked like. And maybe that didn't make it so
hard after all.

Chapter Twenty-Six

HARPER

AS I STARED into the freezer, the only thing colder than the air nipping my face was the creeping certainty that I was, once again, out of dinosaur-shaped nuggets. Not that Finn would accept triceratops-adjacent *chicken fries* instead. Which didn't matter since I didn't have any of those either. God, if only things in life were as simple as finding the right prehistoric poultry.

I pawed past a sticky package of frozen edamame, three separate iterations of blueberries, the last surviving bagel from the beginning of time. No dino nuggets. Not even a pizza, and I nearly always kept one for emergencies. Just an ice pack, probably from Finn's last attempt at the playground monkey bars, wedged where hope should have been.

I closed the freezer with a long sigh and leaned my forehead against a wrinkled paper scrawled in blue crayon. A drawing Finn had assured me was the outline of Florida, and not, as I'd suspected, a representation of an attack shark. It was too quiet with Finn still at the resort Kids Club. Most nights, stillness felt like a gift, breathing space. Tonight, it just pressed in, heavy and empty.

Moving to the pantry, I pulled out a blue box of macaroni and cheese. Our fail-safe, our mutually assured dinner. My mind kept drifting, compulsive and untamable, to Chase. He'd been at the resort most of the day, but we'd only interacted during a site meeting. Just me, him, Jules, and Elena, who was reassuringly competent. There'd been a change in Chase.

HE WASN'T his usual confident, analytical self. He couldn't be, not after the termite horrors, the wall drama, and the emergency shoring logistics. But the difference went deeper than exhaustion. He'd looked right at me. Looked, instead of talking around me, or past me, or at the plans. Then he'd looked straight into my eyes with a small, exhausted smile as he announced, "I'm working on a solution, guys. I'll have more details shortly, but all is not lost. I promise."

Then, when it was all over, he'd pulled me aside. "We'll talk soon, Harper. Properly."

That one tiny moment left a splinter in my side. Because the revised repair costs for Room Block One had landed in my inbox yesterday evening. No positive spin attached—just an email from Chase with two PDF attachments and a subject line that looked as haunted as I felt— *Updated Projections*.

I'd nearly dropped my phone. The final number was obscene. A figure you'd expect from disaster movies, not a family resort already bleeding from a thousand paper cuts. If I really read those numbers straight, we were looking at either gutting the renovation to a sad shadow of itself or putting ourselves into a level of debt I wouldn't wish on our worst Yelp reviewer. Worse, I could picture the quiet, analytic way Chase would've run every scenario, his face as closed off as a safe. And decided this was the truth.

Yet he said he had a solution.

How?

I didn't know how, but I trusted him. That was the bottom line. So I'd smiled back at him and waited to hear how he was going to fix this monumental problem.

I dug a rusty saucepan from under the oven and moved to the sink. Every time I thought we'd settled into something real, the world—Finn's innocent questions, ancient walls crumbling, late-night emails—reminded me just how much distance there still was between Chase and me. How impossible everything seemed right now.

What I missed, absurdly, wasn't just our flirtation or the late-night texts. Or even the toe-curling sex. It was the stupid, beautiful trust we'd found. But after Finn's question about Chase being his dad, I had wobbled. And with the termite disaster, Chase had retreated into architect mode. Solutions, not feelings. I understood, but understanding didn't make it easier to carry the weight of waiting. Just wanting him—wanting us—was starting to feel like trying to hold my breath underwater, hoping the air wouldn't run out before I surfaced.

I was reaching to turn on the faucet when the doorbell rang. I jumped, almost dropping the pan. Staring at the clock, I frowned. Sometimes a worker from the Kids Club dropped off Finn, but I'd told them I'd get him today. I dried my hands on the closest towel, running through a half-hearted mental checklist—nothing urgent I'd forgotten, right?—before heading for the door.

Our entryway was about as fancy as a broom closet in a model home. The table was a little scuffed, but Finn had decorated the corners with sea turtle stickers, which I stubbornly refused to scrape off. Shoes everywhere. I caught my reflection in the glass before unlocking the door—messy ponytail, a ratty, old resort T-shirt, shorts that had probably seen their best days when Obama was in office. Hardly the fantasy image of a woman whose life was going according to plan.

I swung the door open, bracing myself for the usual barrage of solicitor, delivery driver, lost tourist...

Chase stood on my porch, backlit by the last scrape of golden light, looking about ten percent too tall for the doorway and about a hundred percent less guarded than the last time I'd seen him. Instead of his laptop or a blueprint tube, he balanced two big pizza boxes and a brown paper bag against one hip.

He offered a sideways smile, and his hazel eyes darted to mine, then to the pizza, then back again. His hair was damp—probably from a quick shower. His shirt looked fresh too, his pants crisp and clean.

"Chase? What are you—" The question got tangled up in my throat, embarrassed at my own confusion. "I thought you were working late. On... all the stuff."

"Change of plans." He nudged past me, gentle but sure, and walked down the hall to set the pizzas on the kitchen counter. There was a new set to his shoulders.

He rested one hand on the top box. "Figured we deserved something better than emergency budget projections tonight." His voice had that warm edge to it, teasing at comfort, but his eyes were anything but casual.

I tried to cover the complicated mix of panic and gratitude twisting inside me with a quick snort. "Did you bring antacid too? That's about all I've been having for dessert lately."

He let out half a laugh and patted the bag. "Should've known you'd ask. You'll have to settle for cake and... well,

I'll explain." He glanced around. "Where's Finn? I brought pizza specifically to make up for the night of the play."

That made me smile. Something soft shifted inside me —hope, cautious but unavoidably there. "At the Kids Club. I was going to get him in half an hour, but should we go over there now and pick him up?"

He shook his head, more serious now. "No. I'm glad we've got a few minutes alone because I need to talk to you. About the numbers. About… everything."

LEAVING the pizzas warming in the oven, we relocated to the living room. The couch beckoned invitingly, and I flopped down on it. But he hovered in front of it, shifting his weight from foot to foot and not looking at me. Something told me this wasn't about pizza.

Chase glanced at me, then at the lopsided bookshelf in the corner, like he needed a focal point, any focal point, that wasn't my eyes. For once, I let the silence build. My pulse kicked up, but I stayed put on the end of the couch, one knee curled under me, arms around a throw pillow.

"I know you saw the revised costs." His voice was low —steady, but not distant. No spin, no buffer. Just the bare, ugly truth between us.

I nodded, jaw tight. "They're… potentially devastating."

Chase took a breath so deep I could see it tremble through his shoulders. "I spent that first entire night going over every scenario—trying to find a way to keep the scope of the renovation without gutting what matters or burying the resort in more debt. Or me."

He rubbed a hand over his jaw, then slid it into his pocket, as though if he didn't anchor himself, he might drift right out the door. "But it wasn't adding up. Not unless… not unless something gave."

I braced. My mind scrambled. What could we sell, what could we delay, what could I offer? The resort was already running on fumes and legacy. The only thing left to cut felt like blood.

Chase looked straight at me. "I called an old client of mine, Arthur Albright. About my house."

The words hit out of order. The Albright name was attached to an ungodly number of Dove Key properties and half the boats at the marina. What did he have to do with Chase's—

But the rest registered a half-beat later. "You… your house?" My stomach dropped.

"Albright has been pestering me for years to sell. He still wants it. Apparently, the timing's right—my asking price was the highest I could ask for and still sleep at night. He said yes on the spot, and we signed the contract an hour ago. Closing is in two weeks."

Shock rooted me in place. "What? Chase, no! You can't. Your house is gorgeous. There has to be another way… something we can do—"

He held up a hand, gentle but unmovable. "It's just a piece of property. That house… it's what I thought I was supposed to want. Ordered, perfect, detached from everything real so nothing could go wrong. But it was never my home." His eyes were unwavering as they held mine. "Home is right here in front of me, Harper. With you. With Finn. With this chaos we're all fighting for."

He was steady now—voice strong but not defensive. Like he'd rehearsed these words in his head a hundred times and finally meant them.

"You're sure?" Even as I said it, some primal, frightened part of me wanted to pull him close and demand he reconsider.

Chase's expression softened. "Very." He gestured, encompassing the cottage, the resort by extension, the future where we might all belong to each other. "This is what matters. The rest is just walls and rooflines. I design spaces for connection. It's time I stopped hiding from my own."

A laugh snuck out of my mouth, wet and embarrassed. I swiped at my eyes and tried to pull myself back together, but he wasn't finished. Instead, Chase bent and reached into the bag I hadn't noticed he'd brought from the kitchen. He pulled out a small tool belt with the tag dangling—child-sized, red canvas, the kind a kid would wear for *fixing* things. It still had the tag on, a screwdriver and a blunt hammer tucked in the loops.

"I bought this right before the termite disaster." His voice was lower and rougher than before. "Saw it at the hardware store and picked it up without thinking twice. Then I got in the car and almost had a panic attack. Because I pictured Finn with it. And you there, laughing, or telling him to use a level. And it scared the hell out of me."

I swallowed hard, my heart thumping against my ribs as he turned the belt over in his strong, assured hands.

"It showed me how much I wanted this. You. The resort. The family dinners. Even tripping over LEGOs in the dark. It also made me realize I was terrified I couldn't handle it. That I'd screw it all up, let you down, let Finn down."

He squeezed the tool belt in one fist, like it held more than just tools. Then he lifted his eyes and met mine. "But running from that fear would be the real failure." He took another breath, the sound shaky but resolute. "Harper, I'm not the guy who has it all figured out. Not when it comes to this… us. I look at you, at Finn, at the idea of building a real life, and half the time I'm scared to death. Scared I'll screw it up, scared I won't be enough, scared I'll repeat the mistakes I saw growing up. I honestly don't know what I'm doing most of the time when it comes to this emotional territory."

He finally sat down next to me, his hands finding mine and engulfing them. His touch was grounding, real. "But the other half? The part that's stronger than the fear? It knows I love you. God, Harper, I'm so completely in love with you. And I'm falling in love with being part of Finn's life, too. It's messy, it's complicated, and I know I got scared and pulled back when everything started crashing down." His grip tightened. "But I'm all in. I don't want easy or controlled anymore. I want *this*. I want *us*. I don't have all the answers, and I'll probably still get over-whelmed sometimes. But I promise you, right now, I will always find a way, always fight, to make us work."

Whatever air was left in the room disappeared. Some-thing inside me that had stayed tightly locked since I'd dedicated myself to being a single mother—and the walls I'd only reinforced since Jarod left—cracked wide open. No one had ever laid out their dread and their commitment side by side like that for me. No one had ever chosen *us* over the fear.

I didn't mean to cry, but the tears broke loose anyway. Not tears of sadness, but of overwhelming relief, of a hope so fierce it hurt. I slid forward into his space, tangling my fingers in the front of his shirt, needing to feel him solid beneath my hands.

"Oh, Chase," I choked out, laughing through the

tears. "I love you too. So, so much." The words felt like releasing a bird I hadn't realized I'd been keeping caged inside my ribs. "I've been terrified too. Terrified this was too good to last, terrified you'd realize what a mess this all is…"

He pulled me against him fiercely, burying his face in my hair. "It *is* a mess. Our mess. And I wouldn't trade it."

I pressed my forehead to his, laughing a little through the storm. "Brenna told me that fear can keep you safe, or it can keep you lonely." I took a huge breath. "You're right, this is our mess. And I choose it. I choose *us*. I trust you completely." I grabbed his head and pulled him in for another kiss, wanting to prove to him I believed now.

When we pulled back, his hand landed on the red tool belt. He glanced up, green and gold flecks in his eyes searching for mine. "Can I give this to Finn?"

I nodded, barely holding it together. "Right away. He'll… he'll absolutely love it."

Chase drew a thumb gently over my cheek, a touch lighter than air. I wanted to freeze this moment, hold it against my chest and never let it go. "But your house, Chase…"

He smiled, a real one, tired and triumphant. "It doesn't matter. Honestly." Then he barked a laugh. "Though I'll need to start looking for a place soon unless I want to live out of my car."

A wild, brilliant idea hit me with the force of a hurricane. He was selling his house, giving up everything to be with us. Why not go all the way? I bit my lip, my heart skipping beats like an unpracticed drummer. "You know… if you're going to be homeless anyway…"

His eyebrows shot up.

"My cottage isn't nearly as impressive as your place,

and Finn leaves LEGOs everywhere… but there's enough room. If you wanted to move in?"

For a split second, we just looked at each other. The air between us shifted, dense and bright and suddenly open. The look that passed between us was more than yes—it was a promise. No hesitation, no more questions, no defense mechanisms. He tugged me close, laughter rumbling through him, shaking loose months of doubt and distance.

"You're sure?" he asked.

I nodded into his shoulder, feeling freer than I had in years. "Absolutely."

Chase leaned in, pressed his lips softly, reverently, to my forehead. "There's nothing I want more."

We held each other there in the spill of the lamp's glow, exhaustion and hope tangled together, the crisis not magically fixed but now—suddenly—survivable. His promise wasn't a lifeboat. It was a home.

He pulled back slightly, eyes bright. "Don't we have a little boy to pick up? I've got a present for him."

I laughed, pulling him to his feet. "Come on then."

My heart soared as I pictured Finn's face when Chase handed him the tool belt. Chase slipped his arm around me like it belonged there, and for the first time in days— months, hell, years—everything felt right. We were out the door in seconds, the last threads of sunset painting the sky ahead. Even the air seemed lighter, full of possibility instead of pressure.

"Think Finn will be okay with me crashing here?" he asked as we walked toward the resort hand in hand.

I shot him a teasing glance. "You're bringing pizza and presents. He'll probably wonder why it took you so long."

Chase smirked, but I caught the relief in his expression.

Like he couldn't quite believe this was real or that he hadn't woken up.

And as we walked side by side, about to open the door and step into whatever new life waited, it hit me. Sometimes, the best things came when the world forced you to start over. Pizza reheated, hearts full, everything possible.

Chapter Twenty-Seven

CHASE

"THEN THE T-REX SAID, 'I can't tie my shoes because I have stubby arms!'" I kept my voice at a soft, appropriate tone for inducing sleep.

Finn's room was quiet except for my voice and the hush of the ocean breathing distantly. I sat cross-legged on the braided rug, reading from a battered, obviously loved dinosaur book as a tropical-fish nightlight illuminated the colorful pages. Superheroes battled fish along one wall. The rest of the room glowed blue, scattered with pirate ships, plastic sea creatures, and the faintest scribble of green crayon at the baseboard—a guilty memory or unfinished masterpiece, I couldn't tell.

Harper perched on the edge of his bed. For a moment, everything in my life funneled down to this—the soft weight of Finn's trust, her steadying presence, the hush before a promise. I turned the page and smiled at the wide-eyed expression on the struggling T-Rex's face.

She reached over and set her palm against my shoulder. Warm, light, solid in a way that felt like an invitation and a benediction rolled together. I startled a little.

"He's asleep, Chase," she whispered, her smile gone soft and private. Her fingers lingered in Finn's curls as he sprawled in the center of the shark-print sheets, his face slack with sleep.

I looked at the kid. The red tool belt was slung around his waist. He'd insisted on sleeping in it, the safely empty pouches bunched sideways over his hip. At his age, everything important had to come to bed, and in that tiny grip, I saw something impossibly fragile and unbelievably strong.

Trust.

Blind, bottomless, not something I ever thought I'd carry with a child. But there it was, smashing through me so hard it nearly winded me. It wasn't just that I loved him. It was being awed by how much I needed to get this right.

Harper caught my eye and held it. No need for words. There was gratitude in her gaze, but something steadier beneath it. Relief, faith, a dawning realization that the load wasn't only hers anymore. For the first time, maybe, she let herself share the burden.

She eased herself off the bed, barefoot and quiet as dusk. I slipped the book onto the nightstand beside his Captain America figure as he made a small, sleepy sound. The kind you want to pocket for when things get ugly, proof that gentleness exists.

Harper waited for me in the hall, framed by the buttery spill of kitchen light. I watched Finn's chest rise and fall one more time before tugging the door shut with exaggerated care. The click barely sounded, but the feeling hung there between us—something shifting, settling, and binding me more deeply to this little, enclosed world.

Back in the kitchen, the two pizza boxes had been stacked neatly, and the extra pieces were in the fridge and ready for tomorrow's lunches. Harper moved with the kind of practiced calm that made everything feel safe, unspectacularly real. She removed two wineglasses from the cabinet and poured us each a glass of white wine.

"Living room?" I asked, and she responded with a nod.

We settled on the couch that Finn had tried to repair with his tool belt earlier, and I stretched my legs across the threadbare ottoman. The space felt real. Not staged, not curated. Just Harper, just Finn.

And me, if I let myself believe it.

Somewhere in the hollows of this room, I could still feel the echo of Finn's laugh, high-pitched, half-feral with glee when I'd handed him the tool belt, almost holding my breath in anticipation. He gasped, just full-body lit up, like I'd given him the moon. He strapped it over his shorts (backward), spun three times, and announced he was going to fix everything. Declared he couldn't wait to show it to Uncle Eli. Meanwhile, Harper watched it all with a smile on her face.

In that instant—Finn's arms around my waist, Harper's gaze—a truth had snapped into place. The immaculate house, the old life, none of it compared to this. To them.

Zero regrets.

She sipped her wine and leaned her head against the back of the couch, eyes closing for one long beat. The silence felt earned.

"Was there anything else that brought about your decision to sell the house?" Her tone was light, teasing. She poked me in the shoulder, smirking. "Or was it all the termite apocalypse?"

I grinned, swirling the wine in my glass. "Eli might have stuck a cattle prod up my ass, but he wasn't wrong. I ended up verbally vomiting up all the overwhelm and panic I was feeling. And he didn't even run out of the room, so he really is growing. At the end of it all, I knew what I had to do. Selling the house wasn't that tough of a decision."

Harper's nose wrinkled—equal parts apology and amusement. "Yeah, well. I might have had something to do with that prod. There was a… let's call it a minor Coleridge event after you left the meeting room yesterday." She kept her voice light, but her cheeks flushed. "Eli found me sobbing over the table. I gave him the full tear-streaked Greatest Hits—why would Chase shut me out, is it my fault, what am I doing wrong… Very dignified, you can imagine."

I reached for her hand, thumb grazing over her knuckles. Her fingers twined through mine, almost automatically, the kind of touch that grows out of shared nights and mornings. The fact that Eli—Mr. Duct Tape and Beer—had bridged this for us seemed like some cosmic joke.

I squeezed Harper's hand, grounding myself in her warmth, in the simple truth of this moment—no pretense, no noise. Then I let go to cup her cheek in my hand. "That conference room meltdown? That's on me, and you won't have to go through it again. You lean on me now, and we tackle it together. Always."

The promise was more than words. I meant every word, every syllable written in the air between us.

She blinked hard, mouth curving into a tremulous smile. It was the look you gave someone at the exact second the weight dropped from your shoulders. I saw relief there, but something braver too—a hope that she could finally let herself depend on another person. She let out a breath like she'd been holding it for years. "Chase…"

But I didn't want gratitude or anything she felt obligated to say.

I only wanted her, fully, right now.

So I leaned in. She met me halfway. Her lips were soft, searching. Not desperate, not afraid—hungry for comfort, for affirmation. I poured myself into the kiss, my fingers threading through her soft hair.

Her hand curled at the back of my neck. I coaxed her closer, deepening the kiss until her breathing hitched and she climbed unselfconsciously into my lap, knees pressing on either side of my hips. The room faded until it was only the scratch of her shirt against my knuckles, the slide of her thighs over mine, her warmth so close and insistent I could barely form thoughts.

When I finally broke away for air, her eyes found mine, heavy-lidded and dazed, but clear with a sort of easy trust that hit harder than any plea. Moving her gently aside, I stood. And, taking her hand, I led her down the narrow hall to her bedroom. Now our bedroom.

The room was cool and softly lit, familiar in a way that made my chest warm. A hand-stitched quilt lay folded at the foot of the bed, and a novel with the spine broken sat on the nightstand. I wanted to memorize the way her presence had soaked into every fabric fiber, made the air thicker, safer.

We collapsed onto the bed, and I threaded my hands beneath her shirt. Her breath caught, and her hips tilted into my waiting palms. I moved slowly, unhurriedly. There was no rush. I wanted to taste every patch of skin, to make her feel seen.

I peeled away the shirt, lips following every inch of revealed skin. The thin tank top came next—her tips pebbling beneath the soft cotton, a flush painting up her chest. I paused to mouth along her collarbone, relishing the goose bumps that danced across her shoulders. I unhooked her bra and tossed it aside, her chest bare and rising in shallow, expectant pants.

I palmed both breasts, running my thumbs over her peaks, watching them tighten beneath my attention. She arched into me, lips parting for a gasp. My shaft strained against my pants. Still, I didn't hurry.

Her fingers fumbled at my shirt buttons, urgency flickering through her now. I kissed her—slow, messy, tongues sliding, bodies fitting together the way two people fit when they've been lonely for too long. I pulled back only long enough to tug my shirt overhead, shivering when her nails grazed my ribs.

When she was naked beneath me—shorts and panties peeled away, her legs splayed invitingly—I kneeled between her thighs. She watched me, wide-eyed and hungry, but trusting. Vulnerable in the best way. I pressed a kiss to the inside of her knee, then another, mapping my way up, savoring her scent and heat. By the time I reached her slick seam, she was already trembling, desperate.

I licked a slow stripe through her folds, savoring the taste, the way she immediately gripped my hair, hips pressing up in silent demand. I smiled against her, dragged my tongue in lazy circles, teasing as she arched and bucked, her thighs trembling at my temples.

"Please, Chase," she whispered, half-destroyed already.

I swirled my tongue slowly, holding her gaze when she looked down. She closed her eyes with a breathy moan, and I let her climb, then held her at the edge until she was breathless, shaking, her voice a series of broken syllables.

When she tumbled over, her orgasm hit hard. Her thighs clamped around my head, back bowing off the mattress. She bit the inside of her wrist to keep from being too loud. I drank in every sound, every pulse, every helpless buck of her hips. Only when her body went limp did I crawl up, licking a final stripe across her thigh, pressing gentle kisses up her belly, chest, throat.

I lay beside her, hand sliding up her ribcage as she blinked back to herself, skin flushed and glowing, eyes shining with a strange sort of wonder.

"Holy hell," she whispered, still catching her breath, "you don't play fair."

I grinned, nipping her earlobe. Then I rolled toward the nightstand and tugged it open. Reached for the condom box. It was suspiciously light.

I upended it. Empty.

Harper's breath hitched, then broke into an embarrassed laugh. "With all the chaos, I haven't made it to the store."

I propped myself on one elbow, meeting her gaze. "Moving in together does imply exclusivity, right? I'm safe, baby."

"Me too." She didn't look away. "Only you, Chase. God, only you."

I smoothed a thumb over her cheek, overcome with a happiness so raw it nearly hurt. "What about pregnancy?"

She gave a tiny shrug, lips quirking. "It's not prime time in my cycle. And at nearly thirty-five, not a walking fertility charm either." Then, quieter, naked in a way I hadn't seen before, "Is… is that okay?"

A flicker of something flashed through me. A future, maybe—her belly swelling with possibility, this house filled with more kid laughter. But it passed, replaced by a deeper ache, for her, for this. I kissed her, all conviction. "It's more than okay. Look at us. We already have an amazing family."

Relief washed across her features. "I'll call my doctor to get on the pill."

She reached for me and pulled me down to her. This time, when I pressed inside, there was nothing between us. She was hot, tight, the welcome of her body making me groan. I braced myself on my forearms, feeling every small gasp, every ripple of pleasure as she stretched around me. Each thrust was like a homecoming. She wrapped her legs around my waist and kept me close, arms looped behind my neck so our mouths never parted for long.

We rocked together. Slow at first, savoring every draw, every push, every inch buried and welcomed. She scraped her nails down my back, rolled her hips to meet me, eyes locked on mine so I couldn't hide. For a while, I let her lead, my hand clutching her hip, her knee hitched high.

Then, desperate for more, I shifted her onto her side and pushed in deep, hands running from the arch of her hip to the swell of her breast. She clutched at my forearm, moaning as I filled her again and again, chasing the crest.

It felt endless, bottomless—neither of us giving ground. We fell apart together, harsh breaths, muffled, unashamed cries. I rolled onto my back, taking her with me, and she held me close as we shuddered through the final wave. She pulsed around me, body clenching wildly, and I let go, spilling into her with a hoarse groan.

Afterward, we lay entwined with each other, still pulsing, still joined. The room was warm and quiet again. We drifted on the edge of sleep, her head on my shoulder, my hand resting possessively over her heart.

"I love you," I whispered into the small dark space between us.

Her lips curved against my chest. "Good. Because I'm keeping you. I love you too."

I tightened my arms around her and let myself believe it. The world spun down to this bed, this body, this breath. I let myself drift with her, claimed, at peace. Tomorrow would bring what it brought. But tonight, we'd finally made it home.

Chapter Twenty-Eight

HARPER

THE POOL DECK gleamed in the midday light, the custom leaf-motif finish still crisp. Even a month ago, this place had been chaos incarnate—cracked tile underfoot, work crews tramping through puddles, my nerves wound tight enough to snap. Today, there was almost peace in the rhythm of progress. It was similar to the peace filling me.

The air carried the clean scent of new concrete, distant salt, and a hint of whatever Braden was cooking up at Tropical Hops. Where once demolition crews had trailed dust through my dreams, there was only the hum of a drill, a bird call, a half-buried laugh from the parking lot.

Around us, garden beds arched in half-complete curves where sandy soil waited for native shrubs and new palms. Out beyond the deck, Room Block One was once again underway, shoring crew hard at work and the whole renovation back on track with the infusion of cash, thanks to my wonderful, resourceful man. The white paint of the new bungalows down at the end of the beach glowed in the afternoon sun.

Chase walked beside me, arm just close enough to brush mine every few steps, posture easy. He caught my eye as I stared out over the pool, offered a half-smile that made something happy twist in my chest.

We didn't say much, surveying the cabanas and the sweep of the pool edge. There was too much to look at. Every so often, he'd rest a hand on the small of my back, slow and sure, the touch electric in its casualness.

"Feels different now, doesn't it?" he murmured as we studied the final inspection sheet tacked near the pool bar.

"Like we finally turned the corner." I tucked a strand of hair behind my ear and glanced at him sideways. "Bet you never thought you'd be elbows deep in so much contractor drama."

"Or living with someone whose idea of organization is a stack of three color-coded clipboards for every room."

I bumped him with my shoulder, grateful for his teasing. "Like you're any better. I've seen how you organize your side of the closet."

The past few weeks had been a blur of moving boxes, early mornings, and late-night sorting—Chase settling in, us finding our rhythms in life and at work. It turned out blending households was a bit of a dance when one of you was a serial minimalist and the other could never part with anything Finn had ever colored. The sale of his house had proceeded without a hitch, and we'd obtained all necessary signatures to increase his partnership to thirty-five percent with the extra capital he was committing to the renovation.

My cottage was a bit cozier now, and my joke about buying a bigger place might become reality at some point soon. Especially since we'd had to put his gorgeous mahogany desk into storage for the moment. Too many good memories there to hide away in the dark.

The sharp edge of anxiety that had lived in me for too long, the perpetual hum that something else might go wrong, had finally faded to a manageable buzz. Even the clouds that gathered above the trees looked more decorative than threatening, and I could actually hear myself breathing again. Maybe that was just what relief sounded like—wind, hammers, and the burble of water on tile.

I let myself enjoy it, for just a moment. This improbable, hard-earned quiet. The truth was, Chase fit into our days so smoothly I almost forgot it was new. It was the way he squeezed into the kitchen, dodging Finn's plastic trucks, or the way his laugh filled up spaces I'd never known were empty. Finn had accepted him without reservation, treating him like he was the best present on Christmas morning.

I didn't realize I was smiling to myself until Chase leaned in, eyebrow arched. "You're making that face again."

"Which one?"

He grinned. "The happy one. Keep it up."

The familiar sound of footsteps—deliberate, heavy, confident—saved me from replying. Austin appeared at the corner of the pool deck, hands shoved in his pockets, resort baseball hat pushed back, eyes sharp behind that ever-present dark stubble. I could tell by the lack of furrow between his brows that today was—if not a good day—a decent one.

He nodded to Chase, then to me, squinting at the pool and the just-laid sod. For a long beat, he took it in, arms crossed, expression as unreadable as ever.

"Looks sharp, Ashworth," he said, low and just a little gravelly. "You kept the feel of the place but really brought it into this century instead of last." A rare compliment, handed out like a trust fall.

Chase's ears went pink—subtle, but I knew. "That was the goal. Blend the new with the old. Appreciate it, man."

Austin nodded, gaze flitting between us as if registering something about the way we stood a touch too close. But he didn't comment. Instead, his eyes crinkled at the corners and a faint smile raised his lips, the closest thing to amusement you'd get from my younger brother.

He used to be so different…

I sighed and let the thought go. Austin was what events had made him, and we were all grateful he was still with us.

He looked my way. "Have you blocked Ben from your contacts yet?"

I rolled my eyes skyward even as I laughed. "Thinking about it. Who would have thought our big brother would be such a Chatty Cathy? A group text including the world's biggest *PASS* notification followed fifty exclamation points. Plus a selfie so blurry I had to squint sideways to confirm it was truly his grinning face."

Austin's mouth twitched, unmistakable pride in the set of his shoulders. "Aces the exam but still can't hold a phone steady."

Chase nodded. "I knew he could do it."

I grinned, letting some of the old sibling mischief take over. "Now that Ben officially passed his EMT certification test, he's waiting for the state paperwork to start at Dove Key Fire Department."

"Not bad for the family wild card." Chase was impressed, and a little surge of pride wormed its way into my grin. If anyone had earned this win, it was Ben.

Austin snorted. "Maybe now he'll let someone else fix a lawn edger for once."

A wind gust rolled off the gulf, tugging at my skirt. I shivered a little, not from cold, but from the unexpected peace. This was the kind of day I'd been desperate for—the family moving forward, the resort steady, Chase at my side.

Austin tipped his chin, brow furrowing as he sized us up. "Right. Speaking of things paying off… Seems you two agreed to a fishing trip on *Line Dancer* a while back. Haven't forgotten, have you?"

I groaned, half-laughing. "We didn't forget. I just figured you'd be too busy with the new bookings."

Chase slung an arm around my shoulders, squeezing. "We're ready when you are. Name the time."

I thought for a moment. "Maybe a sunset trip? That way it won't mess with your scheduled charters. And Finn could come, too. He's been begging for another adventure with Uncle Austin."

Austin considered, jaw working. "Saturday evening looks clear. Meet at the dock around five?"

"Works for us," I said, already picturing Finn's excitement.

Austin nodded again, an odd softness in his eyes, then started back toward the marina, whistling under his breath.

Chase watched him go, then squeezed my hip. "Sunset cruise with the family," he murmured, low and private. "Sounds perfect."

I leaned into him, letting the solid weight of his arm steady me. "It does. Amazing how things have changed."

"And all for the better," he said quietly, brushing the hair from my forehead. "Hey, promise me something. Whenever you feel like you're drowning in the chaos? Look for me. I'll be right there to pull you out."

He pressed a kiss to my temple, and a gentle, warm light filled me. I let myself look out over the sunlit pool, past the now-back-on-track room block. There was challenge ahead. There always would be. But today, I felt only hope. Saturday, the family, the open water—and whatever the next tide brought us. I was ready to welcome it all.

***

THE LINE between afternoon and evening blurred in a honey-gold wash across the bay, sunlight flickering off the waves and scattering the boat's shadow in broken pieces on the water. I leaned back against the railing, the soft thrum of the engine and the clean, briny sweep of ocean air carving out a space that felt entirely its own. Part workday, part private celebration. Finn bounced at my elbow, life vest snug, the empty tool belt strapped around his waist. He insisted on wearing it whenever possible, especially after he and Chase agreed to build a birdhouse together.

On *Line Dancer*, everything had its place. Tackle boxes were sorted by size and species, rods were propped neatly and securely, and Austin's meticulous touch was visible in the coiled dock lines and polished deck. The air smelled like salt, engine oil, and sunblock. Waves slapped gently at the hull, rocking us just enough that time seemed to slip sideways.

Austin manned the helm, hands wrapped around the wheel, sunglasses perched on his nose. I loved seeing him so relaxed—the infamous wall of silence eased by sunset, water, and family. Out here, he didn't need to talk much. The boat and the sea did the heavy lifting.

Thank God he hadn't lost that too.

I fussed with Finn's hair, fingers tucking loose strands under his cap as he waited not so patiently for his uncle to place the boat where he wanted it so the fishing could begin.

Just then, Austin called over, "All right, Finn. Let's get this show on the road. Time you learned to cast like you mean it."

Finn beamed and hurried forward, the tool belt thumping with each step. "Okay, Uncle Austin!"

Austin's big hands made short work of adjusting the child-sized reel, threading the line through Finn's fingers. He kneeled, meeting Finn eye to eye, and his frown disappeared, replaced by the quiet patience of someone who'd untangled a thousand lines before.

"See this?" He thumbed the drag, letting Finn feel the tension. "Not too tight. If it screams when you hook something, back off a little. Keep your thumb here, just above the button. The rod's gotta be an extension of your arm, not a club. Watch me."

Austin stood and demonstrated with his personal, well-loved rod, his movements unhurried but sure. A flick of the wrist sent the line arcing in a neat parabola before the bait plopped just where he aimed with barely a splash. "You try."

Finn hefted his rod, tongue poked out in concentration. He glanced at me, and I gave him an encouraging thumbs-up.

"Okay… here goes."

The first try was a disaster—the line snared and dropped at his feet. Austin, instead of barking, grunted and kneeled again. "Your thumb's got to be lighter. You're not launching a rocket. You're persuading a fish."

He gently guided Finn's movements, and the next cast landed four feet out with a gentle plop. Finn looked like he'd just solved quantum physics.

I clapped from my seat. Austin smiled, faint but real. "Not bad, kid. You keep this up, I'll make you first mate before your mom."

Finn puffed up with pride. "Can we fish for marlin?"

Austin snorted. "Let's catch a snapper first. Save marlin for next time."

For the next few minutes, Austin moved Finn through the process of casting, reeling, waiting. Demonstrating how to watch the line's movement, telling him about the feel of a nibble versus the current. He pointed out an osprey diving offshore, and Finn's face split into pure awe. Austin didn't fill the quiet with words. He dropped his advice like bait, just where Finn could grab it, then faded back, letting the boy find his own rhythm.

There were too many layers to the way I felt in that moment. Relief, seeing my son glow under Austin's attention. Contentment, with Chase within arm's reach. Gratitude—for all of it, for the messy, blended family that had somehow fallen into place around me.

Austin was explaining the finer points of adjusting the drag. "If you set it too tight, the line might snap. Too loose, the fish gets away. Gotta listen for the click. Feel it in your hands." His voice had that low, steady certainty—the kind you only got from a lifetime of practice. He glanced up once, caught me watching, then looked away so quickly I nearly missed the flicker of embarrassment.

Finn frowned, brow knotting as he listened. "But how do you know?"

Austin paused, expression unreadable for a second. "Sometimes you just do. Fish don't always play by the rules. Best you can do is pay attention and try not to get too impatient."

He tugged the line between his rough fingers, showing Finn how to test the tension. Finn imitated him, biting his lip. The look Austin gave him then—soft, full of something quiet and unnameable—made my breath catch. I relaxed against Chase while Austin and Finn kept up their quiet practice. Chase reached for my hand, thumb tracing a lazy circle across my knuckles.

"You ever see Austin this relaxed?" he whispered.

"Not unless there's a tropical storm and all the tourists are safe or evacuated," I replied, trying not to laugh. "He pretends he's all gruff and crusty, but…" I trailed off, not sure how to sum up the feeling.

"Yeah," Chase murmured. "Guess it's easier out here. He's in his element."

When the sun slipped lower, painting the sky in molten oranges and fading pinks, I enjoyed the breeze while Chase drifted closer to the helm, where Austin checked the depth finder and lines.

"Heard you finished your restoration over on Driftwood Lane," Chase said, folding his arms, letting the gentle sway of the deck rock him into the conversation. "Eli's been bragging it looks incredible. Word is, you scared off the last contractor who tried to put vinyl on your porch."

Austin's mouth twitched, almost a grin, but he reined it in fast. "Yeah. Mostly done. Still some trim work. Place was more bones and bad ideas than house."

"Any surprises?" Chase asked, keeping his tone light and interested. There weren't many old conch homes left, and Austin had fought to save every splinter. I wasn't at all surprised Chase wanted to know all the details.

Austin rolled his shoulders, watching the water roll past. "Plenty. Rotten sills. Wiring from the Eisenhower era. One night, a raccoon got stuck under the floorboards— sounded like a poltergeist. Still, nothing I couldn't handle. If you know what you're doing, these old houses aren't so bad. You know that."

I followed his gaze to the shoreline, where the homes huddled together in the distance, salt-bleached and stubborn as ever.

Austin's face darkened a shade. "Biggest problem now isn't my place. It's that monstrosity next door." He jerked his chin toward a hulking silhouette farther along the beach.

I pushed to my feet and joined them. "You mean the old Heron House?"

Austin nodded grimly. "Yeah. It's sat all but derelict for decades. But I've seen a construction worker over there several times lately. The other day, I was trimming my hibiscus hedge and asked him what was going on. He said Old Lady finally passed away and left the estate to her niece. Guess the niece plans to fix it up." He snorted, unable to hide the irritated humor in his eyes now. "The place is massive. Needs everything. Roof, foundation, probably an exorcism."

His annoyance was oddly endearing. There was a protective streak there—toward the house, the town, maybe even his own battered peace.

I laughed and brushed a stray lock of hair out of my eyes. "Well, it is getting a little cramped over at my place after Chase moved in." I nudged his ribs with my elbow, enjoying the familiarity and rightness of it. "Maybe we should see if the niece would rather sell. We could use the extra space. Finally have enough closets for all your suits and ties."

Austin's eyes flew wide in horror. "That's the last thing you want to joke about, Harper. That place is a money-pit nightmare. Mold, rot, probably ghosts out for vengeance. You want nothing to do with it."

Chase shook his head as a grin escaped. "He's right. I walked through that property for a site consult last year. It needs everything. Even the stilt piles are cracked." He caught our eyes as a decided gleam entered his. "But if you had the right buyer, enough patience, and maybe an architect with a little vision, it would make the perfect bed-and-breakfast or boutique hotel."

Austin shot him a sour look. "A hotel? Next door to me? God, don't say that, Ashworth. It's bad enough thinking about noisy neighbors, let alone tourists hanging laundry off the balcony at all hours. I'll end up moving out to sea."

I snorted. "You wouldn't last a week without Tidal Hops happy hour. Besides, ghosts love a crowd. Maybe they'll come visit you." I turned and poked Chase in the chest. "And as for you, don't even think about it. I was kidding about buying that heap of shingles."

Chase broke into a wide grin. "Agreed. We have quite enough on our plate. Sorry, Austin, but we've been overruled."

Austin only grunted, but I saw the faintest smile tug at his stubble before he turned away, his gaze back on the far-off lights of Dove Key.

Then Finn shouted from the port side, his voice shrill with excitement. "I got one! I got a real one!" He stood planted at the rail, the tip of his rod bucking, reel screaming like the Fourth of July.

Austin, all business now, hurried over and kneeled behind Finn, his arms bracketing the boy. "Okay, hold your reel steady now. Don't jerk it. That's it, just like I showed you." His attention was total—world narrowed to Finn, the rod, and whatever surprise was coming out of the deep.

Chase and I moved to the other side of the stern to give them plenty of room while we watched. Finn's rod jerked again, the reel protesting, and Austin was offering the world's most patient instructions, but it felt miles away.

Austin hoisted the shimmering snapper over the rail, its scales catching the last of the light. "That's a keeper size, kiddo. You want to bring him home for dinner?"

Finn stared at his prize, eyes wide, then shook his head solemnly. "No, let's put him back. He probably misses his mom."

With a nod of approval that said more than his words could, Austin gently twisted the hook free with his pliers. He guided Finn's small hands to hold the slick body, and Chase squeezed my hand as we watched from the stern while Finn leaned over the side, releasing the fish with a splash and a triumphant wave goodbye.

The quiet between Chase and me grew wide and soft, stretched over the gentle slap of the waves against the hull. Austin and Finn got washed up and my brother swept an experienced gaze over the horizon and declared languidly it was time to go home. There was no rush, just a private kind of hush where possibilities waited.

When we returned, Finn slouched between Chase and me, barely awake. Austin stood tall at the wheel, his gaze trained on the Sunset Siesta pier, his profile carved in shadow and a strange, wistful longing. He was a man full of jagged old wounds and silences, the kind you wanted to reach out to heal but were never quite able to.

Chase hugged me a little tighter as the first stars blinked awake, and I leaned back into him, letting the joy be bigger than the worries. Family wasn't always born. It was built, one moment at a time, on a sunset cruise with a child's laughter, a brother's rare smile, and the best man in the world's arms around your waist.

Chapter Twenty-Nine

CHASE

I'D GROWN USED to this—Harper's kitchen in the golden slipstream of morning, the faint scent of toast mingling with ocean salt and fresh coffee. The place looked like us now. My sleek black espresso maker sat next to her battered drip pot, Harper's to-do lists tangled up with Finn's drawings beneath the shark magnet. It felt easy, familiar, the kind of belonging you only notice when you realize how much you used to live without it. A couple of weeks back, I would have worried I was overstepping. Now, in the low hush before the day's tumult, I simply felt settled.

The machine pinged, and I sipped from the rich brew as I contemplated how Harper had gone from a woman I'd known for years to the woman I couldn't live without. I crossed to my bag on the table and opened it. A smile raised my lips at what lay inside. Waiting. Plans were in motion, but I could bide my time.

Her footsteps came next, quieter than usual, slow. I

quickly prepared her cup out of habit. Harper always insisted on plain coffee in the mornings, but I'd started to sneak in a drizzle of honey. The sweetness was more for me. A simple way of loving her.

I glanced up and she filled the doorway in her faded blue robe, hair loose about her shoulders, the light behind her gilding her edges. She was paler than normal, almost wan, and even before she spoke, something in me flickered —a note struck off-key.

"Morning, Sunshine." I kept my voice easy, sliding her mug into her hand as my eyes lingered on hers.

No snappy comeback. Instead, she pressed the mug to her lips with both hands, steadying herself. She managed a weak half-smile. "Sunshine might be a stretch. Maybe more like partly cloudy with a chance of sprinkles."

Her eyes dropped to my laptop screen on the table— my open render of the lobby reno and expansion. She stared at it with a glazed look. When she finally blinked, the gesture looked like it took effort.

"Tough night?" I asked.

She hummed, vague. "A bit. Just work stress. Employee reviews start today. My brain staged a marathon and wouldn't quit." Her lips lifted, but it fell short of a real joke.

I crossed to the fridge. "I know what you need. Let me make you some breakfast. Eggs, bacon, toast. You need it if you're about to take on the full staff circus."

She shook her head, her nose wrinkling a little. "Thanks, but maybe just toast. I'm not hungry. Stomach's a little off."

I stopped, bread in hand, taking her in again. No appetite, the robe still on when she'd usually be wrangling Finn's backpack and arranging to get him from Grandma's. Something nudged at the edge of my brain, sharpening all my internal lines. I fixed the toast anyway, fussing with the dial, giving her space. Meanwhile, my mind ticked over the data—exhausted, not hungry, pale, a bit nauseated. And as always, too ready to blame herself.

And suddenly—stupidly, logically, inevitably—the pieces connected.

I turned around and leaned against the counter. "Harper, are you sure everything's okay?"

She frowned, undoubtedly getting ready to tell me how fine she was. But I held her gaze when her eyes met mine.

I made sure my voice came out careful, gentle, when I asked, "When was your last period?"

The kitchen contracted around us. For a heartbeat, her face was all confusion of wrinkled brow, unfocused eyes, her hand halfway to her hair.

Then her eyes locked on mine. Startled, suddenly still. Then fear tightened the delicate muscles around her mouth.

Time snapped taut.

I didn't say anything more, waiting, not trusting myself to fill the quiet with anything but presence. She blinked. Her gaze darted down, then to her coffee cup as her mind worked the numbers. Her lips parted, but nothing came out. Her shoulders, always squared to the world, seemed impossibly narrow just then.

When Harper's eyes snapped up to mine, they were clear—no denial, no panic, just shock and something bracing underneath. "Okay. You're right. I'm late. A week. Well, closer to two." The words landed between us, heavy and undeniable. She pushed back her chair, steadying herself with both hands on the table. "I need… I need to get a pregnancy test. Like, now."

It was my cue. I didn't hesitate. "Good idea. I'll drive."

My keys were in my hand before I'd even registered

standing up. The thing that mattered was her, what she needed. My heart was pounding, but I didn't let it bleed into my words.

Harper nodded, a breath puffing out of her chest, almost like relief. "Yes. Please. I'll go change."

Outside, the day felt inappropriately bright, the air thick with that pre-storm humidity that always made my skin feel tight. We walked to the car in silence, her in leggings and a big tee, me running through logistics. Grocery store. Main Street.

I glanced over as she buckled in. She stared straight ahead, mouth pressed flat, one hand white-knuckled on the strap of her seat belt. The drive lasted four minutes. It felt like forty. The parking lot outside Island Market was mostly empty, still early enough for a sliver of privacy. Inside, the world looked the same as always with its fluorescent lights and stacked pineapples. Every normal detail seemed offensive in its ordinariness. We went straight for the pharmacy aisle, and she grabbed the first test within arm's reach. I paused, glancing at the sea of boxes. Early Response, Super Accuracy, Over 99% Reliable.

I tried a weak joke as I picked up a white box with pink lettering. "Want me to analyze the data for precision? I'm partial to this one. It has a bar graph on the back."

She gave me a side-eye. Her mouth twitched, almost a laugh, before settling back into something rawer. "If it can tell me yes or no, I don't care if it has Bluetooth."

I wanted to pull her in close, shield her from the world. But this was hers to steer, so I fell in beside her, matching her pace. At the checkout, fate was kind—some kid from up the Keys, earbuds in, half-listening. He scanned the test, looked up, and recognized neither of us, then mumbled the total. I pulled my card, tapped, and glanced at Harper. For the briefest second, our eyes met—both aware of the absurd weight of the little paper bag, the relief that it wasn't Lori from the beauty shop behind the counter.

I opened her car door for her, then slid behind the wheel. The paper bag was clutched in her lap. I reached for her hand, settling my palm over hers on the crumpled paper.

"You don't have to say anything," I said quietly. "But whatever that test says, I'm here."

Her grip on my fingers was tight. I thought of Jarod. The abandonment. The years she'd lived with that particular wound. I squeezed back, every muscle in my body broadcasting,

I'm not him. I won't run.

Back at the cottage, Harper was already halfway to the bathroom before I'd killed the ignition. She held the bag to her chest, moving with purpose, her back straight, every inch a woman refusing to shrink from uncertainty. I found myself pacing in the living room—through the kitchen, by the fridge, back to the couch, then to the small hallway outside the bathroom. Finally, I waited just outside, every part of me restless and wired.

Harper opened the door, watch in hand. "Now we wait a few minutes."

She set an alarm, placed it face-up on the edge of the counter, and stepped into my arms. I held her tight to my chest. Her skin felt warm, shaky. My heart hammered out a rhythm neither of us could ignore.

After an eternity, the alarm chirped.

We moved together, inching into the tiny bathroom. The wand lay on the counter, its window so starkly marked.

Two lines, clear as sunrise.

Harper's face was complicated. Hope, fear, disbelief, maybe the echo of some old, deeper grief all flashed through her. Tears shimmered, unshed. But below all that, there was a steadiness I'd never seen in her before. She looked at me—truly looked—waiting for my reaction.

I reached for the test. It trembled a little in my fingers, but those two lines didn't change. I swallowed as I searched her face, trying to make her see it.

The awe and joy splitting me wide open.

She saw it. The bracing for disaster melted away, second by second, as she read the happiness in me. Something shifted. Her shoulders loosened. Her mouth turned up, slow and wobbly. A breath hitched and left her, almost a laugh.

She trusted me.

She understood I was happy about this.

She knew I wasn't going to run.

The realization hit me harder than anything. Her trust in me was the answer I'd wanted more than anything.

The test slipped from my hand to the counter. I hauled her to me, crushed her tight. For a heartbeat, I lifted her clear off the ground, spinning us until she gasped, half-laugh, half-sob.

"Oh my God, are you okay? This is—wow. This is amazing." My voice was rough, leaking emotion all over the place.

She clung to me, laughing, crying, barely able to catch her breath. "Two lines, Chase! I still can't believe it."

I set her down, cupping her face, brushing her hair back so I could see her eyes. I let every bit of happiness I felt shine for her. "Best news ever. Are you okay? Really okay?"

She stared back, steady as the tide, her voice clear but tremulous, as if letting go of all the old fear at once. "Yes. The idea scared me at first... Old habits die hard. But seeing your face..." She gestured between us, lips twitching. "I'm still a little scared. But I know it's okay, Chase. We're okay."

There was no distance left between us, only the certainty that came from facing the truth and finding the other person exactly where you needed them to be.

I don't know how long we stood there, arms around each other, anchored in a wave of disbelief and dizzy happiness, the echo of Harper's "*We're okay*" ringing louder than any test result. The world outside the cottage could have been spinning or standing still, for all I cared. Here, everything felt brand new.

Harper stepped back, still touching my arm, her gaze drifting to the living room. Finn's LEGO spaceship lay on the coffee table next to my T square. She blew out a trembling laugh and pressed the heel of her hand to her cheek, blinking hard. "Well, I don't need to worry about birth control anymore."

Her doctor hadn't wanted her on the pill, so we'd been using the good old withdrawal method until she got an IUD placed.

"Yeah, guess you were more prime time than we thought."

Her eyes were still glazed as she darted a look toward the bathroom and its life-changing news lying on the counter. "Guess it's a good thing we're on solid footing. And you've moved in already. No one can accuse us of rushing there." Her eyes flicked to the tangle of my running shoes, laptop cords trailing from the couch. "Makes planning a future a little easier."

Then she padded across the room to pick up the LEGO spaceship. "I was thinking about Finn. Should we…" She wiggled her fingers, making a show of glancing at my scattered things, Finn's scattered chaos, the pregnancy test lying in state on the bathroom counter. "Should we make it official? Like, actually get married?"

Her tone was half-playful, but underneath it, I caught the wish. Raw and real, it was a longing for permanence, not just for her but for Finn and the baby we'd just discovered.

A shiver ran through me. Fate making itself known.

And I knew.

I stepped into the kitchen. Fished for my bag on the table once again, my pulse fluttering like it was the very first time I'd ever faced her. I unzipped the back pocket—business cards, a stray pen, a velvet box. I held it in my palm, thumb running over the nap of the velvet.

Harper froze, brow knitting, mouth half-open as she saw it. "Chase... what is that?"

I gave her a look, soft and wide and wry all at once. My face heated, some of that old shyness coming back. "I bought this about a week ago. I've been carrying it around everywhere so you wouldn't stumble across it. I kept waiting for the right idea to strike." I shook my head, almost embarrassed. "Turns out, the perfect moment is standing in the kitchen with a pregnancy test on the bathroom counter."

Her hand flew to her mouth, eyes so wide it felt like the cottage itself was holding its breath. I opened the box. The ring—solitaire, brilliant, chosen for her simplicity and grace—caught the overhead light and glittered.

I didn't get down on one knee. I wanted her to look me right in the eye, both feet on the floor, both of us present in every sense. I held it out, everything I felt stripped down and pure. "This might not be an elaborate proposal under the stars. But my feelings haven't changed. If anything"—my gaze dropped to her stomach, then back to hers, heart thumping—"they just got exponentially more real. I love you. I want to build this life with you. The messy parts, the surprising parts, all of it. Marry me?"

For a split second, she only stared. Then the world snapped into motion. She laughed, breathless, almost giddy, and threw her arms around my neck. "Yes! God, yes!" She kissed me, messy and deep and a little unhinged.

I fumbled the ring from the box, found her left hand, and slid the diamond onto her finger. She looked down, dazed, then met my eyes again, tears shining, her smile stretched as wide as the horizon. We stood tangled up, her laugh trembling through both of us.

She wiped her eyes, still beaming. "Okay, now that that's settled… I guess we should set a date soon?" Her tone shifted from wonder to practical in the space of a breath as she rested a hand on her abdomen. "Like, really soon?"

Elation, as pure and sharp as the Keys sun, surged through me, and a laugh I hardly recognized as my own barked out. I pulled Harper against me so tight I could feel the frantic beat of her heart against my ribs. It was a counterpoint to the sudden, overwhelming calm that settled in mine. Staring down at her, at the slightly dazed, beaming face of the woman who had somehow bulldozed her way past every defense I owned, my entire future clicked into place.

Messy, unpredictable, and more real than any blueprint I'd ever drawn.

I pressed my mouth to her hair, breathing in her irresistible scent. "Anytime, anyplace," I said, overcome with emotion too big for words. "You just say it, and I'm there. Not just for the wedding, but for all of it. The scraped knees, the budget meetings, the quiet Sunday mornings, and whatever comes next. I promise you. I'll always be there."

Epilogue

HARPER

MARRYING CHASE ASHWORTH in the Marathon branch of the Monroe County Courthouse wasn't quite what I'd dreamed about as a little girl. My vision had always involved an ocean view, maybe the good china, certainly more than this odd blend of government antiseptic and whatever fragrance they used to mask the mildew in the corners. But standing next to him, our hands steadily entwined, I couldn't imagine anything righter. Maybe this was what perfect looked like.

Not fancy. Not staged. Just us.

We'd managed to put this all together only two weeks after Chase proposed. The family had been somewhat stunned that we wanted such a bare-bones wedding, though Mom gave me a long, evaluating look. I wanted to keep quiet about the pregnancy a while longer, but Eli had been suspicious the moment Chase asked him to be best man.

Eli had given him a long side-eye and asked, "Did you knock up my little sister?"

And Chase, being terminally honest, confessed immediately. But smart-ass or not, I could count on Eli to keep quiet. And I didn't even need to question whether Jules could keep a secret. Still, they were the only ones who knew.

The ceremony room, if that's what you'd call it, looked like it moonlighted as a place to serve overdue parking fines. Dingy ceiling tiles overhead, paint peeling in one corner, one little fake palm tree. A generic beach print hung on the far wall.

And still, with Chase next to me in a suit—navy, tailored, and making his shoulders look even broader than usual, obviously pressed within an inch of its life—it could have been a palace. His hazel eyes found mine, and the edges of the room blurred a little, my heart doing a ridiculous soft-shoe in my chest. He offered me a tiny, private smile. The nerves sat in the set of his jaw, but his steady, intent gaze was all the reassurance I'd ever wanted.

I had gone simple with my dress. Soft white linen, fitted at my waist, fluttering just below the knee. Nothing sparkly. I'd styled my hair for once, and the waves caught the harsh courthouse light as if determined to stage a little rebellion. In honor of the occasion, I'd bought a new set of makeup and even applied it like I remembered how to.

Eli—God help us—wore a proper button-down shirt, sleeves rolled just enough to keep from looking respectable. And a *tie*. He stood beside Chase, looking almost solemn. No sunglasses. Not a hint of a tan line from the mask of his usual grin. I'd caught the tiniest wink earlier, but right now, he was the very picture of a reliable witness and best man. His hands were clasped loosely in front of him, but there was warmth there too in the tilt of his head, the soft-ness at the corners of his mouth. He looked from me to Chase as if he were seeing a puzzle finally put together. Chase got a quick, subtle thumbs-up. A second later, Eli offered me a smile that was only a little lopsided.

Jules, on my other side, was a study in composure—a pale green dress, hair in an elegant chignon. She squeezed my hand as we lined up, and her fingers trembled a little. "Harper, you two look so good together. All three of you do." It sounded formal, but her voice caught at the end, betraying her. She gave my hand one final squeeze before letting go, eyes shimmering a little too brightly.

Front and center between Chase and me stood Finn. Six years old, pint-sized prince of Dove Key, and a self-appointed ring security detail. His suit—tiny white linen, purchased with only moderate protest—made him look both solemn and a little feral. His hair had already escaped its part, sticking up in an enthusiastic cowlick. He gripped the little navy velvet pillow with both hands, his entire being condensed into this single, important job.

He looked up at me, blue eyes very, very serious. "Mommy, do I give Chase your ring, or does he give it to me first?"

His question ricocheted around the room, pinging off Chase's smile, Eli's barked laugh, quickly stifled, and Jules's soft shake of her head.

I bent and smoothed that rogue bit of hair. "Sweet-heart, when they say it's time for the rings, you hand mine to Chase, and then you give Chase's to me. And no juggling this time, okay?"

He nodded gravely. "No juggling. I promise."

"Good man." I pressed a kiss to his temple and straightened just as the officiant appeared in the doorway.

She was brisk, her smile polished and professional, the kind I suspected she kept in a drawer alongside a collection of Very Official Pens. "Ready, everyone?"

Footsteps echoed as we moved into place. I gripped my rose and lily bouquet, courtesy of Jules, then handed it off to her. I found Chase's gaze and we turned instinctively to face each other and clasped hands.

The officiant cleared her throat. "We are gathered here today…"

Her words washed over me, functional, tidy, doing the job. I heard them, but they didn't quite stick. All my attention funneled into the man standing before me. Chase's fingers brushed against mine, a question and an answer as I squeezed back. Out of my periphery, Finn wobbled on tiptoe, clutching the pillow, his lips moving as he examined the rings.

"… to join Harper Coleridge and Chase Ashworth in matrimony…" the officiant intoned, reading from a script no doubt printed long before any of us decided we'd just make this official before I started showing, and only a month after the fishing trip with Austin.

When it came time for vows, the officiant looked up expectantly.

Chase stepped a fraction closer. He cleared his throat, a sound that was half-nerves, half-clearing the space between us. "Harper, I promise to build a life with you, not just houses. I want every day to be one we put together—foundations, renovations, all of it." His mouth twitched. "Whether it's coastal modern or mid-century stuck, I'll be there for all of it."

My lips lifted in a wild grin that surely appeared more than a little unhinged. He squeezed my hand, his own eyes glassy.

I found my voice, somehow. "Chase, I promise to love

you through chaos, spreadsheets, tropical storms, and slow internet. To hold you up and let you hold me, even when I pretend I don't need it." I reached for a little courage. "To say yes, even when I'm terrified. And to always keep snacks in my desk drawer."

His answering smile melted something in my chest. The officiant appeared faintly amused.

She nodded. "Rings, please."

Finn sprang into action, posture ramrod straight. He offered Chase my rings. Chase took the diamond engagement ring and wedding band, hand steady, and caught my eye again. He slipped them over my finger and lingered, thumb tracing the edge.

Finn gave me his band—thicker, smooth, warm from the pillow. I slipped it on, his fingers curling in mine as if to say, *I'm not going anywhere.*

We both lingered.

The officiant's voice cut through the hush. "By the authority vested in me by the state of Florida, I now pronounce you husband and wife. You may kiss."

Chase didn't hesitate. His hands found my face, fingers strong yet gentle, the faintest tremor betraying all the ways he was feeling what I was. His lips met mine, not rushed, not hesitant, just full. Certain. He tasted like nerves and home.

The room fell away, except for the distant sound of Eli's soft "Woo!"

I leaned into Chase, laughing against his mouth, and his arms encircled me. My whole body sang with relief, with joy, with the ridiculous fact of our love having survived so many unlikely odds. I never thought happiness would smell so much like courthouse cleaning fluid and yet feel like the safest thing in the world.

Sunlight hit me square in the eyes the second we

stepped out of the courthouse, burning off the lingering chill of the linoleum floors and government air conditioning. It was pure Keys outside—palm trees rustling under the breeze, birds waging war over crumbs on the sidewalk, the scent of something grilled drifting over from a café across the street. For a minute, I stood there, letting the new shape of my life sink in, every bit as solid as the bands now warming my finger.

Chase reached for my hand, his palm hot against mine. His wedding band caught a glint of light, almost defiant in its newness. Everything—bustle, traffic, tourists arguing down the block—felt backgrounded by this rush of happiness fizzing through my chest.

Eli was the first to break the spell, of course. He swooped in, clapping Chase on the back with a grin that said brotherhood, celebration, and maybe just a tiny bit of competitive envy. "There it is. Shotgun wedding mission accomplished!"

Jules smacked him in the stomach. "It was a beautiful ceremony."

Eli made a show of crumpling over from her blow, then quickly recovered. "Unreal, man. You got married before me and Jules. I guess I'll have to start crocheting doilies and shopping for rings before you two show me up any further." He held up his hands in mock surrender. "Pressure's on."

Chase straightened his tie and shot Eli a deadpan look. "Doilies would really suit your aesthetic. Maybe a little macramé in your dive shop next."

Jules wrapped me up in a hug so genuine it nearly undid me for the second time in ten minutes. She pulled back, keeping one hand on my arm. "Congratulations, Harper. I mean it." Then she murmured in my ear, "If you need help keeping these lunatics in line, you know where to find me. I have some experience with that."

"I might hold you to that," I whispered back, my throat squeezing tightly. The two of them ambled down the steps, Eli's arm resting over her shoulders.

Finn marched up between Chase and me, the navy pillow held loosely now that it was all over. He gazed up at Chase, brows furrowed, all business. "Okay. I did my job. Now can we get pizza? And can you help me build the birdhouse, Dad?"

The word hung in the air for half a second, as if even the heat and noise of midday Florida paused to let it settle. Chase blinked, just once, then let a slow, beautiful smile break across his face. He bent down, knee to concrete, and tousled Finn's hair, ring glinting against the soft brown.

"You bet, buddy. Pizza first, then advanced avian engineering. Are we thinking standard-issue wren box, or do we go luxury, with a wraparound deck and ocean view?"

Finn pondered for a long, six-year-old second. "We should make it with a pool. Birds need to cool off too."

Chase winked at me as he stood. "That's us. Full-service contractors. You dream it, we build it."

When Chase stood once more, I tucked myself into his side. His arm wrapped firmly around my waist. He didn't say a word, just let his hand drift over my stomach.

Gentle, steady, quietly sure.

My own hand covered his. Underneath everything, the flutter of hope and secret joy pressed between us. For a breathless instant, our eyes locked, all of it understood in the space of that shared look.

He leaned close, mouth grazing the top of my hair. "Ready for the next phase, Mrs. Ashworth?"

The name slipped under my skin and left a trail of

pure warmth. I kissed his jaw, couldn't help the smile that took over my face. "More than ready. Let's go."

The five of us—plus one not fully acknowledged yet—walked down that bright Florida sidewalk together, sun on our faces, future wide open and beautifully unfinished. Our own chaotic, hard-earned joy. Family, in every sense that mattered.

And with every step, I knew.

This was right where I was meant to be.

THANK you for reading BETTER THAN HOME! Harper and Chase were such a fun couple to write about, and I loved the idea of the "Responsible Ones" getting their HEA.

If you'd like a glimpse into **Harper and Chase's happy near-future**, scan or click below to sign up for my newsletter:

Beach Read Update
(www.erinbrockus.com/homebook)

As a thank you, I'll send you a **bonus scene** which

peeks into their lives. This bonus scene gives a little extra context for a big event going on in their lives (wink-wink).

If you're already on my list, I've got you covered! At the bottom of each newsletter is a link to all my free content for subscribers. Just find your last email from me to read this bonus, as well as any others you might have missed. Or you can simply sign up again—you'll have your bonus in a flash.

KEEP READING for a peek at what's next in the Sunset Siesta series…

Second Epilogue

AUSTIN

SIX DAYS AFTER HARPER AND CHASE'S WEDDING

The familiar, yeasty tang of Braden's latest IPA experiment, something he was calling Hurricane Haze, usually settled easy on a Friday night. Tonight, though, even the expertly crafted bite couldn't quite cut through the low-grade thrum of… well, I wasn't sure what it was. Family, probably.

Family always came with a certain level of internal thrum.

I leaned back in the booth at Tidal Hops, nursing my pint, and studied my big sister. Harper was across from me, radiating a kind of quiet, settled happiness that was still new enough to be noticeable. She was sipping water, a small, almost secretive smile toying on her lips whenever she thought no one was looking. Chase was a good man, dependable as they came, but Harper was still my sister.

That protective instinct, ingrained deeper than any fishing knot, didn't just switch off because she'd signed a piece of paper at the courthouse. I eyed the glass of water she was nursing. Harper, who usually enjoyed one of Braden's lighter ales or a glass of wine after a long week, had been clutching her water like it was a lifeline.

Eli, sprawled in the booth beside her, caught my gaze and gave me a subtle smirk before turning back to the diving story he was regaling Harper with. He was in fine form, clearly enjoying himself, and I had a sudden, suspicious feeling he was enjoying something at *my* expense.

"You off the good stuff, Harper?" I tried to keep my tone casual, though Eli's eyes snapping back to mine put me on high alert. "Or did Braden finally brew something you can't stomach?"

Harper's cheeks flushed a telltale pink, and she suddenly found the condensation on her glass utterly fascinating. Eli, damn him, grinned at me.

It clicked then.

The quick courthouse wedding. The water. Eli's smug expression. Harper's sudden shyness. My own internal radar, usually reserved for spotting fish or ominous clouds on the horizon, pinged loud and clear.

"You're pregnant," I stated, not a question. My gaze softened as I looked at my sister. Underneath the usual general manager competence, there was a new, almost fragile shine to her.

Harper let out a shaky laugh, and her hand went to her stomach. "Okay, okay, you got me. How did you guess? I thought I was being subtle."

Eli laughed. "Subtle as a hurricane, sis. My finely tuned shotgun-wedding radar went off the second Chase mumbled something about needing a best man. He looked like he'd just accidentally agreed to a timeshare presentation he couldn't escape. Austin here is just a little slower on the uptake, but he gets there eventually."

"Well, I wanted to wait a bit longer to tell everyone else." Harper's gaze met mine, a touch of apology in it. "At least another month, until we're past the early stage. Things are just… a lot right now. So could you keep it under your hat for now?"

"My lips are sealed," I assured her and meant it. A sharp wave of concern washed over me. She *was* taking on a hell of a lot. "You doing okay with it all?"

She gave me a genuine, if slightly tired, smile. "I'm fine, Austin. Really. Just a bit of morning sickness that seems to think *all day* is a better schedule. Chase is being incredible, though."

I raised my pint. "Well, congratulations, Harp. To you and Chase. And your upcoming fleet expansion."

She laughed, the sound clear and happy. "Thanks, Austin. And not a word to Mom or the others yet, okay? We want to tell them properly."

"Wouldn't dream of it."

Braden swung by the table then, wiping down the smooth wood with a practiced swipe of his bar rag. "Everything good over here, folks? Austin, you look like you've seen a mermaid. What's the big news I'm missing?"

Eli, Harper, and I exchanged a quick, conspiratorial glance.

"Just discussing Austin's latest fishing tales, little brother," Eli said smoothly. "Apparently, the one that got away was *this* big." He spread his hands wide, nearly knocking over Harper's water.

I took another long pull of my beer, warmth spreading through me and chasing away the earlier thrum. A baby. Harper was going to be fine. She had Chase. And she had us.

My thoughts, inevitably, drifted to the noise next door to my own place, and my good mood frayed at the edges. "Speaking of things multiplying, that damn Heron House gets worse every day. The noise is already ungodly. A crew is making it *hospitable*, apparently. Less of a death trap, more like. I found out the new owner is moving in next week."

Eli leaned forward, interest piqued. "Oh yeah, old Lady Lawson's place? Heard someone finally inherited that mausoleum. Who's the brave soul? Or the sucker?"

"Some woman from up north," I said, the words laced with the accumulated annoyance of my recent shattered morning calms. "Holloway. Iris Holloway, according to Cameron down at the lumberyard. Who, by the way, is an idiot for even delivering materials to that place. The house is a hazard."

Harper, ever the diplomat even with a baby on board, chimed in, "Iris Holloway? What a pretty name. She'll probably be nice."

I grunted in response, not bothering to justify that with a reply.

Harper leaned toward me. "Maybe she just needs some local guidance, Austin. Old houses in the Keys can be tricky. You know that better than anyone."

"Tricky? That place isn't tricky, Harper. It's condemned by common sense. And from what Cameron says, she sounds like she's planning on fixing a century of rot with positive thinking and a Pinterest board." I took another giant drink in an attempt to calm down. "He said this Holloway woman was talking about Bohemian whimsy for the porch. *Bohemian whimsy*. On a structure that's probably held together by cobwebs and bad ideas."

Eli was grinning now, that familiar glint in his eye. "Sounds like a project for a capable, slightly grumpy neighbor with a knack for fixing things, Aus. Maybe she needs a consultant. You could offer your services. For a steep price, of course. Payable in silence, maybe."

I shot him a glare that could curdle milk, which he was immune to. Of course. "She can hire her own damn consultants. My only service is going to be filing a noise complaint if that generator starts before seven. Sunny and optimistic isn't going to stop the roof caving in on her head."

"Well, be careful, little brother." Eli's grin widened. He knew he'd gotten under my skin, damn him. "Sounds like this Iris Holloway, whoever she is, might just be the hurricane to your calm harbor."

Harper had a thoughtful, slightly mischievous smile twitching her lips now too. "You know, Austin, a little bit of disruption can be… invigorating. And anyone brave enough to take on Heron House must have some serious grit. Maybe she's what that old place needs."

I scowled at both of them, a united front of sibling amusement I did not appreciate. "Invigorating? Grit? I'd prefer peace. And how about not actively devaluing my property with questionable structural decisions made by someone named after a goddamn flower?"

Harper and Eli both burst into laughter, obviously tickled at the turn of events.

"Calm down!" Harper said. "I'm sure it will be fine."

I finished my beer in one long swallow, the coolness a welcome distraction. "Whatever. As long as her idea of remodeling doesn't involve any actual explosives before nine a.m. That's all I ask."

But I knew, with a sinking feeling that settled in my gut heavier than a waterlogged anchor, it wouldn't be that simple. Not in Dove Key. Nothing here was ever simple. My solitude, the quiet order I'd fought so hard to build and maintain, was already under siege. And I hadn't even met the woman responsible.

Poor Austin is about to get his life shaken up in ways he could never imagine (but desperately needs). The next Coleridge will be Austin in book three of the Siesta Sunset Series, BETTER THAN SUNSHINE. As you might have already guessed, this one is a grumpy-sunshine, neighbors to lovers romance.

BETTER THAN SUNSHINE: A Small Town Grumpy-
Sunshine Romance
Sunset Siesta Series

My new neighbor is a ray of sunshine with a sledgehammer, and she's not just renovating the house next door.

She's aiming it right at my life.

Austin:

My rules are simple—keep to myself, stick to my routine, and never get involved. And here in Dove Key, Florida, they keep the ghosts of my past chained. Until Iris Holloway moves into the derelict mansion next door and breaks all three before she's unpacked.

She's a hurricane of disastrous renovations and off-key singing. Her relentless cheer should be infuriating. She laughs at every setback like a plot twist she's enjoying, and that laugh does something to me I can't afford to name.

I find myself wanting to be the reason for her smiles. Iris came to Dove Key to rebuild. She didn't plan on her grumpy neighbor making it complicated. But letting her in means telling her what I survived—and what I didn't. She thinks she's just fixing an old house, but she might be the only one who can reach the man I locked away years ago.

Escape to the Florida Keys with BETTER THAN SUNSHINE, Book three in the interconnected Sunset Siesta series. This steamy, grumpy-sunshine, neighbors-to-lovers romance delivers slow-burn tension, sun-soaked atmosphere, and a guaranteed HEA.

BETTER THAN SUNSHINE: A Small Town Grumpy-
Sunshine Romance
Sunset Siesta Series

Also by Erin Brockus

SUNSET SIESTA SERIES:

Sunset Charade: A Sunset Siesta Novella

*Available free to subscribers

Better than Never: A Small Town Enemies to Lovers Romance

Better than Home: A Small Town Brother's Best Friend Romance

Better than Sunshine: A Small Town Grumpy-Sunshine Romance!

Better than Yesterday: Book Four coming mid-2026!

CALYPSO KEY SERIES:

ISLAND ESCAPES SERIES:

HALF MOON BAY SERIES:

MAIN NOVELS:

Finding Hope: Half Moon Bay Book 1

Defending Hope: Half Moon Bay Book 2

Rising Hope: Half Moon Bay Book 3

Forever Hope: Half Moon Bay Book 4

Half Moon Whim: Half Moon Bay Book 5 (Standalone)

Half Moon Ember: Half Moon Bay Book 6 (Standalone)

Half Moon Aqua: Half Moon Bay Book 7

Crowning Hope: Half Moon Bay Book 8

The Half Moon Bay Collection Books 1-4: The Hope and Alex Story

ASSOCIATED SHORT STORIES AND NOVELLAS:

Tropical Dawn: A Half Moon Bay Prequel Novella

*Tropical Chance**: A Second Chance Half Moon Bay Novella

*Tropical Hope**: A Half Moon Bay Prequel Short Story

* Subscriber exclusives

About the Author

Erin Brockus writes steamy small-town romance with a tropical twist. Her tight-knit island communities have all the charm and heat of your favorite small town, plus an ocean right outside the door. Her characters are smart, grounded women and the irresistible men who can't stay away from them—the kind of people you actually want to grab a drink with.

What sets Erin apart? Her stories go underwater. Drawing on her real-life passion for scuba diving and international travel, she builds worlds that feel like a vacation you never want to end. Her stories are full of salt air, adventure, and steamy tension that finally ignites.

She lives in Washington wine country with her

husband, who is also a scuba instructor. When she's not sending her characters on island adventures, she's running, mountain biking, or enjoying a good book with a cup of coffee.

Erin Brockus—where passion meets paradise.

www.ingramcontent.com/pod-product-compliance
Lightning Source LLC
Chambersburg PA
CBHW031629200726
48288CB00019B/421